To Nancy —
Your father's be[st] —
We adore him —
See how many
times you
can find Lenny's
name in here.

Deceit

By
J. Tracksler

Best

Joyce

Llumina Press

This is a work of fiction, although certain incidents, some names and places, while real, are used fictitiously. The names of some of the characters were borrowed from friends and again, used fictitiously, you lucky ducks, you.

ISBN: 1-59526-118-4

Printed in the United States of America by Llumina Press

Library of Congress Control Number: 2005904213

Some Thoughts

Big Skip: "Joyce, Use these words in a sentence: "Detail, Defense, Deceit, Deduct, Defeat."

Joyce: "Um, I give up."

Big Skip: "It's easy. Defeat of deduct went over defense before deceit and detail."

Joyce: "Oh."

This book is dedicated to Jack, Adam and Kathy and Matt. Also to Lucy and Dan, Skip and Cheryl, Jody, Christian and Isabella, Jessica, Alexis, and Sasha.

And also to "the girls in The Sisterhood", you know who you are, especially Christa the Goth, Mary from Germany, Tall Barbara, Tuscan Rose, Mona, Rebecca and Mary's own Sara of Gloucester, may she be a best seller!

And a special dedication to all of my classmates at GHS...it has been great to get back in touch...such wonderful memories and rekindling of friendships...

My heartfelt thanks to Robyn Benson, Llumina Editor and Friend.

CHAPTER ONE

Whenever I see a flag waving on a pickup truck, or see the news on TV, pass by a firehouse, or read a newspaper account of what happened on September 11th, I wonder...

Especially when I muse over the horrible statistics about how many people died that day and I remember back...I can't help it... How many others? Two or three perhaps? How many others pretended to die? How many others walked out of the rubble, stunned or hurt, seizing their chance to disappear...perhaps not quite thinking of what monstrous fraud they were going to perpetrate? How many others quietly melded into the smoke-filled morning, never to be heard from again, and let their families and friends, their co-workers, the rescuers and the rest of the world think that they were dead? How many, other than myself?

CHAPTER TWO

A sk anyone; go ahead...Everyone can tell you exactly what they were doing when the planes struck the World Trade Towers. It used to be that people remembered what they were doing when Kennedy died. Then it was where they were when John Lennon was killed, or when the Challenger exploded or even what they were doing when they heard that Kurt Cobain killed himself. No more. Now the quintessential Where Were You and What Were You Doing is September 11th, around 9 AM. I don't think a rock star's death will ever have the same impact, but you never know, do you, what the future might bring? We're a funny group of people sometimes.

Naturally, I remember exactly what I was doing. I was sitting on a toilet, trying to muster up the courage and details on how to do away with myself. I couldn't think of any other way out of my own personal misery. It seemed the sensible solution to my despair, although I wasn't quite sure *how* to do it. It's hard to really kill yourself. I mean, how would *you* do it?

I could break a window and leap out of the 90th floor, in front of God and all of the people I worked with, but the thought of all of my co-workers watching me climb up on the windowsill had a squelching effect on my determination. How would I break the glass? Suppose Zachary saw me? Suppose my skirt blew up over my head on the way down? Or suppose the window wouldn't break and I just looked like a dork?

I *could* go all the way up to the top of the building and somehow talk the guard into letting me out on the observation platform. Normally, you couldn't just stroll around out there, but I just might be able to convince some nice man to let me out for a moment or two. It wouldn't take much time to climb over the protective fencing and jump. Certainly that fall would kill me, but then I'd have the fate of the poor guard to explain to whomever it was that I was going to meet at the Pearly Gates. The poor man would probably lose his job over the whole affair and that wouldn't be fair. And my body would be so, well, you know, *messy*.

I could take poison, but I didn't *have* any poison. Other than lately, I didn't even use aspirin, much less any controlled substance that could be gulped down. I could swallow something like Drain-o, but I'd probably throw up before it was fatal, and then I'd get taken to the hospital and they'd call Ivan and he'd come to the Emergency Room and it would be worse than ever.

My thoughts chased each other like two dogs in the park. Easy to say you'll kill yourself, but *how?* That was the rub. Carbon Monoxide? I wouldn't know where to put the hose and we didn't have a garage anyway. Cut my wrists? I just wasn't that brave. No, I needed a quick and easy out, with no chance of someone finding me before I really died, and no chance whatsoever of it hurting me too much before I gasped my last. I was so despondent. I truly wanted to die, but I just couldn't figure out how to do it. Could it be that Death heard my confused mental ramblings? And laughed and laughed and laughed.

The door to the ladies room opened. *"Shit"* I thought. *"Can't even kill myself without someone interrupting me!"* I had deliberately chosen the deserted ladies room, the one at the rear of the building on the 89th floor where no one but the cleaning staff ever occupied, to meditate solo. I didn't want anyone at Clausen & Chase to see me until I could either end my life or come up with some reasonable explanation as to why my face looked the way it did this morning.

Embarrassed to let anyone see the bruises that Ivan had inflicted, I'd worn a soft, gauzy scarf pulled over my face on the 7:00AM commuter train from Fort Lee, New Jersey to New York. I kept my head down and made no eye contact with anyone. I'd scuttled along the street, wrapped in my scarf and my grief until I got to the North Tower Building. I used one of the telephone booths in the cavernous lobby to call Krissie, my secretary. To give myself some more time, I told her that I was at an unexpected appointment and would be in the office a bit later that morning.

I called Zachary's office next, catching him just before he went to a sales meeting. Oh, how I needed him to tell me how much he loved me! Oh, how I craved the sound of his voice! We had planned this for so long, and now, we could be together forever. It was worth the punches from Ivan, my crooked nose and the way my face had ballooned up.

"Zachary! Oh, Darling, I have to see you right away. I did it, Darling. I told Ivan last night..." I burst into tears. Sobbing and hiccupping, I choked out my garbled story. "He came home drunk, but I told him anyway. He...he was *furious*!" I pulled a Kleenex out of my pocket and gingerly blew my swollen nose. There was an empty, humming lack-of-sound at the end of the receiver. "Zachary? Are you there?" Through the silence at the other end, I heard him breathing. Excited and giddy, I poured out my tale of woe. "He hit me, both times in the face." I sniffed and touched my swollen cheek. "He said he'd never let me go. He told me he'd make me sorry I was born. He said he'd see me in hell first." I cried harder and waited for Zachary to calm me down. I waited a moment more. I could still hear Zachary breathing, but he didn't say anything. "Zachary?" What was wrong? A tiny knot began to grow in my stomach, joining the bruises that I'd already sustained. "*Zachary?*"

Somehow more frightened now, beyond my obvious black and blue trauma, I babbled further into the void, "He shoved me on the floor. He was drunk and out of control. I was afraid to move." My words tumbled over one another as I climbed into hysteria. "He kicked me in the stomach and then left, screaming that I would be sorry." I drew a shuddering breath. "Zachary? Did you hear me? I was terrified! *Zachary?*"

"You little idiot!" His words were clipped and angry. Through the physical pain in my face and belly, I felt an additional punch to my heart. Little idiot? What was he saying? What was *wrong*? What was he telling me? Instead of outraged sympathy, instead of murmured words of consolation, swearing to me that he would kill Ivan for hitting me, instead of assuring me that our love would surmount all of my grief, he stammered and stuttered and then told me that he wasn't going to leave Heather after all.

"*What*? What do you mean?" I could barely speak.

"I just changed my mind. I still love her. Well, I don't love her, but it's just too much of a hassle. I'm not leaving her. It isn't worth the trouble. I'm just never going to see you again. Our relationship is over." His voice was terse – a stranger's voice. "You and I are through."

"But...but..." I could barely breathe.

"Look, Gianna, I'm sorry. Honestly sorry. I thought.... I..."

"*Zachary*!" I wailed in dumb disbelief. "We love each other! We *agreed*!" My voice rose to a screech.

"I know, but I changed my mind."

"Changed your *mind*? What do you mean, changed your mind? We agreed to tell them both last night! Zachary, I got *beaten up*! I could have been *killed*!" My voice rose again to a scream as I lost control. What was he *saying*?

His voice, the voice that had caressed me, planned our future with me, became even more chilly and remote. "I have to go now. I'm sorry, Gianna. I wish...I just couldn't...I can't..."

"You *bas*tard! You can't just hang up on me. I'll come up to your office and make a scene!" I know I was hysterical. My whole life was sliding down into a cess pit. Zachary! What was he *saying*?

He was nasty now, almost sneering at me. "Don't even think of doing that. I'll have the police arrest you. I'll deny everything. We've been so careful. No one ever knew that we were...um...together. No one will believe you. You'll lose your job and I'll see to it that you never get another one in any financial corporation in New York. I mean it." It was a stranger speaking. A cold, horrible stranger. "It was fun while it lasted, Gianna. But it is over. Over, do you understand?" His last words were hissed. I made a whimpering sound. Was this the man I loved? The man I was leaving my bum of a husband for? "Gianna? Are you there?"

"I...I can't even breathe. How *could* you? After all we've... I...Oh, God!" I hung up with a dull click, uncomprehending. I slumped against the wall of the booth, my mouth open, slack with stunned disbelief. My life was spiraling out of control. I tried to take deep, calming breaths, but all I could manage was a whimper. It was all supposed to go so differently. This morning was to have been a glorious beginning for the two of us. So why was I sitting in a telephone booth, crying my heart out?

I huddled in the phone booth for a few moments. What was I going to *do*? Despair settled onto my shoulders and the future, once so bright with promise, dimmed into a dark abyss. I wanted to die.

There was a sharp rap on the glass door. "Are you using the phone?"

"No, I'm finished," I mumbled. "Finished."

I slunk across the lobby, my head hunched into my scarf. I went all around to the back of the building, avoiding the express elevators that would have taken me straight up to Clausen & Chases's offices. I pushed the button for the food service elevator. I didn't want to see anyone. I got off at the 88th floor, then, unable to think clearly, opened the door to the fire stairs and sat down, unable to go any further. My face ached and every muscle in my bruised body was screaming. But my heart hurt more than anything else.

So that was the end. My life was over. There was nothing for me to live for. I certainly couldn't and didn't want to go back to Ivan. Our marriage was a shambles, both before and after I started my affair with Zachary; the affair that was supposed to give me the gift of true love. Zachary was to have been my new beginning. Damn, I *deserved* some happiness. This morning was supposed to be the most glorious morning of my life. I gulped down a sob. Zachary…I shook my head like some dumb, stunned animal and then began to cry again as the pain of this new reality exploded in my brain. Sobbing, unable to stop the tears, I climbed the stairs, pushing myself along the wall, a heap of misery. At the top of the stairs, I saw the generally unused ladies room, the one that was near the garbage elevator. I went in and lifted my head to the mirror.

My eye was swollen, turning a ripe shade of purple, and my nose was mashed a bit to one side. My head and face pounded with pain and it hurt to try to think of how to get myself out of the mess my life had become. I just *couldn't* go into my office looking like this. A story of how I ran into a door just wouldn't wash. Anyway, I didn't want to go into my office. I didn't even want to make a scene outside of Zachary's offices. What was the point? I didn't want to go anywhere. I only wanted to die.

CHAPTER THREE

Whoever it was disturbing my solitary misery flushed the toilet. I heard heavy footsteps walking toward the sink. The water tap gushed. From my toilet seat perch, I peeked through the crack in the door and saw a sturdy back and a bush of red hair. That new woman who worked in Pensions…Vivian Something…She was from England or Canada or someplace like that.

I sat still, huddled on the toilet seat and tried to sniff quietly. *"Please leave! Please leave!"* I implored her in silent urging.

She was taking her sweet time…I heard the snick of her purse opening and through the slit, I saw her leaning in toward the mirror, putting on some additional layer of make up. *Come on! Come on!* I hunched myself into a small ball of wretchedness and vowed to throw myself right in front of the train on the subway tracks as soon as she left. It would be quick and relatively painless, wouldn't it? And I felt it would be permanent. Who cared if my body was ripped apart? It just didn't matter any more. I touched my cheek and felt the pain in my soul.

And then the unthinkable happened.

The sound was incredible. A noise that screamed through the entire building and went on and on and on. The bathroom ceiling crashed down, huge chunks of masonry and tile fell and the room tilted crazily. I was thrown forward, hitting my head on the door to the toilet stall. On all fours, I crouched like a crazed rabbit, unable to comprehend what was happening as the walls and ceiling fell around me. The lights flashed and fizzed and the floor heaved and buckled. I think I must have screamed, but I couldn't hear anything except the earsplitting groans that the North Tower building itself was suffering. Masonry and walls and steel beams crashed around me. Water sprayed from broken pipes and the noise…. the *noise*….the noise…It was alive!

I was terrified, breathing loud gasps through my open mouth, panting almost. My feet and legs were drenched with water. The toilet had exploded behind me. I tried to stand up, but the walls of the stall had fallen in and were crossed just above my head. I know now that they saved me from being crushed under tons of rubble. Acting on sheer animal instinct, I scrabbled under the opening under the door, soaking myself in my frantic efforts to get out.

The room was a shambles. The sinks were tilted crazily, the mirrors broken. That woman...Vivian...oh, God, oh God...she was clearly dead. She lay on her side, her face cut nearly in half from a huge sliver of glass that protruded from her forehead. The back of her head was crushed by a chunk of masonry and a heavy metal pipe lay at a crazy angle across her body. Stuff had exploded from the inside of her skull, and blood was everywhere. I swayed, retching and coughing. A column of water suddenly spouted, bathing her body in a pool of water that rapidly turned a bright crimson from her blood. I gagged again and then lurched into a water pipe as another groaning sound shifted the floor under me. I fell and clutched at Vivian's flaccid arm to lift myself up. Standing, holding on to a corner of one sink that was still affixed to the wall, I looked at her. Her right hand still clutched her tube of lipstick. Her open purse was on the floor, between her feet. Her C&C employee badge was still clipped onto her sweater.

I can't say that the idea came to me then. I don't remember thinking anything at all. I unclipped my own C&C badge, bent down and snapped it onto her sweater. I picked up her purse and grabbed the badge from her body. I dropped my own handbag on the floor. With my mouth open so that I could suck in more air, gagging and coughing, I pulled my scarf up around my head and face, and wrenched open the crazily tilted lavatory door.

I had no idea of what had happened. None at all. Maybe, somewhere down in my subconscious, I might have thought that a bomb had fallen. Or an earthquake. After all, even afterward, who would have believed the reality?

I was in a corridor at the back of the building. There was dust and plaster all around me. It seemed that I could smell smoke, although I couldn't see any flames. I could hear screams and groans and the building itself seemed to cry with terror. There was another loud crash and pieces of the ceiling began to fall, one of them hitting me in the head. I staggered and clutched at the wall, frightened and wailing.

Like some primitive animal, my only thought was to get out. The way to the elevator bank was filled with debris. I couldn't get past it. Turning, I opened the back stairway door. The stairway looked just like it had looked this morning when I crawled up. Had it only been ten or fifteen minutes ago? I grabbed the railing and began to go down. The concrete steps were untouched by the maelstrom and smelled faintly of must. But even as I stumbled down, noting that I had just passed the sixty-seventh floor, then the sixty-sixth, I could hear the incredible sounds of the building breaking up. Loud, heavy noises, crashes, wrenching sounds. Down...down...down, my footsteps thudded. I think I was crying and stuff was coming out of my nose. I wiped my face with the sleeve of my coat and saw dust and blood. I heard echoes and booming noises and voices screaming and I thought I could hear the crackling sounds of a fire. I sniffed at the air, but couldn't smell any smoke now. There was no one at all in the staircase with me. The sound of my footfalls careened crazily off the empty walls. My breath was coming in hoarse, screaming gasps. My sobbing turned into a steady snuffle. Down...down...down.

I fearfully opened the door into the lobby. All was pandemonium there. People were screaming and moaning, bleeding, lying dead, pushing, grabbing, crying and dying. Chunks of the building were lying in heaps and each crash brought more debris to the floor. A huge scream, from the bowels of the building itself, assaulted the air and people stopped, covered their heads and echoed a scream back. The building tilted and glass from a thousand windows crashed on the other side of the lobby. I saw bodies fall and blood spurt where the glass cut several people in two.

I wish I had been a hero. I wish I had helped someone. But I was numb and only wanted to breathe air that wasn't filled with death and danger. Those who were still able formed a river that was pushing toward the doors. Someone screamed to get out. Someone else yelled that the building was falling. I know I was screaming myself, but I couldn't separate my cries from the cries of the others. I was caught in the tide of hysterical humanity and was spit out on the sidewalk with thousands of others whose only thought was to get away.

The river of people moved into the street. And then we turned as one and gaped at the North Tower. Way up, up in the vicinity of where I worked, there was a huge hole in the side of the building. Thick, black smoke and sheets of fire had burst out of the crack in the building. It was...incomprehensible. I saw the heads and torsos of people leaning out of the windows. I think they were calling and crying and screaming, but the building itself was making so much noise that they couldn't be heard. One man leaped out of a window. His body turned in graceful cartwheel circles as it careened through the air. I couldn't see over the heads of those in front of me, but a collective moan went up. There was a sound...so loud...like a melon splitting open. I didn't realize what it was then, but now I know it was the sound of his body smashing into the street. I looked back up in the air. Flames and smoke hemorrhaged out and I knew it must be exactly what Hell really looks like. Had I really wanted to die a few moments before?

I turned and ran.

CHAPTER FOUR

I flagged a taxi after I couldn't run any longer. I was almost too dazed to look around me, but as soon as I slammed the door, I noticed that people on the street were not acting normally. "Where to, Lady?" The driver asked.

"Uh, um. Uh, drive toward 5th." I couldn't think of what to say and sat forward on the seat, my entire body rigid and tense.

"You tell me when, Lady". He cheerfully whistled as he slammed the lever of the meter down. His radio played a combination of static and foreign sounding music. Whatever had happened out there, my cabby...I looked at the picture in his license and a wooly black head looked back at me...Muttar Freebody...didn't seem to be aware of it. I looked out the window. People were yelling and screaming and grabbing one another. Shaken, I sat back, trying to get my head to think coherently. I looked down. The black purse was in my lap. Her purse...Vivian...I wondered what had happened to my own handbag. Had I left it in the toilet? I thought so...but it hurt my head to try to remember. Thank goodness I had Vivian's. A hysterical bubble of laughter exploded from my lips. She sure wouldn't be needing it any more. I opened it up and took out her wallet.

Vivian Morrison. Oh God, Vivian. Lying broken and dead and full of blood and water. Vivian. To block out the thoughts of her, I concentrated on the contents of the purse. She lived at 129 East 73rd Street, Apartment 2A, and there was a wad of twenty-dollar bills folded into the wallet.

I looked at her license and her picture. She was 30 years old, a beefy, full-faced woman with frizzy red hair. She wore big, square red-rimmed eyeglasses. Not pretty at all. She had brown eyes like me, was 5'7", about my own height, and weighed 180 pounds, almost 50 pounds more than I did.

I should be mourning for her. But I barely knew her. I felt nothing. Nothing at all. I shuddered and tried to remember what I knew about her. I knew she worked for Dan Vanderwall in the Pension Depart-

ment. That she was a new hire…maybe been at C & C for a month or
so. I remembered Dan bitching about her. What had he said? "She's a
bull dyke if I ever say one. Big, husky babe. Just got her from…"
Where? England, maybe. Maybe Ireland. Or Canada. "Yeah, I think
she came from Canada." He wasn't really interested in her. "No family. Funny sort of accent. And I can't say I'm impressed with her
skills." Dan had laughed. "She's a loner, and what else would she be
with those looks? Raggedy Ann hair and those red rimmed spectacles.
I wonder if she thinks she looks like Sally Jesse Raphael!" He laughed,
nastily, and made the prophecy that she'd be gone in a few weeks. He
was so right. And Dan? Had he survived this horror? I shuddered,
huddled back in Muttar's smelly back seat.

I rummaged in the bottom of the purse and came up with a ring of
keys and the oversized, red-rimmed glasses. I put them on, wincing as
the sidepieces imprisoned my swollen forehead. I was slightly far-
sighted, and the glasses were nearly perfect for me. I blinked and
began to think. Hard.

"Muttar!" I rapped on the Plexiglas.

"Yaaas?"

"Let me off on the corner of Lex and 72nd, please."

"Yaaas," He nodded, bobbing his head. "The Lady says street
number Seventy Two. I take her there, I do, I do."

I stared at the back of his frizzled head. The world was coming to
an end and I was in a cab with a Rastafarian Hennie Youngman.

He drew the cab up with a tap on the horn. I gave him a twenty,
telling him to keep his day job. He bobbed his thanks, not understanding anything except a fine tip. I got out and swayed with emotion and
fatigue. Muttar drove off, waving his thanks, totally oblivious to the
peculiarities of this horrendous morning.

Not so the rest of New York City. All around me, people were jab-
bering, grabbing one another, running around, looking at the sky, and
crying. Perhaps it really *was* the end of the world. So be it, I shrugged.
Maybe God was taking out His frustration on us all.

My body was on automatic pilot. I trudged to East 73rd, and then
east along the block to number 129. It was the fifth doorway off First
Avenue and there was no one around. I opened the street door and was
in a drab lobby painted the shade of green that all low to medium in-
come lobbies are painted in New York City. It was decorated in
moderate graffiti with two bicycles chained to the metal staircase. I
went up, knocked on the door of 2A and waited breathlessly for a few

minutes, noting that there was no name on the name-slot on the door. I tried two keys before I found the right one, and then I let myself into Vivian Morrison's apartment.

I was in a short hall. I turned a corner and could see the entire apartment in front of me. A kitchen to my left, a bathroom straight ahead, and a living room with a pull-out bed folded out for sleeping to my right. It was a pigsty. There were clothes dropped all over the floor, an unmade, disgusting-looking sofa bed, dishes piled in the sink, food-encrusted pots and pans on the stove and I didn't have the strength to look in the bathroom. I was so caught up in the filth of the room that I nearly forgot what had happened. Nearly.

I kicked out at flannel shirts and jeans and clunky-looking shoes on the floor, dumped stuff from a chair and pulled it in front of the television set. Vivian was some housekeeper, I thought, wondering if she was really a lesbian. Whatever her sexual persuasion, she was a pig. I found the remote control and figured out how to turn it on. The breath whooshed out of me as I watched the mind-bogglingly unbelievable total destruction of the building where I had worked.

Then, incredibly, a few moments later, I saw the plane hit the second Tower. Like the rest of the world, I began to cry.

The television swam before my face as I realized just what had happened. *Zachary*! Ohmygodohmygod! All of my friends and co-workers! They all had to be dead! Ohmygodohmygod!

I found myself on the floor, lying on top of a pile of dirty clothes. I lay still with my nose pressed into a fleece jacket, stunned with reality, trying to process what I had just seen, what I had just run away from. I sat up and faced the TV screen and the horrors it continued to spew.

As I watched, random thoughts twisted through my semi-conscious mind. No one could survive this, could they? They all were probably dead. Zachary, Dan, Krissie, Sharon, certainly Vivian, Mr. Clausen and Mr. Chase...the Hispanic guys in the cafeteria...the girls in Payroll, everyone. There was no way that anyone could have survived such a horror. Ohmygod. Every single person at C & C. Every single person on the 90th floor.

Everyone except me.

But...my identification? Who...? And all the dead bodies? And all the devastation? I stared at the television. The drumbeat started in my head:

Who would know that I wasn't dead? Ivan? No one. Muttar? No one.

Could I....? Could I...? Could I be someone else? I began to laugh, nearly hysterical. *Me?* Someone *else*! I stuffed my fists into my mouth. Could I be stocky and redheaded and have red-rimmed glasses and be Vivian Morrison? Perhaps.

While the images of planes and the Pentagon and destruction flickered just out of focus, I thought it through. I didn't really look like Vivian, but who would know? Most likely, no one was left at C & C to say what she looked like. No one was left to say what I looked like. Who would know I wasn't her? Supposedly, she didn't have a family. Was there some kind of lesbian lover in her life? I giggled, half-hysterical, my head pounding and shock setting in. No problem with the people at C & C. There probably wasn't *anyone* left at C&C. Hell, C&C itself was gone! So who was to say that I hadn't died too? Gone! Gianna St. Clare was gone. She wanted to die, didn't she? Well, she did! And wouldn't Ivan be pissed! And Zachary, oh, God. Was Zachary dead. Dead! Zachary, my love. Certainly he was dead, you idiot, I scolded myself. There was no way that anyone could have escaped that horror. He sure was dead, the bastard. Poof! Gone! Together with me...myself...I was dead, too. Except I wasn't. All of a sudden, I erupted, sobbing, weeping and groaning, grabbing at the fleece beneath me and ripping it to shreds.

I *was* dead. I might as well be dead. My head turned, pillowed on Vivian's fleece, and I stared at the television set. After watching the images over and over and over and over again, I sat up and then struggled to my feet. If I were to make a success of this, I'd better begin right away.

I took Vivian's license photo out, put her glasses on and went into the bathroom. The glasses really changed my entire face. I held my hair up off my shoulders and peered at myself. What would happen if I cut my hair...my glorious long, swishing, smooth, chestnut, source of vanity, Zachary-loved-to-run-his-fingers-through hair? Suppose I colored it red and got a perm....could I get away with it? Maybe.

Before I could change my own mind, before I could think of the ten thousand reasons why I shouldn't be doing this, never mind that it was fraudulent, deceitful, illegal, immoral and whatever, I grabbed Vivian's purse and rummaged through it.

I learned that she banked at Chemical Bank, that she was blood type 0+, as was most of the world, including me, and that she wore a dark red colored lipstick. Two books of matches and a Marlboro cigarette lighter led me to think that she'd been a smoker, although there were no cigarettes in the purse. I rummaged in her drawers, hoping not to find cockroaches or dildoes, and found her bankbooks and bank statements. She wasn't poor, this Vivian Ann Morrison. I also found a stash of money, more than three thousand dollars in cash. My state of mind was so hyped up that I never stopped to think just why she'd have all this money. This discovery would explode at me later on. I opened her passport. Vivian Ann Morrison, born in Canterbury, Kent, England. I found her Immigration papers, her Naturalization information, her new Social Security Card and a key to a security box at Chemical Bank's 5th Avenue Branch. What I didn't find were any family photographs or any letters or any signs of another human being that she might know. No lesbian lover. No nothing. And, oh, yes, neither did I find any cockroaches nor dildoes.

I saw a brown leather fanny pack hanging on the back of a door, transferred Vivian's C&C badge, checkbook, wallet and keys to it and strapped it to my waist. I put her glasses back on, took five hundred dollars, and let myself out the door.

I walked over to Lexington, and then went downtown. New York had stopped. There was hardly any traffic on the streets and people were huddled around any kind of store that had a television set. I didn't see any pigeons or squirrels or cats or dogs. I was the only one who seemed to be going anywhere. I walked until I saw a sign that said "Super-Cuts. No Appointment Necessary" in red neon script. I don't even know what street I was on. I went in.

Every hairdresser and all of the customers except two ladies sitting under dryers were clustered around a small television set. "Can I get a cut, color and perm?" I asked, tapping one of the beauticians on the shoulder.

"Now?"

"Right now."

The woman shrugged. "World's comin' to an end and she wants a perm." she said to no one. "Who wants to do her?" she asked the group without taking her eyes off the set. It was playing the video tape of the plane hitting the second tower. Over and over and over. In a moment, one of the girls nodded. Keeping one eye glued to the television set, she absentmindedly shoved me to a chair, all the while telling me, in a high, wondering voice, about the terrorist attacks. For now we knew a tiny bit about what had happened.

"I can't freakin' believe it! I can't freakin' believe it!" she squealed. "Geez! What is the world comin' to?" I shrugged sympathetically. I was completely unable to answer her question. What, indeed?

Cheryl…that was her name…blinked a few times when I told her what I wanted her to do to my hair. "Geez. Are you sure?" She pronounced it "shoo-wa?" "You got such lovely hair." She pronounced it "haaaeh." I assured her twice of my sincere intent, lay my head gingerly back and closed my eyes. I tried hard not to think of anything as she shampooed, cut, globbed thick goo, rinsed, cut some more, rolled and applied another round of smelly, thick goo, unwrapped and brushed.

"There!" She pronounced it "they-ah." And twirled me around so I could see the splendor of me. I looked….I looked like an older, beat-up version of Little Orphan Annie. Dispassionately, I saw the reflection of a battered face, not horrible, not awful, but certainly not like I used to look. The red-rimmed glasses put the finishing touches on. I didn't really look like Vivian's picture, but sort of like a smaller, thinner and prettier version. Someone looking at me would only see the vividness of the hair and the distinct redness of the frames of my glasses and wouldn't look too far beyond. I wondered in a small thought if that was why Vivian looked like that.

"Exactly as I wanted it." I complimented her. I appreciated the fact that she hadn't asked me about my black eye and bruised nose and added another twenty bucks to the tip.

"Are you in a play?" She asked as she pocketed the money without even looking at it. "Are you an actress?"

"Sort of." I replied, and exited the shop.

CHAPTER FIVE

I t was hard to find a cab. There wasn't much traffic at all. Only a few cars and a truck or two rolled by and so I began to walk downtown. At 51st Street, I spied a cab coming down the street. I waved it down.

"D'ja heah?" The driver asked me. I nodded. "Fuckin' A!" the driver ejaculated, shaking his head sorrowfully. I agreed. "Goddam sunaofabitch!" He continued. "Where to, Lady?" I guess they all say that.

"As close as you can get to the Twin Towers." I instructed him.

"Ain't no Twin Towers anymore, Lady," he kindly explained to me.

"I know." I said, wondering if he'd believe me if I told him my story.

He deposited me about twenty blocks away from the destruction, in front of a yellow-beribboned police roadblock. "I checked on the radio, Lady. This is as far as you can get." He looked curiously at me, but didn't ask me why I wanted to go closer or why I looked the way I did. I paid him and tipped him well. After all, this was a special day. For both good and for bad. A very special day.

Even twenty blocks away, I could feel the devastation of the explosions. The air was thick with smoke and a fine, white dust. There was rubble on the road, small pieces of concrete, paper, and who knows what else. The air seemed to pulse with a menace punctuated with tiny pieces of debris. At every corner, where the winds of New York whistled around corners, little scraps of – what were they? – paper? Ashes? Whatever, they began to float down, settling on the sidewalks with the rest of the flotsam and jetsam of a busy city. Although I saw a lot of policemen, no one tried to stop me as I made my way closer to the disaster. People were clustered in groups, some covered with dust and dirt, some dazed and bleeding, and all of them talking, gesticulating, and holding on to one another. Police and firemen were running here and there. There were black, rubber fire hoses coiled on the ground and men were beginning to set up barriers.

The destruction escalated as I got closer. The air was thicker here, and it was beginning to be difficult to see more than ten or twenty feet ahead. Every person I passed was covered with white, chalky dust. People's eyes stared out like skeleton sockets, not believing what they saw. Some walked by like animated zombies, staring straight ahead, lurching in a funny gambol. Others grabbed onto to every human being they passed, clutching, holding, perhaps trying to affirm life. I passed several people on the ground, some moaning and hurt, some of them apparently dead. Debris covered the streets. Large, jagged pieces of metal, some still smoking, lay thrown around as if they were pieces of a child's Tinkertoy set. Chunks of concrete with wires sticking out were tumbled all over the street.

What the hell was I doing going back here? I couldn't have told you. I still have no idea of why I came back. Perhaps the criminal returning to the scene of the crime? You tell me.

I became aware of strange sounds…the shrieking of ambulances, the warning hoots of fire engines and the groans and screams from those who were pinned by the fallen buildings. Even the buildings themselves seemed to make noises. Strange creaks and grating noises. The wind keened through their windows and rattled at their doors. They might almost be alive, these concrete monoliths. They reminded me of great wooly mammoths or mastodons watching the ice age devour them. Was this what it was like at the end of the world?

I passed a man with a carton of water bottles. I suddenly discovered that I was thirsty. He wordlessly handed one to me and I drank it straight down, spilling the water over my blouse and skirt. Vaguely I noticed that I, too, was now covered with the soot and ashes. The man took the bottle back and asked me if I wanted to help by giving out water to those who might want some. I nodded, unable to speak. My throat had closed up and I felt as if I never would be able to talk again. He handed me two six-packs of water. I stumbled closer, handing the water to anyone that I saw. Passers-by grabbed at the bottles and drank in great gulps, with the water gushing too fast to be consumed, spilling over their mouths and running in rivulets over their chalk colored clothing.

I bent to help a man whose leg was imprisoned by a steel beam. He leaned forward, helping as best he could. Fortunately for him, the beam was a small one. Summoning all my strength, I managed to lift the beam enough so that he could slide his leg out from under it. "God bless you. Thanks." The man gave me his hand and I helped him to stand. "Goddam day," he said. "Be careful, girlie," and limped away.

I was very close now. There was frenetic activity around me, with firemen yelling and bellowing, police running, New Yorkers screaming and pointing and shoving. A group of people at the corner of the street were gathered around a large heap of rocks and metal. With grunts of effort, they worked feverishly to free the hapless people who were trapped underneath. I gave the rest of the water away and began to help them, lifting rocks, pieces of metal desks, ceiling tiles, a picture of someone's wife and children, a clock, and jagged pieces of glass. We grunted and sweated and cut ourselves. But there was no way that we could stop. At last, we reached the six people in the center of the debris, crouched under a large beam of some sort. I presume that it saved their lives, although I could see one man – I think it was a man – who was just outside the cave made by the beam. He was dead. I'm sure that he was dead.

The people saved by the beam gave a cry. We cheered, with tears streaking our filthy faces. All of the people were moving, groaning and cursing and crying, but moving, all except the one man, and I left them and went even closer.

You could barely see to walk. Ghostly images of people loomed suddenly in front of me and then, just as suddenly, disappeared back into the swirling shroud of mist. The only light came from the column of flame that seemed to engulf the entire end of Manhattan.

Again, if you asked me why I was there, why I went back, I don't think I could tell you. I just wanted to get closer. Even closer.

"Look Out!" Someone screamed, and an entire wall of rubble fell to my left. I staggered with the pulse of the implosion. My insubstantial body was blown off its feet and I was thrown through the air, landing with a thump on the rubble-strewn sidewalk. I think I blacked out. I couldn't move. I couldn't breathe. The dust choked me and my legs were pinned by some heavy thing. I screamed.

Strong arms pulled at me. "Easy!"

I tried to tell them how thankful I was. I tried, but my throat was sealed.

"We've got you!" They dragged me out, three men that I didn't know and would never see again.

I lay on my back, dazed and barely breathing. Another man, dressed in what might have been a black jumpsuit called to some others, "Here! Here's one that's still alive!" I couldn't seem to open my eyes nor could I seem to move. Gentle hands slipped a stretcher under me and I felt my self lifted in the air. Was I dead now?

A woman with chapped, rough hands loosened my filthy jacket and blouse, keeping up an inane one-sided conversation with me, telling me that I was fine now. That I'd be safe now. That everything was OK now. "Can you talk?" she asked. No. I couldn't. I couldn't breathe, I couldn't see, I couldn't feel and I felt myself slip away into oblivion.

CHAPTER SIX

I couldn't see. Couldn't move. Was this the punishment God had sent me? Was I paralyzed? Blind? Ohgod. I drifted back into the darkness. Someone was babbling....Lips were dry...My head hurt...

"She's coming around." A voice penetrated. I tried to speak, but my mouth couldn't form the words. I felt the darkness rush in again.

Another voice. "Hush, sweetheart. You're safe." A soft, cool hand touched my forehead. Something warm and watery wet my lips. I licked at it, thirsty as I had never been thirsty before.

And another voice. "Vivian? Can you hear me? Vivian?" *Vivian*? Who was Vivian?

I opened my crusty eyes. Vivian! My mind snapped back. "I...I..."

"Can you take a sip of water?" I nodded and pain flashed behind my eyes. I gasped with the effort of cutting through the agony in my head. I coughed and pain cut through my chest.

"Easy now. Here, I'll hold a cup to your mouth. Just let it wet your lips. Don't take too much." I let the blessed coolness bathe my mouth. "OK?" I nodded, careful not to move too quickly this time. I licked my lips slowly. The voice came again. "Now take a small sip." I sipped. "Better?"

"Better." Was that *my* voice croaking?

"How are you feeling, Vivian?" I blinked, lowering and raising my eyelids, giving myself time, relieved that at least I had remembered that I was now Vivian. I guess I wasn't dead yet. I was still able to lie.

"I feel awful." Yes, it was my voice. Croaky, barely able to converse, but my own voice. At least I could speak. And I could see and hear. Now, could I move? I lifted my head slightly and looked around. Obviously, I was in a hospital room. "The building fell." I said in a childlike whisper.

There were three women...nurses or doctors... clustered around me. One of them was dressed in blue operating room scrubs, one had a top printed with rainbows and the third had a top with teddy bears on it. Teddy Bear gave me the cup again and I drank thirstily.

"I'll give you more in a few minutes." I gave her a grateful smile. The nurses, or doctors or angels or whoever they were, glanced at one another and collectively smiled back at me. "Thank God that you're all right." I wiggled a foot, then the other foot. I tried to move my right arm and found that it was attached to a tube that snaked back over my shoulder. My arm, where I could see it, was bruised and bandaged. It felt weird, like someone else's arm.

"Do you remember what happened?" Blue asked me.

I closed my eyes for a moment, gathering my thoughts, or what was left of my thoughts. I was better prepared now. "I was in the North Tower. I work..." I hesitated, unsure of how to phrase it correctly, "I worked for Clausen & Chase. The big financial company. We had nearly all of the offices on the 90th and 91st floors." My head started to pound. "The plane hit our floors. There was a huge bang and then fire and smoke. The building was mortally wounded. Like some big animal." Blue watched me carefully as my voice began to spiral out of control. I gulped some air and forced myself to breathe slowly. "What happened to everyone else there? What...? Is anyone else alive?"

They looked at one another again, wondering if I was strong enough. "Thousands of people were killed," Blue told me, taking hold of my hand. "I don't know how many were able to get out alive. There were hundreds of passengers on the planes." The planes. I shut my eyes in pain and thought about the planes. Pointing into the air, hitting the building. The planes. OhmyGod.. Her voice cut through the images in my mind, and then replaced them with one even more horrific. "And then another plane hit the Pentagon building in Washington." I nodded dully, watching her as she spoke. The images flickered again and then faded. I know now that my mind was reacting like a wounded animal, shutting out the pictures that I was unable to deal with. I concentrated on Blue, squinting to watch her mouth, hanging onto her words. I figured that she was the doctor. Her uniform was the most professional looking of the trio. She touched my shoulder. "Another plane crashed in Pennsylvania, too. They don't know what happened there."

"How terrible." I stared at the white sheet that covered my body. Terrible? What a silly word to describe what had happened. I sucked in my breath trying to say something meaningful, but my voice and my mind didn't seem to be working in concert. Pitiful sounds emerged. "I...I can't take it all in." I looked up at each of them. "How could this happen?" I began to cry.

Rainbow shook her head. She bent toward me. "Can you remember anything else, Vivian? Can you remember what day this is?"

I wiped the tears with my fist. Rainbow pulled a Kleenex out of her pocket and gently dabbed at my face. "Try to remember. What day is this?" she insisted that I answer.

It hurt to think. I closed my eyes and squeezed out some thought. "What day? Um…" I could remember. I could. "The day of infamy," I joked feebly, only I wasn't joking. "No, I do know. It's the 11th." Rainbow looked pleased. She made a tick on a piece of paper that she held in her hand.

"And what is your name?" I blinked, wondering if this was a trick. Perhaps they already knew that I was an impostor.

"Vivian…um," For a moment, Vivian's last name was gone from my head. I exhaled and focused, and it floated back to me. "Uh, Vivian Morrison. My name is Vivian Ann Morrison."

"Good!" Rainbow smiled, checking off yet another accomplishment for me. "Can you remember your address?"

"Uh," I thought furiously. "East 73rd Street. Apartment 2A." Please God, don't let her ask me the street number. I didn't know it.

"Great. The unasked for detail of the apartment number got me through. "And who is the President?"

"George Bush, but it was touch and go there for a while." I tried a real joke. Rainbow laughed.

"Poor man. Can you imagine being the President today?"

"What will he do?"

"Only God knows. The whole thing is unbelievable." Teddy Bear pulled a stethoscope out of her pocket and leaned over to listen to my chest. "Hmmmm?" She stood up, smiling. "Other than the mess you've made of yourself, a broken nose, lots of bruises and a possible concussion, you seem OK."

"I don't feel OK." I was just snapping out all these amusing responses. A regular stand-up comedian, wasn't I? Even though I was lying down. "What happened to me?"

"You have awful contusions to your face and all over your body…" She gave me a sympathetic look and a gentle pat on my shoulder. Little did she realize just when some of those contusions had been smacked into me and by whom. She was presuming that all my bruises and wounds had been suffered in the disaster. They had been, but in a different disaster. She continued, "Your nose is fractured." I closed my eyes so that she couldn't see the temporarily forgotten hatred for Ivan that sprang back full-blown as I remembered what had happened last night "We've re-arranged the septum back to the way it was, or at least the way we think it was. We looked at your license photo to see how your nose was, but you've obviously lost a lot of weight since then." I nodded, careful not to have my head fall off. She just assumed that the license picture was me. Thank God for small miracles. "We did the best we could. Your whole face is bruised, and you'll have to be very careful about the nose for a few weeks. Don't bump it or blow it hard or it will start to bleed again." I pulled my left arm out from under the sheet and touched the tip of my nose with my finger. I only felt gauze and a curiously numb tingle. Careful not to shake my head too hard, I nodded again.

"You've had some smoke and dust inhalation and the concussion. You've got bruises all over your body, but those are superficial."

"Even so," Blue chimed in, "They're going to hurt like hell for a while."

"But I'm alive," I whispered.

They fed me. Some kind of broth, and then some Jell-O, and then a cup of tea sweetened heavily with sugar. I tried to eat a saltine cracker, but it hurt too much to chew. "We'll give you more to eat tomorrow. You'll be hungry then." Rainbow took the tray away.

"Is there someone we can call? Is there anyone that you want to talk to?" Blue came back in with another clipboard. "Is there anyone who should know you survived?" She watched me as she held a pen in the air.

I tried to think. Who could I call? No one. I thought harder. Was there anyone who...? No. No one. I shook my head sadly and began to cry. She knelt at my side, giving me a Kleenex. "There's no one?"

"Only the people at Clausen and...." The tears rolled down my cheeks again. "I don't think they are still...Everyone is dead, I think. I...I... just came to the United States from, um, ah, Canada a few months ago. I don't know anyone in my apartment building except to say good morning to. I only know the people I worked with. Is there anyone else...here...I mean? Is anyone left alive from Clausen & Chase? Anybody at *all*?" My voice rose to a hysterical squeak. Was I hoping that there were some survivors, or was I hoping that they'd all died? I couldn't answer my own question.

"I'll check. People were taken to eight or ten hospitals. People are still being brought in and there are still many people trapped under the rubble. I don't know how long it will take to get them all out." I remembered that enormous pit of hellfire and flames and choking smoke. Surely no one could still be alive in the middle of that. "Everything is in a state of great confusion still." She had tears in her own eyes. "I can't believe what happened." She gestured to the television set hanging on the wall. "Do you understand the enormity of the devastation?"

"I saw...I saw the building fall down." I knuckled the tears from my eyes, thinking of how I planned to kill myself only a few hours ago. Was it only a few hours ago? I shut the door to my imagination. My nose was running and I tenderly dabbed it with the tissue. It hurt like crazy. Everything hurt like crazy, but I simply had to get through all of this. I felt like Scarlett O'Hara. I'd think about it all tomorrow. But not now.

"Do you remember how you got out?" Was this the trick question? "Do you want to tell me about it?"

"I was on the floor below where I work. I had...I needed to use the bathroom." I was thinking furiously, trying to explain plausibly, but not to say too much. She nodded, sympathetic. She didn't seem to be questioning anything that I said, only trying to understand what had happened. I continued, leaving out quite a bit. "I felt the explosion and was thrown onto the floor. There was another woman in the bathroom. She was killed right away." Blue bit her lip. "In an instant. The whole wall and the mirrors crushed her head. I saw her. She was lying on the floor and a pipe had burst and the water was mixing with her blood and it was gushing all over the floor." I tried to sit up. "She...she..." My agitation was palpable. "There was no way that I could help her." I pushed at the sheet, trying to get out of bed. It was obviously to them that I was getting upset.

She soothed me, pushing me gently back into the bed. She smoothed the sheets, her voice was gentle and sing-song, like a mother shushing a child. "Did you know her? The woman in the lavatory with you?"

I paused. "No." I drew the word out. "I'd seen her around the office, but I don't think...She wasn't anyone that I'd ever spoken to. I worked in Human Services. In the Pension Department. I think she might have worked in data storage or some other department. It was a big company. Hundreds of people worked there..." I hunched my shoulders. "I don't know her name. Poor pitiful thing."

Blue nodded sighing with compassion, satisfied and unsuspecting. "Then what happened?"

I told her that I managed to get to the street, about the debris, the endless flights of steps down, about the deafening noise of the build-ing, the fires, the creaks and groans of the metal structure. About the dead and the screaming and the man who jumped out of the window. I thought I wouldn't want to tell anyone those things, but I couldn't seem to stop. Blue held my hand and smoothed the bruised skin of my arm, listening and listening. Finally, I wound down, sobbing and hic-coughing, drained.

She stood up. "I'm going to give you a pill that will help you to sleep tonight." She turned to leave and then turned back. "And another one for the pain. You can have one every four hours. Doctor Merrill thinks you'll need them. And I agree."

"Who is Doctor Merrill? I thought you were the doctor?"

"Not me." She laughed. "I'm just the nurse. Doctor Merrill was the one wearing the teddy bear shirt. She wears the loudest scrubs in the hospital." I nodded, thinking that I wasn't so smart after all. "Brightens up the whole operating room."

"She's a surgeon?" I wanted to know.

"Trauma surgeon." Blue told me kindly. "Most people think she's a pediatrician." She rolled her eyes. "Goes to show you, doesn't it?"

"It certainly does," I glumly lay back.

"Do you want to watch the television, or would you rather not? It might be disturbing." She paused.

"Please put it on." I wanted to know what was happening. "I need to know if anyone I know survived." She nodded, as if I had just passed some kind of examination, and plugged the television on.

I watched, together with every person in the world. I saw the whole of the devastation. Each time they ran the endless shots of the first plane slamming into my building, my body jerked. It still didn't seem real to me. The way that plane plunged through tons of steel and con-crete, like a knife cutting through a stick of butter. And then the second plane, relentlessly swooping and aiming, and the collision. And the people…and the way the towers, one by one, collapsed like a stack of wooden blocks kicked by a small child. And the shivery thought that a group of human beings had planned this….and were willing to kill themselves and thousands and thousands of oth-ers…..ohgodohmygod. The television set flickered and the voices droned on, solemn and sad. Finally, dulled by the sleeping pill and the images, I slept.

In the morning, I was stupefied to discover that I had slept all night and had to be awakened by the morning staff. They told me that the doctors and nurses who stayed all day and night to care for the maimed, burned and broken bodies, had to be forced to go home and get some sleep.

"They wanted to stay and keep working. But, they were dead on their feet," my morning nurse told me. "Like the firemen and the rescue workers. They don't want to leave. They're all heroes. They have to be forced to go home, to eat and sleep, and then they can come back and search some more. They don't even want to do that. They say that they just can't go while there is a chance that maybe one person is still alive." She turned the television on again and sat on the foot of my bed while I ate my breakfast of cream of wheat, toast and a poached egg. We were both silent as we watched the awful news roll on and on. We learned that at least ten firemen who had gone in to help others escape had been killed themselves. A priest had been suffocated by falling debris when he went into the rubble to give Last Rites to the dying. When would the tragedies stop?

You'd think that I wouldn't have been able to eat, but the human body is a funny thing. I was surprised that I was so hungry, but I ate every bit on the tray and asked for a second cup of coffee and another piece of toast and butter.

"You're doing fine." She grinned and took my tray. "I think they might let you go home today."

"Really? I can go home?"

"I think so. You have a lot of boo-boo's, but nothing terminal." She turned at the door. "We can use the bed, as long as you're really OK, and we feel that you are really OK." She walked out and then, a moment later, stuck her head back in. "But don't think because we are sending you home that you're all cured. Not by a long stretch. You're going to have a few weeks of recovery. Especially with the concussion. Be a bit careful about your head. Try to take it easy. I'll be back with a little more food in a minute."

I watched as George Bush, Rudy Giuliani, Donald Rumsfeld, and George Pataki tried to fathom the horror and explain it to us. I saw news clips from most of the world leaders and then Tony Blair came on camera to assure the United States of his support. Tony Blair...I gasped and sat up suddenly, almost ignoring the stab of pain that pulsed through me. *Tony Blair*! From England! *England!* My mouth dropped. What a mistake I'd made! Tony Blair! Just *listen* to him! He spoke like an *Eng*lishman! Of course! I closed my eyes. An Englishman! "Damn!" I cursed my stupidity out loud. What a *huge* mistake I'd just made!

My head hurt as I tried to think. It was such an effort. I squinched my eyes shut and tried to concentrate. Vivian! From England! Shit! Had I ever actually spoken to Vivian? Had I heard her voice? I seemed to remember saying hello to her, but couldn't remember how she sounded. Did she have an English accent? Of· course, she had an English accent! She came from *Eng*land, didn't she? I hit myself in the head and yelped in pain. But hadn't Dean said she lived in Canada? Canada. A Canadian accent wouldn't be an accent like Tony Blair's, would it?...I tried hard to think of why she or I might not speak like Tony Blair...Uh, maybe she grew up in, um, Switzerland. Maybe her mother and father were in the diplomatic corps and she spoke American just like everyone else in Switzerland who might have gone to American schools. Or Canadian schools. Was that plausible? I groaned and lay back, gnawing on my bottom lip and wondering how I was going to rectify this little blooper of mine.

After a moment, I shrugged. What was done was done. With a little luck, I'd never see Doctor Teddy Bear again and perhaps Nurses Rainbow and Blue might not come on until nighttime. And from now on, I'd try to modify the way I spoke to give myself a little accent that might sound Canadian. Or English. Or whatever the heck Vivian had been.

I started right in. I'd need to practice. When the little nurse came back in with my coffee and toast, I made my first attempt. "Thanks awfully." I said, hoping that was the way an English person might graciously accept a bit more breakfast. As she left the room, I called out "Ta Ta", and then had to put the cup down on the table while my poor sore body jiggled with laughter at my idiotic acting.

Ah well, it would either pass muster or not.

My clothes came back to me in mid-morning. "They were awful. We was gonna throw them away," the brisk housekeeper told me. "But we thought we'd try to clean them up." She held up my blouse. "It came out OK, huh? Not beautiful," she rubbed at a stain that looked suspiciously like dried blood. "We did our best." She folded everything and put the pitiful bundle on a chair. "The shoes," she shrugged, "We don't have any idea of where they disappeared to."

"They look fabulous," I said in my new, slightly clipped voice. "I know you did your utmost". She patted the little pile. "Thanks awfully." I nodded, regal as the flipping Queen. She grinned and departed, hopefully thinking that I must have come right off of Piccadilly Circus. Or wherever.

The next hour brought some new visitors to my room. Two people who worked for the Red Cross and for some organization called Operation Relief Recovery. A tall, older man, dressed in impeccable clothing with a thin mustache and grey hair and a younger woman, crisp in a blue suit with a white ruffled blouse. They introduced themselves to me as Major Gerald Summers and Tracey O'Malley, and explained the roles that Operation Relief Recovery and the Red Cross would be taking in the upcoming days to help me and the other survivors and the families of those who had perished.

"Such a bloody tragedy." I knew that *bloody* was an English-type of swear word. "Is there news of survivors? Are you able to tell me if any of my friends or co-workers are alive? Was anyone able to get down in the lift?" I tried to make my A's broad and inject as much Brit as I could into my sentences.

They shook their heads, the two of them sorrowful. "We're compiling lists, but it's much too soon to know anything at all," Tracey told me, her shining dark hair swinging forward. "They're still bringing people out of the buildings. A lot of people haven't been able to talk, so we don't know who is where."

Major Summers harrumphed. "People are searching all of the hospitals looking for their loved ones." He smoothed the wings of his mustaches. "It will be weeks before everything is straightened out." He made another noise in his throat. "I don't know if…I mean, there may be some who are never found."

I prayed to myself that a certain Gianna St. Clare would never be found…or that her identification would quickly be found…or…what did I want? I tried a question. "Has there been any communication with the offices of Clausen & Chase?"

"There's really no one that we can talk to at this time." I could see that she was trying to be diplomatic. Offices? *What* offices? How the hell could anyone talk to someone at Clausen & Chase? Clausen & Chase had been blown to Kingdom Come. I blinked and thought of Zachary. I wished that he'd been a little nicer to me this morning.

"We're here to help you today with getting yourself home and settled." Major Summers pulled a sheaf of papers out. "We have clothing and shoes if you need them and I have authorization to give you emergency cash if you need it."

I told them that my clothes were "a bit careworn, but nonetheless wearable. " I'm not sure…I mean, I'm not certain about the shoes." I thought that "careworn" had a certain British panache and that "certain" sounded more English than "sure". This was going to be hard. "The housekeeper told me that my shoes have been misplaced."

Tracey went out to check on the status of my footwear and the Major and I talked about the events of the past twenty-four hours. Neither of us could believe it all. He told me that there had been a tremendous outpouring of generosity already from all over the nation. "People are calling and sending us money, food, clothes and offering shelter." He tugged at his collar. "I ..am...ahem... overwhelmed at the generosity and sympathy." Both of us had tears in our eyes.

"I'm so...lucky...fortunate...to be alive. I can't quite take it all in." He patted my arm and harrumphed that chance was a funny thing, wasn't it. What fickle fate put me in safety and obliterated all of my co-workers? What chance, indeed.

Tracey returned carrying a pair of Birkenstock-like sandals, a small pile of new underwear, and a few packets of pantyhose. "Your shoes have gone. Who knows where. I got these," she held up the sandals, shrugging. "They can be easily adjusted and at least you can get home in them." She put the sandals on the floor. "I think we can get you decently covered until you can get back home. I think I got your size OK." She pulled the panties out and held them up for inspection. Major Summers harrumphed again and turned his back on us, walking over to the window in a show of embarrassment. Tracey winked at me and bustled around, examining my skirt and blouse. "They look acceptable. At least until you can get home and change into something clean and comfortable." I thought of the mess at Vivian's. There was no way in Mesopotamia that I would put any of her clothes on me.

"We'll have some kind of a coat here in an hour. They tell me you can go home in a cab after lunch. The doctor will be here to see you and then we'll arrange for the cab." She peered at me. "Do you think you can manage at home?"

I thought about the messy apartment and nodded emphatically. "I'll be fine. Can the cab stop at the grocery store for while I pick up a few things? Um, tea and crumpets and um, Bovril." I sounded slightly demented, even to myself.

She smiled at me, a genuine smile. "You can do anything you want with the cab. Keep it as long as you need it. It's already been paid for." She peered worriedly at me. "You say you have enough money?" I nodded. "Are you sure?"

"I have enough. I just ...um...cashed a check."

"Well," she looked doubtful. "If you're sure? All right. If you need anything at all, call me or the Major. Here's my card and another one with the major's number. If we're not there, just leave a message and someone will get right back to you. I mean it, Vivian. Money, household help, rent money, electric bills, whatever. We don't know what will happen with your job. I don't know when you might get paid…if ever." My eyes widened. I hadn't really thought of the practical implications of having your livelihood blasted out of existence. Literally. "The Red Cross is here to assist you and Major Summers and the people at Operation Relief Recovery have the funds to keep you functioning until there is some normality in your life." The thought of cleaning Vivian's pigsty almost made me beg her to send me a team of cleaning people, but, after a nanosecond, I knew I couldn't have anyone connected to the Red Cross see that place as it was now.

"Perhaps after a few days, when I've rested and feel more, um, like myself, I'll think of something I need. I just can't fathom anything this moment." I thought that "fathom" had that British ring. I knew I needed some help with this British stuff. First, I needed a British dictionary or something like that immediately if I was going to get myself through this deception.

Tracey dipped her head. "Be sure to keep any and all receipts for anything you buy. You'll be compensated for anything you need to purchase. I'll be calling *you* tomorrow. I want to be sure that you all right." The Major finished looking out of the window and returned to my bed. I thanked them both with sincerity. Who knew what I might need in the near future? Or what friends, even people as remotely connected to me as the Major and Tracey.

"We are the lucky ones," the Major confided. "Operation Relief Recovery is the practical side of the help offered. Our job is relatively easy and our clients are usually grateful." I nodded. *I* certainly was grateful. "There are teams of Red Cross administrators whose job it is to visit the homes of those who perished." He bowed his head. "Imagine the sadness in trying to help a widow with six children, or a bereaved husband left with a baby."

Ivan. Someone like this would be visiting Ivan. Telling him about my death and asking him if he wanted money. I blinked at the vision and had to will myself back to say good-bye to Tracey and her Major.

I fell back on the bed. Son of a gun! Ivan would be a widower! I closed my eyes in pain at the thought. Would he be sorry that I died? Would he be bereaved? I snorted at the thought. Ivan would be in hog heaven. He'd play this to the hilt. The role of a sad, mournful husband, left to manage all alone. I laughed aloud! Ivan would eat it up! What a great opportunity I was giving him! Ivan, who lost his thirteenth job last month. Ivan, who couldn't get past the afternoon without getting drunk. Poor Ivan! Poor Ivan indeed!

My marital musings were interrupted. A new doctor, a young man this time, with the name "Geoffrey Geiger, MD", pinned to his shirt appeared. His gift to me was a handful of small plastic vials filled with pills. Pills for the pain, pills to help me sleep, pills to keep infections at bay, pills to keep my lungs clear…lots of pills. Dr. Geiger gave me instructions, gave me copies to prescription refills, made sure that I understood the dangers of taking too many pills at once, and wished me good luck. I awkwardly signed a release form. I guess I was free now.

Another nurse came in and helped me to dress. I was amazed at how weak and shaky I felt, and was grateful for the assistance. It was difficult to lift my arms into the blouse, and I never would have been able to manage the ill-fitting bra and panty hose without her. She brought me a used navy blue duffel coat to wear home. Evidentially, my gauzy scarf and suit jacket didn't make it out of the laundry. I thought I would be able to walk out, but they forced me to use a wheelchair, and I acquiesced, saving my small store of strength for the ordeal of making Vivian's apartment habitable.

My cabby this time was a woman; a large, Black, lovely lady named Zandra. She wore a bright turban on her head and sported a crazily patterned jacket. Her face was kind and sympathetic. Her practical advice was helpful. "Relief Recovery is payin' me, dearie. You need some food shoppin'? Some clothes? Where you wanna go first?"

We settled for a small grocery store on Lexington where I bought milk, bread, peanut butter, butter, eggs, tea and coffee, cleaning supplies, soap and three other bags of groceries. Zandra went in with me, helped me to shop, and carried all the bags out. "You kin pay me extra if you want," she said. I agreed. She looked strong and I thought about what else she might be able to assist me with.

Our second stop was at Bloomingdale's, where we valet-parked the cab, a new experience for Zandra. I used one of Vivian's checks, apologizing about the way I wrote the check and signed my name. The clerk was so horrified upon hearing about my ordeal that she wouldn't have noticed if I'd written the check in Sanskrit. We bought two bath towels, two face cloths, four dishtowels, a bathmat, shower curtain, shampoo and cosmetics, two feather pillows, a navy blue Ralph Lauren blanket and a set of pink striped sheets and pillowcases. Zandra was enjoying herself immensely and insisted on toting all of the new possessions. "Now to the clothing department. I need one or two things."

We emerged to our cab laden with several sets of underwear for me, a fleece pullover, two new nighties, a robe, three pair of slacks and four sweaters. I had discarded the rags in which I had left the hospital and was dressed, head to toe, in new, clean clothing. On my feet were a pair of brown tasseled loafers. I left the Birkenstocks in the dressing room together with the other used clothing. Oh yes, and we bought a new dress and a peach colored slip for Zandra. What fun! Bloomingdale's was delivering three more pairs of shoes, a topcoat, a raincoat and a bevy of socks and panty hose tomorrow afternoon. There was only so much we could carry, after all.

The last stop was at the Barnes & Noble store. I quickly found a copy of a dandy item called "*British, A to Zed*". The book translated words like *truck* and *apartment* to words like *lorry* and *flat*. I'd have to really study if this deceit was to pass muster.

As we parked outside the apartment, I put a proposition to Zandra. "Do you want to make five hundred dollars this afternoon?" She goggled. "I was away for a few weeks before all of this happened. One of my old college friends needed a place to stay. She turned the place into a filthy mess. I meant to clean it yesterday, but I don't think after what happened that I can manage to do it myself. I just don't feel well enough."

"I can clean anything for five hundred dollars," she assured me stoutly.

"Wait until you see it," I said dryly. "You might want more."

She didn't want more, although I often wonder what she really thought about it all. She did all the cleaning while I picked up all the clothing, shoes, make up, and what not and packed it all away in big, black, plastic bags. I wanted to go through it all again in the next few days, to be sure that I wasn't throwing away anything that might help me out in the future. Zandra cheerfully accepted a gift of the dirty sheets, towels and pillowcases. "I kin wash em when I get home. Ain't nothin' wrong that hot water and soap won't fix."

"Good luck." I wished her.

At nine PM, the apartment looked pretty good, and I was swaying on my feet with exhaustion and pain. Not that I had done much in the way of work, you understand. Zandra had scrubbed and cleaned in yeoman fashion. I gave her six hundred bucks and my fervent thanks. She took the money and tucked it into her pocket. "Your friend," her broad face was expressive, "Some pig." I agreed. She tsked dolefully. I kissed her cheek and she drove off, both of us delighted with our bargains.

I checked the telephone answering machine. No one had called. No one had left any messages. No one, at least up to now, was wondering where Vivian Ann Morrison was. I was thankful.

Aching in every joint, barely able to function, I slid my battered but clean body into the freshly-made bed and lay back on the soft, new pillows. I took a pain pill, an antibiotic, a muscle relaxer and a sleeping pill and tried to think of what Ivan was doing now. I wondered if he'd give me an opulent funeral. In three minutes, I was in dreamland.

The shrilling of the telephone woke me. The room was in darkness and I stumbled, whacking my knee against a table, as I tried to answer it. Frantically, I grabbed at the receiver, trying to think of what to say.

"Uh, hello. Um, hullo." Hullo sounded a little more British. There was no sound from the other end, although I could hear someone breathing, a stillness and then a snuffle…someone was there. "Hullo? Hullo?" There was a click, as my unknown…I mean Vivian's unknown caller hung up. I replaced the receiver and noticed the thumping of my heart. Who the hell was calling her? Any why had they hung up? Was there some secret code that Vivian used when she answered the telephone? Or was it a friendly telemarketer? Nah, much too late.

I was thirsty and my mouth was dry and furred with the residue of all the pills I'd taken. I shuffled to the kitchen and took a Coke out of the refrigerator. I held the cold can up to me forehead and then rolled it, tracing a path of chill, back and forth. Ahhh. I popped the top and took a cold, fizzy sip. Much better. I swished another mouthful and rolled the Coke around in my mouth before I swallowed it.

I took stock. My entire body hurt, my legs, my face, my head, my hands, my ears. What time was it anyway? I glanced around. There was no bedside clock. How the heck had Vivian known what time it was? I went back into the kitchen and saw a wall clock. Three thirty in the morning. Who called me? Definitely not a telemarketer. "I'll get a clock tomorrow," I mumbled aloud and then the telephone began to ring again. I grabbed at it. "Hullo?"

This time, the click came right away. I held the receiver in my hand and stared at it, too worn out to be worried and frightened.

CHAPTER SEVEN

I awoke, sweaty and miserable, jolted again by the telephone. I grabbed it, every movement of my body hurting like hell. "Hullo?"

"Ms. Morrison? Vivian?" A man's voice, deep and professional-sounding…no one that I had ever spoken to before. Was he calling *me*, or was he calling Vivian?

"Yes. I mean, yes, that's me. I am Vivian." I made myself sound as British as possible.

"I hope I didn't wake you. This is Oliver Church." Who? I squinted into the phone and sat up carefully. "Oliver Church. " It was as if he'd heard me thinking. "I'm with Operation Relief Recovery. A nephew and co-worker of Major Summers. Is this a bad time to call?"

"No. No." I babbled, so relieved that it wasn't Vivian's best friend, or lover, or whoever called last night. "I'm just getting up." I eased my aching body out of the bed and padded barefoot into the bathroom.

He laughed, this Oliver Church. Again, a deep and infectious sound. "Good. How are you doing today? Feeling any better?" His voice was delicious, and I smiled into the receiver.

With the grin still on my face, I cautiously lowered myself onto the toilet. "Better than what?"

He laughed again, such a nice laugh. I got my scrambled mind into order. "Much better, thank you. Much better than yesterday, I suppose. I…I had a bad night. Didn't sleep too well…I'm feeling rather dreadful. Uh, my flat was rather noisy. Um, the lorries and the traffic kept me awake…"

His concern flowed through the receiver along with his velvety voice. "I'm so sorry, Ms. Morrison. Or can I call you Vivian?"

He could call me that, you bet. As a matter of fact, wasn't that what this was all about? I tried to stop a giggle, but it bubbled out. "Certainly, Mr. Church. You all have been so decent to me; you could call me anything you liked." Except Gianna St. Clare, that is. I stuck the receiver under my chin and tried to wash my mouth out. I felt sweaty and clammy and a little nauseous.

"Oh, please, my dear. Call me Oliver. As we are going to be colleagues, we should be on a first name basis."

"Colleagues?" And what was this my dear stuff?

"You are on the top of my list," he explained, and then he actually burst into a few verses of an old Cole Porter tune, "You're the top, you're the Coliseum...da de dah, dah de dah da deum.." He laughed, this man with the voice and the bubbly personality. "I'm going to be your counselor, to help you through this ordeal." As I gulped down two Super Excedrin's, he told me a bit more about his organization. It had been founded by Oliver's Uncle Gerald, Major Gerald Summers, a former war hero, to assist those who were victims of disasters. "We're the social workers who take over after the Red Cross has ministered to some of your needs. We'll be working with the families of some of the people who died in this tragedy, as well as working with those like yourself who somehow managed to survive."

As he spoke, I took courage and looked into the bathroom mirror. A wild red-headed stranger looked back. She looked dreadful, whoever she was. Her face was puffy and her nose was bandaged. Her cheek, forehead and chin were blistered with black and blue splotches and her disheveled red hair stuck out in an electrical-shock fashion. Was this me?

Mr. Church...Oliver...my new best friend...talked on. "I'd like to set up an appointment today with you, if possible. We'd like to get you checked over by one of our own doctors once more, just to make sure that you're as good as we hope you'll be." I found to my dismay that I was crying. Oliver paused, perceptive. "Are you crying, my dear? Are you OK?"

I snuffled and wiped my face. Everything felt tender and bruised. Hell, everything *was* tender and bruised. "I'm bearing up." There, that certainly sounded pip-pip. "It's just a bit overwhelming."

"Try not to worry. We're here to care for you."

I felt a bit better and warmed by his kindness and concern, limped into the kitchen and poured myself a glass of orange juice.

"Here's what I want you to do," he continued. "Let's make an appointment...say eleven this morning?"

"That's fine, uh, first rate, uh, with me."

"Good. I have your address listed as ......" I rummaged among the groceries we had bought yesterday and located a bag of coffee. I brought out the Mr. Coffee machine and noted that Zandra had scrubbed it well. Shit! I'd forgotten about filters. I rummaged through the cabinets and listened to Oliver's soothing voice as he outlined our morning's activities. He needed my driver's license or some other form of identification, my pay stubs, information as to my financial needs. My rent information, my utility bills, insurance information and a few other things. I wrote down all he said and prayed that I would find all of these things somewhere in Vivian's desk. The orange juice made my throat feel better. I presumed that the Excedrin's were finally getting into my bloodstream. Somehow, I would face the day.

I washed up, finding myself singing "...You're the Louvre Museee-um..." It was nice to be awakened by such a cheerful call. Heck, I felt so cheerful that even my bruises seemed less lurid.

However, amid all this early morning upbeat gaiety, I turned on the television and was again assaulted by the carnage shown over and over again. I felt sick once more and astonished and humbled at the peculiar circumstances that had me sitting in the apartment of a total stranger, alive, while almost everyone I knew had been burned to ashes. I couldn't watch or listen any more.

The telephone rang again. I stiffened and looked at it with anxiety. Would it be my mysterious caller again? Or some lesbian friend of Vivian's? Gingerly, I said my standard opening, "Hullo?"

"Good morning, Vivian. I hope I haven't waked you."

"Uh, no. Good morning." A woman's voice...

"This is Tracey. Tracey O'Malley from the Red Cross." Whew. Tracey! Relief flowed through me. "How are you feeling today? A bit better?"

"A bit, Tracey. Thank you awf'lly for inquiring." Veddy veddy British, I thought.

"Marvelous. I understand that Oliver Church has called you and you two will be meeting today, right?"

"Yes, Tracey, he's rung me up. We've booked an appointment for later this morning."

We chatted for a moment. She told me that there had been hundreds and hundreds of injured people at the hospital. Some, like myself, with minor injuries, and some who would never make it.

"We've been very busy. Trying to put families together, trying to find a lost daughter, a sister, a dad. Some of the situations are pitiful." She sighed. "However, you, Vivian, are one of the good parts. Your name gets a star." I could feel her grin through the telephone wires. "We're going to discharge you from the Red Cross and move your case from our files to those of Operation Relief Recovery, but if you need us for anything, please let me know." I assured her that I would, we exchanged goodbyes and mutual comments of sorrow at the plight of the more-injured victims.

I needed some coffee. I thought I remembered a restaurant on the corner of Second Avenue. But first, I gingerly took a sponge bath, ouching and oohing as I lowered myself into the warm, soapy water. My entire body was covered with black and blue patches, scratches and bruises. No wonder I felt so horrible. I dressed in my new clothes, again ouching and groaning as I managed to put on a bra and get a tee shirt over my head. Stupid woman that I was, I should have realized that I needed a shirt that buttoned up the front so I didn't have to struggle so hard to pull the thing over my head. Nonetheless, I finally was dressed.

There wasn't much I could do about my face. No make up could disguise it. I looked like death warmed over. I managed to gather my new bushy hair into a loose bun and when I put my red-rimmed glasses on, no one, not even my beloved, ha ha, Ivan would *ever* recognize Gianna St. Clare from the visage that stared back at me. So much the better, I supposed.

I made the bed and straightened up the room as best I could, putting everything new away, hiding the fact that all my clothing was bought yesterday. Methodically, I looked through Vivian's desk, finding her sheaf of paperwork from C & C, including her insurance information and the paperwork that showed that her paycheck had been electronically deposited into her checking account. Another file held her lease and rent receipts, another, her monthly bills. I gathered these things up in a pile for the velvet-voiced Oliver.

I put on a pair of the kitchen rubber gloves that Zandra had used for cleaning (what was I afraid of finding? Cockroaches? Germs? The ever-possible dildo?) and went through the trash bags that were filled with Vivian's clothing. Ugh. Ugly stuff. How could anyone wear such...yuk!...homely, utilitarian stuff? And the shoes! She must have had the biggest, broadest feet in the entire United Kingdom! I patted and searched through every item, turning out the pockets of the heavy pants and shirts and clunky, masculine footwear that she seemed to favor. If she had any lesbian love life at all, she certainly was the butch in the relationship. Even her belts were embellished with chrome studs. I wondered for a moment, if possibly she had a motorcycle stashed away downstairs somewhere. This Vivian was weird! But there was nothing to really give me any clues to her inner self. Other than three matchbooks, a quarter, and a New York Lottery scratch ticket...a loser...there was nothing. I bagged everything up and piled the bags in the hallway. While I was doing this, one of the tenants from an upstairs apartment came down the steps. He was an older man, wearing a grey fedora-type hat and clad in a blue woolen overcoat. He was stooped and heavy-set. He looked foreign, maybe Jewish or middle European. I smiled at him and wished him a good morning, praying that he hadn't known or ever spoken to Vivian. He touched the brim of his hat and muttered good day. I scuttled back into the apartment, grinning to myself. New York. What a wonderful place. No one knows anyone else.

The kitchen clock said nine-thirty. Good, that gave me some time. The apartment looked neat and all of my purchases had been put away. Ooops, almost all! I gasped and grabbed my "*A to Zed*" and hid it under my pillow. In my eagerness to leave nothing that might give my deception away, I checked the bookcase and Vivian's music collection. Funny taste. Most of the cassettes were of bands or groups that I had never heard of. Heavy metal stuff. Maybe they were British groups. I shrugged. Whatever. There was an automotive magazine on the bookcase and a two-week old copy of Newsweek. Nothing else. No books, no photographs, no personal items. Only a big ashtray filled with corks and beer caps. I got out another trash bag and threw out all of the cassettes and the automotive magazine, the corks and debris in the ashtray, and three bright red lipsticks, some thick, sludgy foundation cream, four razor blades, a tube of hair goo and a hairbrush…ugh!… that had escaped my eagle eye the day before. I tied the bag up, got my fanny pack and went downstairs to find a newspaper and everybody's early morning buddy, a cuppa joe.

The day was a grey one, dreary and overcast. I wondered if the haze overhead was still part of the debris, blown by the wind, left over from the building crashing down. People on the street looked weary and frightened and hurried along, not meeting anyone else's eye. Ah well, this was New York. Still, it was different today. I could sense a menace lurking in the very air.

At the corner of Second and 73rd, I saw the welcoming steamed-up windows of Bernie's Delicatessen. I opened the heavy glass door and was assailed by the smell of bacon and coffee. The place was half-filled and most patrons were watching the TV set that was bolted to the wall or reading a newspaper. I picked up The New York Times,

The Post, and a copy of The Wall Street Journal, ordered the world's largest coffee, bacon, toast and two eggs over medium at the counter in my best British accent, and sat at an empty table.

The man who had taken my order was eyeing me in a wondering fashion. Was that because he knew Vivian and was trying to figure out who I was? Or was he just stunned by the poetry of my black and blue face? I shrugged and buried myself in the papers.

The waitress, heavy-set and about forty years old, with "Anita" written on her nametag brought my breakfast to the table. "Geez, honey," she offered. "What the hell happened to you?"

"I...I, um, was in..." I gestured helplessly at the TV.

She sucked in her breath. "No shit! Ohmygawd, are you OK?" I nodded, a bit wary. Had she known Vivian? "Geez," she breathed out. "I think I recognize you...that red hair and glasses." I shuddered in fear... "Ain't you the limey woman? I seen you here before."

She *recognized* me! Glory be to the Father, Son and Holy Ghost! She *recognized* me! I picked up my fork, trying to still my heart's tattoo. "Yes," I gulped. "I, uh, live in the flat..." I gestured out towards the street, thanking the red hair and the glasses, Anita's simple gullibility and the realization that people saw what they expected to see. "What *hap*pened?" She pulled out a chair and sat down. "I mean, I hope you don' mind me askin', but, ohmygawd..."

I dipped my toast into the warm yolk and chewed. It felt wonderful, sliding down my throat, buttery and smooth. I smiled at Anita, my new best friend who *recognized* me. "It was awful. The lift wasn't working. I managed to find a staircase and climb down. Then, when I got outside, I was hit by flying debris and was taken to hospital." I remembered, perhaps from some Agatha Christie novel, that Brits said "to hospital" and not "to *the* hospital" as Americans would. Anita gasped and put her hand gently on my arm. Her face expressed nothing but kind wonderment.

"Hey, Nita!" The man behind the counter yelled. Anita waved at him and patted me again as she got up.

"I'm comin', Bernie. Hold your horses." And to me, "You rest here, um...Don't rush. Take it easy. Thank God you're OK. Um, I don't remember your name..."

"Vivian Ann," I said, with a firm nod. "Vivian Ann Morrison."

I found I was ravenous and finished the platter, wiping the vestiges of egg with the last piece of toast. I looked up to find that Anita had spread the news and I was the subject of every customer's interest. I smiled, wan and tremulous, acknowledging their sympathy and most everyone smiled back, saluting my ordeal. I noticed two men at the table near the window. One was thin and bald; the other was tall, muscular and exotic-looking. The muscular one held his coffee mug up to me in a silent salute. I ducked my head and gathered my papers, leaving Anita a five dollar tip.

She had been worth it to me.

As the man behind the counter (I guess he was Bernie) made change for me, I wandered to the magazine rack and chose a Time, a new Newsweek, and a Good Housekeeping magazine. I browsed through their small stock of paperbacks and picked up two mystery books. As I turned to pay for them, I was aware of someone behind me.

"You were in the Towers?" It was the muscular man. I turned. He was big, maybe 6 foot four or five with an almost oriental face. Sort of Hawaiian-looking; slanting, dark eyes and jutting cheekbones. Handsome son-of-a-gun. He was dressed in jeans and a Yankees jacket and the jacket strained over his well-built shoulders. Behind him, his thin companion still sat at the table, watching us.

"Yes. It was awful." I smiled, and it came out a sad one. He nodded with some kind of understanding.

"Yeah, we," he thumbed back to his thin friend, "were down there for two days and two nights."

"Down there?"

"Yeah, we're New York City cops. Narcotic detectives." My mouth made a big "O". "We've been working straight out doing what we could. Trying to get people out." I noticed now that his face looked lined and tired and that his slanted eyes looked weary. He stuck his hand out and I juggled magazines to take it. We grasped hands and his touch was warm and solid. "My name is Kenji. Kenji Hutchinson." His paw engulfed mine.

"I'm Vivian... Vivian Ann Morrison." His face was definitely foreign. Dark-complected, with white, even teeth. Muscular and testosterone-filled body, with thick, slightly wavy hair cut short and brushed up into a sort of longish crew cut. Devastating, like some exotic animal. A panther, dark and sleek and dangerous. I stopped myself from staring and gathered what was left of my wits around me.

"How...how bad is it down there? It was just...like hell, I think, when I was taken away." His eyes took in my bruises. "I don't remember too much. I was in hospital and just came home."

He was somber. "It *is* like hell."

"Are you two all right? Tell me…"

He shrugged and again I was mesmerized by the movement of his shoulders. "Hard to explain, Vivian Ann Morrison." He grinned and looked embarrassed as we both realized that our hands were still clasped together. We jumped apart and dropped hands. Under all my black and blue skin, I could feel another color…a red blush, staining my cheeks. He…Kenji…seemed a little uncomfortable too. Could it be that he might find me attractive? Bruises and bandages and bushy hair and all? Or did he simply feel sorry for a person who was as beaten up as I was?

His thin-faced friend joined us. "Oh, Lenny. Um, this is Vivian Ann, uh, Vivian Ann Morrison, did you say?" I nodded. "This is Lenny." Lenny and I nodded at one another. "Uh, we gotta go now."

My eyes asked if they were going back to the disaster area and they both nodded. "We gotta do what we can…you know, every minute, you could save somebody, you know…"

"Thank you," I touched each of them. "Thank you for this." I didn't mean to start crying again, but…well, I just started to sob.

The eyes of every customer in Bernie's eagerly watched. Such a story they'd have to tell… "Yeah, she was one of the survivors! Honest. She was all banged up and she met these other two guys, cops…they were going back down. Yeah, I remember her from the neighborhood…Man, can you imagine? She crawled out of the building. She looked like a truck ran over her. She was crying. It was heartbreaking, ya know."

Lorry, my mind corrected their imaginary conversations. She looked like a lorry ran over her.

"Hey, hey," Kenji put his arm around me. Anita came over to us.

"You go home now, Vivian Ann, sweetheart. Get some rest." Anita patted my hand and gave me a paper bag. "There's a toasted bagel in here for you from us," she waved towards the counterman. His beefy face broke in two and he smiled at me with a wave of his spatula. "You eat it later with a nice cuppa tea. I know you English people love your tea."

Again, I grabbed at her lead. "Thanks awfully, Anita. A cuppa is simply tip-top."

"Can we see you home?" Kenji and Lenny asked. I nodded, why not? I craved companionship. Like every other American, the tragedy seemed to have brought all of us together with some new appreciation of humanity.

The two men escorted me across the street and to the doorway of my apartment. We all shook hands, instant friends in this tragedy. "Take care of yourselves, please," I urged them. "Be careful."

They joked for a moment, downplaying the danger, but we all knew how serious this horrid thing was. "We'll see you tomorrow morning, OK?" Kenji stopped down and kissed the side of my cheek. "We'll be at our regular table and we'll save you a seat." I nodded, overcome with emotions.

"Rest easy, Vivian Ann," Lenny waved to me, his face serious. Kenji just looked at me, smiled a sort of lopsided smile, and turned away.

I stood there, watching them, as they hailed a cab and went back to the inferno.

CHAPTER EIGHT

M using at the amazing twists and turns already happening in my new life, I climbed the stairs to 2A. I passed yet another neighbor, a thin, kerchiefed older woman. She gave me a stiff nod, and I smiled at her and wished her good morning. She looked a bit startled. Was it because I spoke to her, or because I looked like scrambled eggs three days old?

I checked the phone as soon as I got in. No calls. I tried to think. What was I going to say if and when some real-Vivian's friend -person called? I'd try to mumble my voice, make a big thing of the disaster and plead that my concussion had left me without much in the way of memory. What the heck else could I do?

I scattered the magazines and books around, trying to make the little apartment look as if I'd lived there for eternity. "There," I said out loud and sat down to scan the newspapers. The entire half of each paper featured nothing but the disaster. I read for ten minutes. It was nearly time for my visit from velvet-voiced Oliver Church. Almost on cue, the buzzer rang and I opened the door to the second gorgeous man that I was destined to meet this morning.

He was tall, with that kind of thick, straight blond hair that goes with expensive prep schools and old time money. He wore knife-pressed chinos, tasseled loafers that gleamed, a navy blue belt with embroidered sailboats skimming around, a blue and white checked button-down shirt, and a wide, toothpaste-ad smile. "Hullo," I mumbled. "Top of the morning."

His blue eyes crinkled. Lord, the man was beautiful. "Hi, Vivian Ann Morrison." His laugh tumbled out. "You've got to be Vivian. Your poor, sweet face…" His finger traced a hot little path down the side of my cheek. I didn't mean to, but I gasped and stood aside, ushering him in. Could I fall in love twice in one day? I felt sweaty and hot and bashful. What was *happening* to me?

He took in every item at a glance. Thank God for Zandra and her cleaning. I sucked in my breath and gathered my wits about me as best I could. "How are you managing?"

"Oh, moderately well." I mentally kicked myself for the Irish Top O' The Morning goof. "Can I get you a cup of tea?"

"No, thank you. I figured that we'd do the paperwork stuff here and then we'd go out and grab some lunch." I nodded, like some puppet and sat on the freshly-made daybed. "OK?" The puppet wagged its head in agreement. "Good. Business first, and then some relaxation and getting to know one another." I felt hot and then cold and then hot again. He was so good-looking!

He plopped on the canvas chair and opened his briefcase on the coffee table. The briefcase matched his shoes. Supple, shiny expensive chestnut-colored leather. Again, everything gorgeous, just like the owner. I pulled the pile of papers that I had gathered together and he began the interview.

It went well. The questions were easy. Name, address, telephone. Social Security Card, Naturalization Papers, License, Insurance Documents. Rent receipts, telephone bills, electric bills, cable TV receipts. He put them all in a file folder and promised "I'll have these copied today and get your originals right back to you." Again, I nodded. "Now, what do you think you spend a week on groceries? Two hundred? More?"

My face must have shown my confusion. "Two hundred?" Two hundred? Would a single woman spend two hundred dollars on groceries? Mentally I went back to life with Ivan for comparison. Ivan had always handled all the money in the family, taking every cent I made and giving me an allowance of seventy bucks a week for transportation and lunches. When I needed groceries, he'd give me a hundred or two. If I were single and living in expensive Manhattan, what would I be spending? I badly wanted to give the right answer, and so I shrugged.

"Um, I guess."

He touched my arm. "No big deal. Let's say three hundred. This is an expensive city."

He wrote something on his pad. "Now, how about incidentals? Cosmetics, medical supplies, cleaning things?" Again, I was flummoxed.

Again, he helped me out. "We'll put down another two hundred for those things."

"All right," I was subdued. "It, um, hurts to try to think. I, ah, have a bit of a headache…"

His smile could melt the Polar Cap. "Take it slowly. There's no rush, and if you can't remember something, we'll just let it ride and get back to it another time." His eyes crinkled and I almost swooned at the thought that, yes indeed, there would be another time. "OK. And transportation costs? Taxis. That kind of thing?" I looked dazed and he frowned. "Don't worry about it. I'll just estimate here." He wrote down another two hundred dollar notation, then looked up and smiled. The man had a dynamite smile. Could he hear the excited thumping of my heart? The heart that had been yearning for Zachary just a day or so ago? I guess he couldn't hear, as he asked me, "And incidentals?"

Incidentals. What else could be left? I presume I looked even more puzzled as he gave me the benefit of that warm, intimate laugh and counted on his fingers: "Entertainment. Going to the movies or a show. Clothes. I know you lost what you were wearing on the eleventh. Beer and wine and such. Dinners out. Lunches. Little things that you might need, like oh, perhaps a new saucepan." We both chuckled and my nervousness began to subside. "Who knows? A pedicure. Girl stuff."

"I do need a new bedside clock," I ventured and he wrote it down. Could I fall in love so quickly with a handsome man who was prepared to give me my every wish? A clock? A pedicure? All the groceries I might ever want? Perhaps. Perhaps.

"Good. I think we'll put three hundred down and make your weekly stipend an even thousand dollars. Plus your rent and utilities…um, let's say another thou…no, maybe twelve hundred more…" He wrote busily while I gawped, amazed at the way this kind of thing went.

"Is this the way this sort of thing goes?" I had to ask.

He finished writing out the form, signed it and tore out the carbon copy. "Actually, Vivian Ann Morrison, this is our first brush with this kind of disaster. Usually, we're doing a family that has been burned out of their apartment, or flood victims, or survivors of a famine in Ethiopia. This flying of airplanes into buildings is rather new for us." His handsome face was thoughtful. "I'm sort of treading water until I get a better feel for it all."

"Oh," I said, my voice small and meek.

He then took a checkbook out of his briefcase and uncapped his gold pen. I knew he'd have a gold pen for this sort of thing. This man had solid gold everything. He looked up at me. "How about, instead of giving you a check, that I just give you the cash? Would that be easier?" I thought about a check. Payment to Vivian Ann Morrison. To me. One more piece of confirmation.

Then I realized that I didn't have the faintest idea of where my, um, Vivian's…bank might be. I didn't want to get into a corner, so I agreed that, certainly, cash would be just jim-dandy. "Do you always carry, um, that much money with you?"

The velvet laugh spewed again and once more, my traitorous heart beat a little faster. What kind of a woman was I? Ivan left in the past, Zachary dead only a few days, and here I was, blushing and stammering like a school-girl over this handsome specimen in my apartment, um, I mean my flat. The handsome specimen answered me. "In some case, yes. I have a lot of clients who don't have bank accounts."

"I do have an account," My voice was stiff.

"Naturally. But I have the money here, so why don't I just give it to you." Naturally, what else? He reached into the briefcase again and pulled out a soft leather case. It was stuffed with cash. Big bills, little bills, lots and lots and lots of moolah. He counted out two thousand, two hundred dollars and handed it to me. It was heavy in my hand. All those bills. I took two hundred and put it into my waist pack. The other two thousand, I put into the top drawer of the desk. "I'd rather you had a little too much money than not enough." A good philosophy, I agreed.

"When we find out if you are ever going to get a paycheck and what will happen to your insurance benefits and such, we'll do a re-evaluation." He stood up, looming over me.

"Enough of all this paperwork. Let's get out of here and grab some lunch. Then, I'm going to drop you off at the office of the doctor that works with us." He saw the alarm in my eyes. "Just a simple check-up. We want to be sure that you are on the way to recovery. Major Summers was a little worried about your concussion." I touched the side of my head with my hand and blinked. "Are you up to all this?"

"I'm…I'm fine. My head hurts a little and I felt a bit dizzy this morning when I tried to remember all that happened." My mind was churning. I wanted to set up, just in case, a scenario that might cover any questions that I couldn't answer, whatever they might be. Perhaps the doctor might not be as nice. Perhaps he might see under my façade and try to expose me as the charlatan that I was. Liar, Liar, Pants on Fire.

Oliver's face showed concern. "Don't you feel well? Are you dizzy now?"

"N..no. I'm fine, but…When I try to think of what happened, I can't seem to quite remember. It's as if I'm looking back and there's a curtain over my memory. I can't even think back…I mean, I was trying to think of the names of my co-workers…I can't really think of them. I remember some names, but others are a complete blank."

"That's natural, Vivian Ann. Lots of people who are in very traumatic situations sort of shut down. It's a form of mental self-

preservation. You can't manage what happened, so you shut it out."
Again he touched my arm in a solicitous way. "You should tell Dr.
Giggi about it."

"Dr. Giggi?"

"He's the man you'll be seeing today. He's an expert in trauma.
He'll make you feel a lot better." He stood up, looming over me.
Hmmm, how many men would there be today who loomed? "Come
on, let's get you something to eat."

We went to the 21 Club. Oh frabjous joy and expense! I'd never in
my wildest dreams thought I'd ever eat there. I tried to be blasé, but I
know that Oliver could sense my excitement. Perhaps that's why he
took me there. It truly was a spiffy place. Black wrought iron façade
and all those cute little jockey-men dressed in differently colored racing silks lining the steps. Soooo upper class New York. I was certainly
awed.

Oliver, naturally, was familiar with the maitre d' and the two of
them made tsk-tasking noises about the tragedy. He, the maitre d',
handed us to a waiter who ushered us into the room. There, we were
met with a phalanx of other waiters. With the kind of reverence that
only a snooty waiter can give, if they want to, the waiters practically
carried us to a corner table. I looked around. Even today, a few days
after the worst disaster to happen in the history of New York and while
the horror was still strong with us, the restaurant was filled to capacity
with well-heeled and hungry patrons. .When I peeked at the menu, I
had a hard time not to gasp. The prices! The prices were insane. Iced
tea was eight dollars. A hamburger, albeit with French fries, was forty
dollars. Forty dollars! My cow!

Oliver put down his menu. "I'm having a martini. This has been an
eventful day for me...meeting you." I know I began to blush. "If
you've never had it, the chicken hash is sublime." Who was I to turn
down sublime?

"Fine. Chicken hash for me, too. But no martini," I waved my
hands. "I have about seven different drugs in my system. Some to
make me feel good, some to make my pain go away, some to do this,
some to do that. I'll have an iced tea." Oliver laughed, as if I'd said
something really witty. He beckoned one of the waiters over and
picked up them menu again.

"And maybe some oysters to start?" He looked over the top of the
menu at me, his eyebrows asking. I nodded again, what the hell. I
think, although I was too embarrassed to re-look, that the oysters were
in the seventy dollar range. What the hell.

During the meal, and the oysters were marvelous, and the chicken hash *was* sublime, Oliver gently queried me on my life. You know, all the books on How to Catch a Man tell you that you should always ask the man about *himself.* That guys adore you showing an interest in *them.* That a girl should deflect the conversation from herself to him. Well, those books would have been proud of me. Every question he asked, "So tell me, Vivian Ann, what made you decide to come to the US? What was your life like in Canada? Tell me about yourself?" was parried by me looking sweetly demure and turning the question back.

"What did you do at C&C, Vivian Ann?"

"Oh, the usual financial stuff. Boring, mundane work. Tell me, Oliver, how did you get into this line of work?"

Then followed a ten minute informative session on Oliver's induction into what was originally his Uncle's business. Actually, I learned a lot. Gerald Summers, after leaving thirty years of military service, became hooked up with a division of the Red Cross that assisted famine victims. When Red Cross funding dried up, Major Summers continued to assist those people who had suffered as a result of disasters, finding financing with grants and private patrons who operated philanthropic non-profits. Oliver, upon graduating from Yale (I knew it, I knew it) with a dual degree in Finance and Human Services, went to work with the newly christened Operation Relief Recovery. I gathered that much of the Major's work now consisted of finding funding for his "orphans", while Oliver did much of the actual interviewing and processing. They had a spiffy office in downtown New York, several secretaries and accounting personnel, and traveled all over the world helping others.

A few things I did answer.

"Why did you want to come to America, Annie?"

Annie? My eyes flew to his and he blushed. "You just don't look big enough for a grown up name like Vivian Ann." His dimples showed and my heart pounded again. I laughed, a little uncertain, a little nervous that he might think that the name Vivian didn't fit me. He laughed with me and settled back against the leather seat. "So, what brought you here?"

"I'd always been keen to travel to the US. My parents were teachers at the American School in Switzerland (I thought that this bit of fluff had a lot of potential). I spent most of my time with American children growing up." Laugh by me here. "Sometimes my mother despaired that I was completely losing my English accent and spoke like an American." A little more laughter. "It drove my mother barking mad." I played with my fork, pushing cubes of chicken around my plate. "Then, after both my parents died several years ago, I came to Canada. I didn't actually like it there, so a few months ago, I thought I'd come here." A big smile crossed the table. "And I'm glad I did." A piece of chicken up to my lips and a switcheroo of subject. "Are you ever depressed by the plight of the people that you help?"

He'd answered thoughtfully…and I was off the hook again. Those advice-to-a-girl books are filled with wisdom. I think this sort of thing always works. Men *do* want to talk about themselves.

When the bill came, I tactfully looked at my fingernails. As we were escorted out, I again mentally gaped at the careless expense of the patrons. I saw tables groaning with caviar platters (I think the menu listed them at $95 for the domestic kind), more oysters, thick porterhouse steak plates (I don't remember what they cost, but I know it was near the one hundred fifty dollar mark). Was everyone in here a millionaire?

Oliver's cab dropped me off at a posh 5th Avenue medical office building and told me that Dr. Paul Giggi's quarters were on the third floor. He promised to be waiting at the door in two hours time, and we waved goodbye.

Dr. Giggi's office was sleek, expensive and discrete. His receptionist could have been a Vogue model, whippet thin, with a helmet of gleaming hair, cut in a glamorously atrocious way, and then spray painted, I suppose, with purple dye. Oh so chic. Her dress seemed glued onto her skinny body. I could actually count her ribs and her hipbones stuck out like those on an anatomy class skeleton. I was awed by her glamour. Only when she opened her mouth and showed me her Bronx accent was I able to relax a bit.

I was ushered into a modernistic patient room and divested of my clothes by a friendly, heavy-set nurse, dressed in a starched uniform with a nursing cap in her head. No new nursing look, with colorful scrubs in here. No sir, it was as if Sister Bertrille herself had come flying through the door to minister to me. She was nice, though, funny and adept and took great care not to hurt me. She tsk-tsked over my bruises and bangs, took my vital signs, made me pee into a plastic cup, and told me that the doctor would be with me in a jiffy.

And in a jiffy, a short, vital man breezed through the door. Handsome, dark hair worn slightly long, devastating moustache, deep dark and piercing eyes. No whites or operating clothes here either. No, our Dr. Giggi was outfitted in a suede jacket, butter-yellow shirt and muted grey-green slacks. Nice. He greeted me and shook my hand, holding it a moment longer than necessary, and then picked up my sheaf of medical records.

As I watched him read, I marveled anew at the choice selection of men folk I had met since the walls fell down. Here I was beforehand, the battered wife of Ivan St. Clare, reviled and smacked around; then the discarded lover of Zachary Jacoby. In one memorable day, I had set eyes on the exotic Kenji Hutchinson, the suave and handsome Oliver Church, and now, the cosmopolitan Dr. Paul Giggi. Not bad. Not bad at all.

It hit me suddenly. Zachary. Dead! I must have gasped involuntarily, for Dr. Giggi put down the papers and watched me with keen medical interest. My gasp turned into a storm of weeping as the game I was playing became real again to me. Dead! They were all dead, and I was dead too.

"Tell me about it..." His voice was intense and hypnotic. Even through my sobs, I felt a prickle of fear. I would have to be very, very careful here.

"I had gone down the lift. I needed some paperwork that was in the mailroom, which was on the floor below Clausen & Chases' office. I stopped into the ladies' room at the back of the building. I was..." I stopped and looked down, pretending to be embarrassed... "I was in the, um, ah, toilet, ah...when there was this awful, awful noise. The toilet walls protected me," I made a tent out of my fingers, showing him the amazing way that I was still alive. "I fell to the floor and all hell broke loose. The ceiling came crashing down...." I found that I couldn't stop talking. Some small part of my brain was still functioning, allowing me only to tell him what I wanted to tell him. "One of the women who worked with me...I can't remember her name...Gianna somebody, I think...she was dead on the ladies' room floor..." I described the cries, the screams, the terror. That much was real, vivid and real and the rest of the story was almost true. He listened, tapping his gold pen against the side of my folder.

When my torrent of words and weeping stopped, he stood up. "You've been through quite a bad time, Miss Morrison." He pushed a button and Sister Bertrille appeared. I guess Dr. Giggi didn't trust himself to be alone with me while he listened to my chest with a stethoscope. Or perhaps he'd been slapped with a sexual harassment suit once, or perhaps, and most likely, he didn't *want* to be slapped with one and was taking no chances.

The examination was swift and efficient. "Not much wrong with you physically, Miss Morrison. Lots of superficial contusions, but you're a healthy woman and those will quickly disappear. But I'm concerned with the lump on your head." I gently touched it and winced a little. "Your broken nose will heal, but you might find that it isn't as cute as it once was." I resisted touching my nose even though I wanted to. Sister Bertrille gave the back of his head a peculiar look, washed her hands and disappeared again.

"You say you can't remember some things from before the disaster?" I nodded, sad and wan. "Why don't you get dressed and then come next door to my office." He grinned and I felt the punch of his masculinity. He reminded me of some darkly handsome Italian movie star. I just couldn't remember his name...maybe the concussion had affected me more than I knew.

"How did it go?" Oliver asked, after ushering me into the back set of the cab he had waiting. I grinned at the attention I'd gotten all day. I might even get to like this kind of thing. So many men and all so nice to me.

"He was kind. So sympathetic. He made me feel better about my lapses of memory. Told me that it was something that happens to a lot of people in a traumatic situation." Oliver nodded sagely and reminded me that he had made such a pronouncement at lunch. I turned to him gratefully and told him that he was just as smart as Dr. Giggi.

"I know you have so much experience. I'm grateful that I have you to assist me." He smirked slightly and tried to look humble.

"I give all of my clients the best attention I can." He was a wee bit pompous, then, he grinned at me. "Especially, when they're as sweet as you, Vivi-Annie." I think I also smirked and tried to look humble too. "Well, are you tired, or do you want to do a little shopping? I remember that you need a bedside clock."

As girlishly as I could, without being overwhelmingly coy, I gushed that I had completely forgotten and wasn't he clever for remembering. We both laughed then. He took me to a little shop called Fishs Eddy, and told the cab to wait. We went in and I bought a darling one-of-a-kind alarm clock, shaped like a sailboat, and, unable to resist, I also bought a tablecloth, four napkins and a trivet. Armed with our bundles, we returned to the cab. "I also need a package of coffee filters," I told him, and the cab made one more stop before it brought me home.

"I can't stay to have dinner with you," Oliver told me. "I know that was presumptuous to say, but I want to have dinner with you." I couldn't think of anything to answer, so I just stared at my shoes.

"I...I...I'll call you tomorrow and see how you are doing, if that's all right with you." I looked up at him and nodded. For some reason, I felt like crying again. Perhaps he could sense this, for he touched my arm oh, so gently and was gone.

As I unlocked the door, my telephone...or should I still say Vivian's telephone, was ringing. I picked it up gingerly. "Hullo?"

Heavy breathing. Then a click. I sat down, holding the receiver to my chest. Was there someone stalking Vivian? What was it all about? No one, *no one*, could know that it was me who was here. It had to be someone who was trying to frighten her? An old lesbian lover? A disgruntled co-worker? A stalker who was harassing red-headed women? A burglar who was checking to see if anyone was home? Who? What was troubling her? Had I changed my own set of insurmountable problems for Vivian's? And which ones were worse?

CHAPTER NINE

I t was good to be alone. I turned on the television, made myself a cup of tea, and settled down to watch the devastation that still enveloped the end of Manhattan. I watched as firemen and policemen with dogs on leashes entered into the gates of Hell, hoping, praying against fast-diminishing odds, that any human being might still be alive, buried under all that rubble and concrete. I looked in vain to see if I could spy Kenji or his skinny friend among the brave men and women who searched the rubble. I watched the fires, and the smoke and the wretched horror that man can do to man.

The announcer talked about the potential victims, putting the number in the thousands. I shuddered as he mentioned Clausen & Chase, and Manhattan Financial, which had been on the floor above C&C. His voice mournful, he told the world that almost everyone who had worked for those companies was dust. Infinitesimal, smoldering particles of rubble. Zachary…no pieces of Zachary left. Everything and everyone gone. Except me.

A pathetic array of mothers, fathers, sisters and brother, friends, husband and wives appeared on the TV screen, holding a picture of a missing loved one, hoping against hope that someone might have seen a glimpse of Sandra Cunningham, or Shadeen McQuade, or Peter Johnson, or Juan Martinez. Anxious people spoke, pleaded. "He's about six feet tall. Reddish hair. Thirty years old. Was at a breakfast meeting at Windows on the World. Perhaps he's in a coma in some hospital. Please call 212 - ------- if you have any information."

And then, I sat up, riveted…Omygod! It was Ivan*! Ivan*! On *tele*vision! Ivan! He held a picture of me and was speaking…. "She's my beloved wife. Gianna. Gianna St. Clare. I don't know how I can live without her!" I sat back, my mouth in an astonished 'O'. Son of a bitch! Son of a bitching *bitch!* How could you, Ivan? How could you feast on my death! We hated each other. Hated! Beloved wife, my ass!

It was amazing. In just a few days, I had almost forgotten about being Gianna St. Clare. I was jerked back into the reality of my former life. I got madder. Beloved wife? Shit! "Tell them about how you beat me up!" I yelled at the television. "Fucker! Tell them, you…you…you…*bas*tard!"

Ivan's lying face pretended profound sorrow. "I'll be here until the last stone is turned, waiting for my Gianna." The reporter's professional face took on a look of professional sympathy. He turned to the camera.

"That was Ivan St. Clare, husband of Gianna St. Clare. Gianna worked, um, uh, works for Clausen & Chase. If anyone had any information, please call the number on your screen." The reporter shifted gears and smiled. "And now, a few words from our sponsors…"

I fell back onto the cushions, my cup of tea spilled and unnoticed. I sat there, almost catatonic, while the television screen warned me about the horrors of not brushing properly. And then I began to laugh. It was so damn funny! My laughter turned. Tears ran out of my eyes, I doubled over, unable to stop my hysteria, until I ran out of breath. Gasping and mewing, I slumped down, hugging a pillow to my chest until utter fatigue and stress put me to sleep.

Some sound wakened me and I sat up, sweaty and cotton-mouthed. In the dark, I padded into the bathroom and then into the kitchen for a sip of water. I don't know why I peered out of the window…perhaps a devil drew me to look, I don't know. There was a man down there, right across the street, watching my apartment. I drew back, afraid that he could somehow see me, but the room in back of me was dark, and there was no way that I could be seen…or could I? I crept to the living room window and peeked out, careful to only show one eye. Yes! He was there, watching. It was dark and the street lights didn't quite reach the doorway where he was sheltering, but I could discern a faint silhouette… thin and short, wearing a long overcoat and a fedora kind of hat. Who the hell was it? Vivian's old boyfriend? The father of Vivian's old girlfriend? Having a man watch your apartment in the middle of the night does peculiar things to one's imagination. I watched him, and he watched my apartment for a long time. I sighed and looked at my new clock. It was 3:30 AM. I ducked under the window sill and got into bed, wide-awake and shivery. At 3:45 AM, I got back out and went to the window. He was gone, whoever he was.

I awoke with the sun shining in the window. I looked out again, frightened and wary. Other than a garbage truck...ooops, lorry, six cabs, seventy-five people walking, four pigeons pecking for crumbs and a dozen cars in the street, there was no one out there.

I brewed myself a cup of coffee and made a list for shopping. A few new blouses, some books, and a few CD's for music to keep me company. My face, in the bathroom mirror, looked as bad as it had yesterday. My hair was scraggly and bushy, my face still swollen. I sighed, then shrugged and sat at the table, drinking my coffee and studying my "*A to Zed*". My words for the day were *bonnet*, for the hood of a car or truck and *football* for soccer. I learned that a small sewing kit was called a *housewife*, but pronounced "hussif", but perhaps that might not come up in ordinary conversation. Whispering "*the lorry has a bonnet*" with fierce concentration, I went out to breakfast at Bernie's.

Anita greeted me with rapture. Again, I guess people see what they expect to see. She truly thought that I was Vivian Ann, and thus, to her, I was. No one as of yet, had any suspicions whatsoever that I wasn't Vivian Ann Morrison, ex-employee of C&C and British woman.

I peered around. Kenji and Lenny were not there and my heart plummeted. I was looking forward to seeing them...well, to be honest, I was looking forward to seeing Kenji.

The man behind the counter – Bernie - waved at me and asked me if I wanted my regular. Amazing, I'd been there once before, and already, I was a regular. I smiled and nodded and sat down with the paper. I was getting good at all this deception.

Small wonder, I said to myself. Haven't you been deceiving everyone since you were a child, Gianna? I snorted. Gianna? Even that was a big fat fake! I stared at the front page of the New York Post and remembered...

I was born in the Italian section of Chicago. The dirt poor area, where the tenements lean into one another and the smell of frying peppers and garlic permeates the concrete. The bastard daughter of Rose Sottosanti. Gina Sottosanti. That was how I started my life. Skinny and mouthy, with scabby knees and long, gangly legs. Teased...after all, every family on the block knew that my mother whored around and that I had no father. "*Gina, Gina Sottosanti, wears a droopy, dirty panty!*" Children were merciless. I was in a lot of fights, even won a few, and learned quickly to keep my problems to myself. There was no one to listen to them anyway. I was a burden to my mother and she let me know, every day and in plain, street-wise words, what a pain in the ass it was to have a daughter. Especially when I began to get bigger and she had to explain an eleven year old daughter to the myriad of men in her life who thought she was ten years younger than she actually was.

She made up a story that she was a teen-aged bride of a man who had died "in the war". I don't think anyone believed her, but she persisted in her little lie. One night, when she had much too much gin, she told me that I was the product of a five minute screw at the train station. "He was a good-looker, though. I think his name was George...or Glen...some name that began with G. That was why I called you Gina."

Rose was wiry, with bushy black hair and snapping black eyes. She had enormous breasts for such a thin woman. I presume that I took after my father and that he had thick, chestnut hair and warm brown eyes. That much he gave to me. I, too, was thin and I, too, even at eleven, had Rose's breasts, "I think he had money," Rose reminisced as she drank another glass down. "He gave me a hunnert dollars and called me his dollbaby."

In the morning, she smacked me because she had heard that I had played hooky again from school. I hated school, hated Rose and hated everyone. I lied and cheated and stole money from a teacher's unwatched purse. I was miserable and delighted to make everyone else's life miserable too. In some childish bravado, I told my classmates that my father was a prince and that he had to hide his true identity because his enemies would kill him if they knew he had a daughter who might succeed to the throne. When they laughed at me, I told them that they would be sorry when I got all the money that was to come to me when I got to be twenty-one.

They jeered at me, and I learned from it. I learned that a lie, to be believed, had to be somewhat plausible. I promised myself that my lies would be better prepared in the future.

When I was twelve, my mother met Joey Tesso, a small-time hood and bookmaker. The two of them were well suited. Both drunks and both worthless. She even got Joey to marry her. She paraded up and down the street, her wedding ringed hand held high, finally a respectable married woman. No one on the street was fooled, even though Joey bought her a Cadillac convertible. Baby blue, it was, and as long as a battle ship. Still, the neighbors sniffed. They knew, Cadillac or no Cadillac, ring or no ring, that Rose was a whore.

Joey was pleasant and distant to me for the first few months, handing me a wad of cash whenever he wanted to be alone with my mother. I kept my distance. His snakey eyes scared me.

In the summer of my twelfth year, Joey began to notice that I was growing up. He began to touch me, just a light touch on my waist, or a casual arm across my shoulders. He made me nervous and I always tried to crab away, repulsed by I-didn't-quite-know-what.

My mother noticed too, and she and Joey began to have screaming matches, culminating in Joey beating her up on a regular basis. She, in turn, took her frustrations out on me, shoving me and punching me at every opportunity, calling me a little whore, even though I avoided Joey as best I could. I tried to hide my burgeoning breasts, and walked hunched over, with my arms crossed. Even so, he still gave me glances.

In the ensuing year or two, he stalked me, getting bolder and bolder. One night, when Rose had passed out from drinking and Joey was still able to ambulate, he came to my room and raped me. Although I fought and bit him, I was no match for his lust and strength and he smacked my face until I could no longer fend him off. And after that, he came often, each time more brutal than the last. I quickly learned that it was much better to lie still and get it all over as fast as possible. If I tried to fight, tried to squirm away, he beat me until I was almost unconscious – and *then* he would do what he wanted.

I waited and bided my time. I left school. The truant officers came to our house and tried mightily to get me back into the classroom. Rose greeted them with indifference, Joey with ferocious cursing and threats. I presume that the burden of problem children was a huge one in that section of Chicago, and somehow, the truant officers gave up on me.

I got a job, simply to get myself away from the house. It was at the local library, shelving books and dusting. To my astonishment, I loved it. I took every opportunity to stay as late as I could at the job, hiding myself in the dusty stacks and reading every book I could get my hands on: novels, romances, philosophy, medicine, history. They all slid down like sugar candy to my starved soul and brain. I began to plot and dream about some kind of a future. One that didn't include either Rose or Joey. I looked for some opportunity to change my life, and behind the desk, stamping books in and out, Dame Fortune heard my prayers.

Each night, about six o'clock, a young man appeared at the desk. He was tall and thin, with floppy brown hair. His clothes were neat and expensive-looking and his pale blue eyes gleamed appreciatively behind his glasses when he smiled at me. It was a different kind of smile from the shark-like grin that Joey sent my way. This young man, whose name I learned was Lucian Josephs, smiled at me as if he really liked me. I was flattered and intrigued. We began to talk and become friends.

I learned more about him. He was twenty years old, but, with his boyish smile, looked as if he were still a teenager. He was the only son of a prosperous factory-owner; his father was Jacob Josephs of Josephs' Fine Furniture. Lucian was in his last year of college at a small school in Mountainview, Indiana. Western Indiana Teachers' College. He wanted to teach history. His father wanted Lucian to follow him and take over at the furniture factory. Lucian thought that all of this was an insurmountable problem. I knew better. *Joey* was an insurmountable problem. Lucian and his father would one day work their little disagreement out amicably. I didn't verbally venture this sudden wisdom to Lucian, but commiserated with him. Lucian and I began to see a bit of one another, going for coffee or ice cream after the library closed. He looked at me with calf-eyes. Although he never touched me in any way, he told me that he was in love with me.

I liked and admired Lucian and envied his life as a college student, able to sit in libraries and read, go to classes and soak in learning. He was sweet and kind and polite to me. I told him huge lies about my family. People like Lucian would never, ever, understand about people like me and Rose and Joey. I told him that I was an orphan and that I lived with a strict aunt and uncle.

The weeks went by and Lucian was distraught that the time had come for him to return to school. How could he leave me, he almost cried.

I thought about it and told him that I would go with him, back to Mountainview, Indiana and his school. No one had to know. He was thrilled at this little bit of deception and we made plans together. Lucian left on a Monday, driving his car, and leaving me with two hundred dollars. I was to follow on Friday, taking the train from Chicago to Evanston, Illinois, and then a bus that would bring me to the little college town of Mountainview. Oh, and by the way, Lucian thought that I was eighteen and had graduated from high school. Lies, you see. I was beginning my life of deception. But what else could I do? Stay in the house with Rose and Joey. No. No way. I would either become impregnated with, ugh, Joey's baby, or wind up killing him. No, I had to lie somehow. Those were easy lies. And Lucian was gullible and had no reason not to believe me. I was learning the fine art of deceit. Even in my innocence, with not much training in deception, it worked.

On Thursday night, after Rose and Joey had gone out to a night-club, I packed every scrap of clothing that I owned. I knew where Joey kept his bookmaking money and I took every cent that he had in his· little blue plastic case. More than fifteen hundred dollars. I also took the book that had all of his records in it. Just before I walked out the door, I burned the book and slashed every single one of Joey's expensive suits and shirts. I wanted to destroy my mother's stuff, but, in the end, I didn't. I don't know why.

I lugged my suitcase to the train station and took the 10 PM sleeper to Akron, Ohio. I felt terrible about Lucian, but I didn't love him at all. I liked him, but that wasn't enough. I often wondered, in the years that passed, if he ever went into business with his father.

CHAPTER TEN

I got a job, waiting on tables, at a coffee shop in Huntsville, Ohio, a small college town that might have been just like Mountainview, Illinois. I rented a room over the bakery that was three doors down from the coffee shop. I liked waiting on the customers and made a decent wage, as I was willing to work hard and was pleasant and accommodating to all of the people who came to eat there.

I told everyone that my name was Gina Josephs and that I was an orphan from Boise, Idaho. Fortunately, no one ever asked me anything about Boise, Idaho, as I had no idea whatsoever, where it was or anything about it. My introduction to Deceit 101 progressed as I began to learn that a simple lie, told often enough and authoritatively enough, became well-accepted as the truth.

After three months, I took a better job at Hunt College, a small, pleasant liberal arts school with an excellent reputation. The college was at the outskirts of town. I worked in the Registrar's Office. Back then, in those much simpler times, no one asked for identification, social security cards or proof of anything. I was accepted at my word. After all, hadn't the professors and the Dean known me from the coffee shop?

I bought myself a bicycle and rode to work every day. I found out that I could, in my spare time and days off, sit in on some of the classes, and thus, I learned a lot about business, improved my reading skills, and even learned how to type. I began classes to learn about the new office phenomenon, computers. I took every opportunity to educate myself, after all, I was alone in this big world. . Not only alone, but alone with no background, no family, no one to help me. I was going to become a new person, shed the skin that I hated and despised. Forget about Joey and Rose and the children who teased me. I had a new identity and she was a lot better than my old identity. I was never going back.

I lost the horrible accent that I had absorbed at Rose's knee, and began to speak like an educated person. I read every book that I could find, took a class in Beginner's French, and tried to improve every aspect of my life. I dated a few men and made a few friends, but I was always aloof and no man touched me physically or emotionally. At least not then.

The college was advertising for a professor in the Business School. There were many applications, and one of my jobs was to prepare a file on each applicant. One of the applications was from a woman named Gianna Lewis. Kind of, sort of, like my own first name. Miss Lewis was born in Philadelphia and was a graduate of Penn State University. She was several years older than me and had three years of teaching experience at the University after her graduation. She had an exemplary transcript with a grade average of 98.7 percent. She had sent in a copy of the transcript, her teaching certificate, and glowing letters of recommendation. She was what I might have been, if my birth circumstances had been different. Her file made me think...dream...I set the file aside for a day or two, but then, when asked, included it in the pile of files for Dean Gervase's perusal.

The next day, I opened a letter from Gianna Lewis' father. Gianna and her mother had been killed in a train wreck and he was, sadly, informing Dean Gervase that she was no longer, obviously, applying for the job. Tsking, Dean Gervase tossed the file into the waste basket and wrote a kind letter of condolence to Mr. Lewis.

So this was what Fate was. I retrieved the file. On a sheet of Hunt College stationery, I wrote to the Office of Vital Statistics in Philadelphia, identifying myself as Gianna Lewis and asking for a copy of my birth certificate. Naturally, I knew her date of birth from the transcript information she had sent. I explained to the people in the Vital Statistics office that I had lost my original certificate and needed a copy for my new endeavor as a professor at the college. I used my own address as hers. In two weeks, I received a certified copy of Gianna's birth certificate.

Armed with my documentation, or perhaps I should say Gianna's documentation, I took a bus to the Social Security office in Cincinnati. I told them that I had lost my purse. Could I please get a copy of my Social Security card? "Why certainly, Miss Lewis. It will be mailed to your address in three weeks." The nice man took the envelope that had contained the birth certificate, copy of her diploma, and various other forms of identification and copied my address from the front. I thanked him prettily and took the bus back home, but not before I bought myself a new skirt and blouse from Stern's Department store in downtown Cincinnati.

When the Social Security card arrived, I put it and the birth certificate into the file with all the other documents and letters and placed the whole thing at the bottom of my underwear drawer. It was my ace-in-the-hole for my future when I made my next move.

I was jolted out of my revere when Kenji and Lenny and my breakfast arrived at the same moment. I forgot about my machinations so long ago as I saw them come in the door. My plummeting heart lurched upward and stuck in my chest as both men greeted me with tired smiles and sat at my table. Two women in uniform trailed after them. Kenji touched my cheek and asked me how was I doing. I said that was keeping a stiff upper lip, as well as a stiff neck and, as a matter of fact, I was sort of stiff all over. Laughing, he introduced me to the policewomen. "These ladies have been down at Ground Zero with Lenny and me." Jessie King was the African-American one, a tall, rangy woman with a short afro, green eyes and a wicked grin. Carmencita Blue was a lighter shade of tan, Hispanic, with a long, black pony-tailed hairdo, dark eyes behind sequined harlequin glasses, short and a bit plump. Both women gripped my hand hard, squeezed with sympathy and told me that they had heard about my ordeal.

"Oh, thank you, but I was only lucky. At the right time, I was using the loo." I laughed a little. "You four and the rest of you firefighters and police are the true heroes. I'm astonished and humbled at your courage." And I meant it sincerely. Then I did a tiny double-take. "Ground Zero? What does that signify?"

Kenji and Lenny sat back and let the women talk. "That's the name that the firefighters have given the World Trade Center disaster area." Carmencita yawned. "I need some coffee." She stuck her chin out in the direction of the counter. "You owe me, Len. Go get a couple of bagels and some Java."

I craned my neck to see what had become of my breakfast. Then, struck by a memory of a British TV sitcom I'd seen, the one about that lady, Hyacinth Bucket...no, no BooKay..., I ventured, "And where's my breakfast? I'd murder for a bacon buttie." Everyone looked blank. I laughed at them and told them it was a well-known line from a BBC comedy. "It means that one is ravenously hungry."

"Mmmmm-mmmm!" Carmencita agreed. "I could use one a them bacon things too. Go on, Lenny. It's your turn today."

Good-naturedly, Lenny took orders and ambled to the counter. My plate, heaped high with eggs and bacon, was whisked in front of me. Anita greeted the newcomers, "You guys are terrific. Boss says breakfast is on him today. Sky's the limit." She patted Carmencita's shoulder. "Least the old fool can do."

They convinced me to start eating, although I insisted on sharing my hot toast with everyone. "I'll have a piece or two of yours when it arrives." I sat back, whacked away at my eggs, and listened to them talk about the horrors and small triumphs of their night.

As we all got up to leave, I tried to pay for my breakfast. "You're included in the freebie," Anita assured me. "His nibs told me to rip up your check too." We left Anita the best tip she'd ever received, thanked Bernie profusely and gathered our stuff to depart. Kenji pulled me back for a moment as we all exited.

"I can't get away for a few days, but can we have a quick dinner on Thursday?" His exotic eyes made my insides gooey. I nodded. "Can I have your phone number and I'll call you, just to confirm?" I nodded again, dry-mouthed, and wrote my…uh, Vivian's number, on a napkin. Fortunately, I had memorized it by now. He wiggled his eyebrows, touched my swollen cheek with a finger, and trotted after the rest of the group.

I brought my newspapers home. The little red light was blinking on my answering machine. There were three messages. Two hang-ups with breathing and one call from Oliver asking me to join him for dinner tomorrow night. Brushing the heavy breather aside, I grinned. Oliver and dinner Wednesday night, Kenji and a little dinner Thursday night. I made a short list of things to buy. The last items were a wall calendar and a small appointment book.

Oliver picked me up at seven. He was wearing a dark blue blazer, with shiny brass buttons that had some kind of emblem on them. Yale, perhaps? He wore grey slacks and a pale grey turtleneck sweater made of some light, silky wool. He looked great and my heart beat a faster tattoo when he greeted me. I wore a pale green suit that I had bought four hours ago in a small boutique on 5th. It had a sheer, paler green sleeveless sweater and the jacket hung open and looked good on me, even with my bruises. The pale green and the fading purplish blue of my cheeks matched in some strange way.

Oliver brought my folder back and left it on my desk. "OK, Annie-Bananie, where do you want to go?" he asked. I shrugged and told him that anywhere was fine. "Chinese?" He asked and I nodded with happiness. I adored Chinese food.

We went out into the street. Just before I got into his car, I thought I saw a small, thin man lurking in the doorway across the street. I stopped, but the man turned and walked away. Was it the same man? He was wearing a fedora, but lots of men wore fedoras. I watched him as he walked out of sight.

Oliver touched the small of my back. "Are you all right?" He opened the car door for me. Naturally, the car was a Porsche. What else would it be?

"No, I'm fine. I just thought I saw someone I knew…" I bent and slid into the low slung auto, showing about ten inches of nylon clad thigh for Oliver's inspection. Dang, how does a girl get into this kind of car gracefully? If she has good legs, I told myself smugly, for my underpinnings were satisfactory, she gets in just like I did! I settled back as Oliver walked around the car and squeezed himself behind the wheel. The soft, cushioned leather hugged around me. Goodness, it certainly would be easy to become accustomed to luxury like this.

'"We're going to The China Palace, OK?"

"Brilliant" That was one of the words I studied this afternoon. Brilliant and Hoover and Barmy. Hoover was when one vacuumed and barmy meant crazy. Soon I'd be bilingual.

I shifted a bit in the car, turning toward him. "Oliver, do you take every client out on the town?"

"No," he laughed. "Only special ones." I raised my eyebrows and sat back to enjoy myself, hugging my arms around my stomach.

The dinner was superb. This man just automatically did everything with perfection. We'd gone to a smart, private club afterwards had champagne, and danced to a jazz combo. Oliver held me lightly and was careful not to hurt me or tire me out. My battered body glowed when he held me. The spots where he touched me - my hands, my waist, and my thighs, as we bumped into one another - felt on fire with a lovely, warm glow. And when he walked me upstairs and I wondered what might come next, well, nothing came next. He only smiled that devastating smile at me and told me that he'd had a marvelous time and that he'd call me very soon. "Goodnight, Sweet Annie," he winked and was gone. As I brushed my teeth, I puzzled at his insistence in calling me by my, um, Vivian's, middle name. It made me feel…odd. Nice, but odd. Very nice, as a matter of fact, but still…odd. I spit into the sink and told myself to relax.

I got into a nightgown and switched on the television set. The devastation was still showing on every channel. I turned the sound down, depressed again, and made myself a cup of tea. I took the documents out of the folder that Oliver had returned to me. Hmmm? My driver's license wasn't there. I squinched up my face…had I put it in there? Yes, I distinctly remembered sliding it on at the last moment. Whatever happened to it? I shrugged. I had no car…or Vivian had no car, or didn't seem to have one anyway. I could find no evidence of a registration, no car keys, and presumed that there wasn't one. Maybe she had gotten a license because she was going to purchase one. I shrugged again. I'd call Oliver in the morning and ask if the license had somehow been left in the copier. I put the rest of the documents back where they belonged and then stopped for a moment, looking at the bankbooks and the key to the safe deposit box at Chemical Bank. Maybe I should stop by there tomorrow and see what was in the safe deposit box. I finished the tea, shut the telly off and got into bed.

I awoke at 2 AM, used the toilet and drifted into a half sleep…In the drifting swirls of my memory, I was back at the college, beavering away, answering to the name of Gina Josephs…and then Aiden came into my life.

He was a professor of English, an Irishman who had come to the US to work on some sort of American Literature project. He saw me, wanted me, and I saw him and lusted for him, perhaps seeing in him some way to erase the memory of Joey's hands and…other things.

Aiden O'Sullivan, for that was his name, was tall, craggy and bearded, and spoke like a poet. I had never seen anything like him. He wore brown checked, earthy suits, made out of heathery wool, and had horned-rimmed glasses and a thin aesthetic face. All the college women, even the ones that were homely and fat and had beards almost as prodigious as Aiden's were thrilled with him, tittering and flirting with him whenever he poked his fascinating face into the offices. I, young and innocent, if you didn't count Joey, and I didn't count Joey at all, was putty.

He...well, he *romanced* me. Read me sonnets, spoon-fed me Shakespeare and W. H. Auden and Yeats. Prepared little feasts for me in front of the fireplace at his apartment, oysters and foie gras and instructed me in the selection of fine wines. I was besotted and completely out of my depth. I adored him and probably would have committed murder for him.

I succumbed physically to him on the third afternoon that we met. The room was strewn with roses and Aiden had put thick, chunky candles on every surface. Their waxy glow lit the room with dim shadows as Aiden recited a verse from Kahil Gibran and I was an easy and willing conquest. With only Joey to compare with, Aiden seemed to me to be the perfect lover. Joey had been brutal, intent on hurting me, while Aiden only touched me with light, tender touches. The act of sex wasn't quite what I expected, but I, in my ignorance and youth, thought that the fault must be mine.

With my office keys, I went to the locked-up section of the college library, the section where they kept *special* books. Books on human sexuality. The ones that you kept away from the children. I needed their information, *now*! Fascinated, I poured through every sex manual that I could find. None of them seemed quite right to me. There was a lot of amazing information, but nothing that fit my own situation.

You see, it seemed to me that I should be feeling something more...something explosive, something that made the angels sing, but, other than a general sensation of pleasure, nothing much happened. I mean, his touch felt good, maybe like stroking a kitten feels, but it wasn't...quite...what I thought it would be. Or maybe I just didn't read the right book.

I thought that it was my inexperience. That when I learned something more about life, that I would finally get to that moment that the books told me about. But no matter. I adored him. I was in love with love, with romance and poetry and there was no one to talk to, nor anyone to advise me. I could never tell any of the people that I worked with about our affair. Thus, I humbly submitted to Aiden's ministrations and his touch and considered myself the luckiest girl in the world. He was my god and I was his slave.

Foolish me, I didn't think that anyone at the college knew about our little romance. Again, innocent chump that I was, I thought that we were discrete, and, perhaps, some of the glamour was in the clandestine meetings, secret glances and touches.

The sky fell on this little Garden of Eden. It was on a Monday morning...Aiden had been away for the weekend. He told me that he'd had a research project in Akron. I'd hinted that I would have been delighted to accompany him, but he told me no, that he'd be busy all the time and that I'd be bored. He promised to buy me some special present. There was nothing for me but to be satisfied with the expectation of a gift and Aiden's return. He had told me several times in the past that he hated women who whined.

Anyway, on that Monday morning, when I arrived at work, I noticed a few stifled giggles and odd glances coming my way. I'd shrugged it off; perhaps I was imagining things. I'd missed him, and at the first possible moment, made some excuse to go to the English Building so that I could, at least, see my beloved. His classroom was closed and dark and a white card thumb-tacked to the door told me that "Mr. O' Sullivan's classes have been cancelled indefinitely."

I went back to my office, puzzled. Heather Gobienski, one of the other girls who worked in the office, snickered when she saw me. "Looking for someone?" she asked, and then burst into laughter.

"What do you mean?"

"Looking for lover-boy?" When Heather laughed, she snorted. I usually thought it was disgustingly funny, but right now, her glee seemed sinister.

"I don't understand what you mean." I tried to be nonchalant, but something wasn't quite right. Heather laughed again, this time, covering her mouth and nose with her hands.

"*You'll* see," she winked at me and I jumped, startled.

The office door opened and Dean Gervase came in. "Ah, Gina," he said. "Can, um, you please come into my office?" Heather's eyes were wide with nasty curiosity. She bit at her bottom lip as she pretended to be busy with the files.

"Certainly, Dean." I went to the door ahead of him and the two of us walked down the blue carpeted corridor and into his private study. I was nervous and apprehensive. What the heck was going on?

The Dean seemed nervous too. He seated himself at the large ornate desk and I sat in one of the chairs that were usually occupied by a parent who was called in to discuss the failing grades of a son or daughter. He coughed, "Um, Gina, some word has reached my ear that, uh, you..." He coughed. "You and, um, Professor O'Sullivan have been, um, seeing one another." I blushed and felt sick. I couldn't say a word. I huddled in the uncomfortable chair, afraid to move.

"Is this true?" He thundered at me. I squeaked in fright and managed to nod yes. His face got red and angry. "You little fool!" he hissed. "Don't you know that he...he..." Suddenly, he sat back, shook his head and blew his breath out. His anger was gone, and in its place was pity. I was ever more frightened.

"I don't understand..." I began.

"No, I'm afraid that you don't. He slumped in his chair and reached for his fountain pen. He uncapped it and looked at it carefully, then he re-capped it, as if it was the most important thing in the world. With great concentration, he returned it to the wooden stand at the front of his desk. He sighed. "I shouldn't be mad at you, Gina. You're young and innocent and I don't think you really understood what was going on."

I suppose I looked puzzled. I certainly *was* puzzled.

"Gina," he continued, "There are some men who...they are not...they..." His sentence broke down completely as he watched my bewildered face. "Ah, child, perhaps none of this is your fault. You are very young." I sat still and listened to my heart thump. What *was* it?

Dean Gervase blew out his cheeks and slammed his hand down on the desk. I jumped and almost ran out of the room. He held his hands up, as if in surrender. "Professor O'Sullivan was arrested yesterday. He was found in a bathhouse in Akron, having illicit sexual conduct with a young man." I shrank against the fabric of my chair. Even with my tender years, I knew, sort of knew, what he was saying. "The young man...uh, really a boy...was um, eleven years old." I must have gasped. Someone gasped at any rate. "It has been reported to us that this wasn't the first time that this sort of thing has happened with Professor O'Sullivan." I don't know how I breathed. My chest hurt and my eyes were dry, sandy sockets. "He, um, has been arrested before, in, um, Boston, for, um, the same sort of thing with a nine year old boy." He slumped back.

I didn't know what to do or say. *Aiden?* A little boy? How...how?

"He is, naturally, dismissed immediately." Dean Gervase looked uncomfortable. "And you, we must also terminate you. I'm sorry, Gina. But you cannot work here any longer. Our school cannot tolerate this kind of scandal. I'm sorry." He stood up and I cowered in the chair. "You can pick up your check at Mrs. Halvorson's desk. She has it ready for you. You understand, naturally, that we cannot give you any sort of recommendation." His eyes were expressionless. "Good day, Gina".

CHAPTER ELEVEN

I called the offices of Operation Relief Recovery. Oliver wasn't there, but I spoke to an efficient sounding secretary, Sarah Somebodyorother, who promised to look and see if my license was lying somewhere, "Perhaps it's still in the copier." She chirped. "I'll call you back."

I waited for a half hour and then, hungry…what is that they say about eating Chinese food?…went out for my breakfast and Kenji-sighting at Bernie's. Although the place was jumping and Anita greeted me like a long lost buddy, none of the policemen or women was there. I ate a splendid, but solitary meal of corn cakes and maple syrup, bought the papers and went back home. The blinking light on the telephone answering machine greeted me and I found, via a message, that my license was nowhere to be found. I shrugged, perhaps it was for the better.

I then called Information for the number of the Motor Vehicle Department, called them and found out that a lost license can be replaced easily. "Just come down to the office on 38th Street, bring a photo identification and a utility bill or a phone bill…something with your name and address on it…and a check for twenty five dollars, and we'll issue you a new license." Obviously, this happened a lot in New York City.

Getting a new license was easy. I had all the documentation ready, and the girl at the counter was held in thrall by my account of escape from the World Trade Center. I don't even think she looked at the passport picture. In less than an hour, I was back at home, the proud possessor of a new license in the name of Vivian Ann Morrison. Just like the old license, except *this* one had *my* picture on it. So maybe it had all been for the best.

I made myself a sandwich and sat down with the paper. The news…indeed, still the *only* news, was the Trade Center Tragedy. As Carmencita and Jessie had said, the burning towers were now known as Ground Zero. I read with horror of six firefighters who had been trapped in the flames and rubble as they tried to find even one more human being who might still be alive in the inferno. And another priest, traveling along with the firefighters, giving the last sacraments to the dying was also buried in the rubble. One more statistic. I sighed, feeling hollow and empty.

On page two there was a story about the donations that were pouring in…millions and millions of dollars…from total strangers, kiddies who gave their pennies, children who went door to door, collecting dollars, everyone, it seemed, was opening their hearts and wallets to help the families of the dead and injured. I wondered if anyone had contacted Ivan yet. And then I turned the page.

There he was! A quarter of a page large. Ivan! My mouth dropped open and I began to read:

"I can't believe she is gone. My beloved wife, Gianna. How can I live without her?"

Ivan St. Clare, above, opens his heart to our reporter." was the headline.

The text went on in much of the same vein.....*loved her....can't live without her beautiful face...searched the rubble high and low*...and then the article told of an attorney from the law firm that represented Clausen & Chase… *"He told me that there was a large life insurance policy in her name and that Mayor Giulliani had declared that a special law had been rushed through the Legislature that exempted all of the survivors or spouses of the victims from having to wait the customary seven years to collect the insurance monies."* My eyes narrowed. My salary doubled was the life insurance that C&C had on all of its employees. It could have been more, but Ivan was too cheap to have me apply and pay for the better benefits. I laughed. Cheapskate! He could have had more! Still, I mused, old Ivan would wind up with one heck of a lot of money. I sat back on the chair, anger beginning to grow. Ivan didn't deserve spit! But what could I do about it? Suddenly appear, like a wraith returning from the grave? No, I was too far into my masquerade to go back now. I thought of Ivan's drunken stupors, his rages and of the many times he'd hit me, kicked me and worse. I remembered how he'd told me that he never wanted children. That if I ever dared to forget my birth control and slipped up, he'd kick me in the stomach until baby was aborted. I wondered if anyone watching television and seeing Ivan's overly-pious face would believe that little story. No, I laughed in rue; I could never go back now. I was stuck as Vivian Ann Morrison. Hell, I even *liked* being Vivian Ann Morrison better than being Ivan's battered wife, and I didn't even have to go through the grimness of a divorce. No, a little voice inside me whispered, you only had to go through the latest version of Hell.

My eyes glazed and I shushed the little voice.

I did like it. I liked changing my life yet once again. Liked becoming another person. Liked leaving my problems behind, like an old coat that I didn't want any more. It was fun, wasn't it?

Like when I became Gianna Lewis.

I let my mind drift backwards again…

I'd stumbled from Dean Gervase's office, aware now of the pointed looks and stares from the office girls, unable to look at Heather and her snorting laugh. I'd packed…there wasn't very much…and in my handbag, ready to use, was my new identification. Goodbye Gina Josephs. You were a nice, innocent kid. Stupid, gullible and innocent. And hello to Gianna Lewis, wiser, intelligent, a college graduate, ready for anything.

I cashed my last paycheck, and put the extra check that I had picked up at the administration office, facing their averted eyes, in my purse. Fortunately for me, including the week-in-the-hole money, the check also included an additional two weeks of vacation money. I guess Dean Gervase had been as accommodating as he could be. I couldn't really blame him. What else could he have done? I couldn't have stayed. I'd have been a living, breathing, daily reminder of how it pays to check references, again and again. However, I knew from my small amount of experience that rarely *did* anyone check references in any depth. That was how I was going to be able to pass myself off as Gianna. Luck would be with me this time.

I just caught the bus as it left from the station. Where was I going? Who knew? The bus was heading east, and I was going with it. I slung my suitcase up on the rack, settled back and ate a Mounds bar that I had stuffed into my pocket. I watched Ohio go by and vowed never to come back. Never. I examined my heart. Had it been broken? Was I going to shoot myself because of Aiden and his disgusting penchant for little boys? How did I feel now, now that I was the laughingstock of the entire school? Actually, I felt pretty good. No wonder there were no fireworks when he made love to me. I chuckled, despite my weary soul…when he was touching me, he was probably fantasizing about some seven year old kid. Pervert creep! I learned a bitter lesson. Never again would I be bowled over by passion. I'd do a lot of checking on my next love's background. I wouldn't be fooled or be made a fool of again. Ever.

The bus thundered through the night and in the morning, we stopped at a depot in Harrisburg, PA. Harrisburg. I looked out the window and saw a fine looking old brick building with a big sign over it that said "Harrisburg Public Library". I'd always loved libraries, as I said previously. I took that as an omen. Harrisburg. Sounded fine to me. I heaved my suitcase down, said goodbye to the driver and looked around.

I liked what little I could see of Harrisburg. Not too big, but big enough in which to disappear, not too small, but small enough to be friendly. Lugging my suitcase, I went to the Harrisburg Public Library and spoke to the elderly librarian at the front desk. She kindly directed me to a bulletin board that had cards and notices pinned onto it. Tractor for Sale, Hardly Used. Needed, Man to Pick Corn. Wanted, Speedboat, Fiberglass Preferred. Quiet Room for Rent (Woman Only) by the Week or by the Month. Aha. I copied the telephone number down, called from the pay telephone at the drug store across the street from the library and made an appointment at two o'clock to see the room and be interviewed by a Mrs. Lovatt.

It wasn't hard to find 52 Brookside Drive. The house was a big one, with gables and turrets and porches. It was on a pleasant, tree-lined street fronted with large houses that had once been filled with Harrisburg's wealthy early residents. The street was served by the bus line that could take me directly downtown and into the business districts. Many of the houses now were business offices, doctors, attorneys, dentists. Some, like the Lovett house, had been turned into respectable rooming houses. I liked the fresh-painted look of the house. It was old, but elegant, spick and span, and Gianna Lewis would certainly be happy there.

Mrs. Lovatt also had her own share of personal porches. She was a huge woman, more than six feet tall, with a double chin, large bosom and an immense rear end. She was clad in a yellow sweater and men's dungarees, her abundant grey hair screwed up into a careless topknot. I liked her on sight.

"I got a single room and a two-room suite, Miss Lewis," she told me. "The single room has a fold out couch and shares a bath with two others, both women." She eyed me to see if I had any comment on her statement. I gazed back at her, waiting. "The other is a sitting room and a bedroom and has its own bath. Naturally, the two rooms are more expensive." She named two prices and I thought about the cash that was all that I had. She rolled on, "Your breakfast and dinner are included in the prices. I run a clean, orderly house here. No loud party-ing, no messing around with the men guests." I looked a bit startled. She explained, "Full up, I got six women here and six men. I keep the women on the second floor and the men's rooms are on the top floor. I expect them to stay that way."

"Other than you and the friendly librarian, I don't know anyone in Harrisburg," I told her. "I don't know any men here at all." She nod-ded, her mouth firm. "I need to find a job, and I think I will want the two rooms with the bath." I did some mental arithmetic. "I'll take them today and pay you for one week. If I can't find a job by the end of the week, I'll go into the smaller room. Will that be OK?"

She pulled at her bulldog chin. "Well...I haven't got anyone else looking at the rooms, so if no one else comes looking this week, that's alright with me." I nodded and we shook hands on it. "What kinda work you looking for?" She looked me up and down and I felt as if I were being sized up.

"I graduated from Penn State. After graduating, I taught at the uni-versity. I can type, use a computer and do bookkeeping and any kind of office work." I shrugged. "I have great references and I am sure that I can find something right away." She humphed and told me that after I unpacked, I could come down, have a cup of tea and read her news-paper in the kitchen to see what the classified ads were offering. I handed her a wad of cash and accepted her kind offerings with glad cheer. Whatever test Mrs. Lovatt had given me, I think I passed with flying colors.

The Harrisburg Clarion's classified section listed perhaps seven-teen jobs that fit my qualifications. Several of them, the ones for working at the local college, I discarded. I felt that a college just might check my – or rather Gianna's – references, and I didn't want to have my past looked at with such scrutiny. A smaller office or something a bit off the wall might suit me better, at least until I established myself here. I circled three that seemed more interesting and thanking Mrs. Lovatt for her tea and hospitality, took the bus back to the library.

The friendly librarian, the elderly woman whose name tag told me that she was Miss Cardin, remembered me from the morning. I intro-duced myself, "I'm Gianna Lewis." I really don't know how the original Gianna pronounced her name, maybe Gee-Anna, but I had de-cided to use the Italian pronunciation, *Joh Nah*. Start as you mean to go on was my motto for my future.

I confided that I had found a wonderful place to stay and thanked her for helping me. She and I spoke for a few moments, and she told me that she had been born and raised here in Harrisburg, had taken a job shelving books when she was in high school, taken Library Science courses at Harrisburg Junior College, and here she was, still at the same place of employment after nearly fifty years. "I never married," she said, "The Library and the books are my children now." She laughed and I caught a glimpse of the shy, sweet girl that she had been. "Some people might say I could have done better, but I love it here." I nodded. I, too, loved libraries and I told her about my job, naturally moving the library from the reality of Chicago's dismal streets to some fictitious splendor in Boise, Idaho.

I told her that I was seeking employment and needed a typewriter to bring my resume up to date. "Is there a place where I can rent one?"

Miss Cardin dimpled. "You can use the one in the cubicle of the Reference Room." She pulled a pink card out of her desk. "You'll need a library card, but as you are now a resident, that will be no problem." She gave me a pen. "Just fill this out...don't worry about the phone number part...you can fill that in at a later date."

I grinned at her and thanked her profusely. I filled out the pink form, signed it with a flourish...Gianna Lewis. Miss Cardin looked at it. "My lands," she exclaimed. I wouldn't have known that you spelled your name that way. I figured you would spell it *Jonna*." We both laughed and I said that I was named for my Italian grandmother. I figured that no one need know that I really had been named for the first initial of a man that my mother screwed with for one brief moment.

"Italian," Miss Cardin looked at my long, chestnut hair and raisin dark eyes. "Yes, I can see the stamp of the Mediterranean on you." She harrumphed as another customer plunked a stack of books on her desk, finished filling out my card, stamped it and handed me yet another little piece of paper that would cement my new existence. How easy the deceit was. Almost natural.

Armed with my library card and Gianna's resume, I typed up a letter. I thought a lot about just what kind of a job I was going to lie about having since Gianna's resume ended with her three years of teaching a year ago. What had Gianna done since then? It couldn't be too technical or be in some field that needed specialized experience. No one would believe that I had worked in a law office, for instance, nor a dental office. I just didn't know the jargon, nor did I quite have those kinds of skills. No, I needed something simple, yet something with some stature. After a few moments, I began. The letter stated that after teaching at Penn State, I had returned to good old Boise and

worked for the past year as an Office Manager at The Boise Empo-
rium, a fictitious department store. I knew a lot about offices, and I
figured that I could bluff my way through any interview.

I returned to Miss Cardin's desk and thanked her again. I bran-
dished the letter and the classified section of the paper. "Now, I need
your expertise once again." She beamed, pleased that she had helped
me. "Do you have a copy machine, and do you have a pay phone? I
want to make a few copies and then try to set up some interviews for
tomorrow."

"There's a Xerox machine in the little room next to the lobby.
Copies are ten cents apiece." She gestured towards the left. "And when
you're done, you can came here and use my telephone to make local
calls."

I set up three interviews for tomorrow. The first one at 10:00 AM
was at a medium-sized pharmaceutical office. They needed someone
to do billing. Not fascinating at all, but hey, it would at least be a start
and money in my pocket. The second was at an architect's place of
business. They needed a Girl Friday and I would see Miss Pedersen at
noon. The third was at a grocery warehouse. They wanted office help
and would interview me at 3:30.

Miss Cardin was eager to hear about the interviews. She pursed
her lips. "Come back and tell me what happens," she urged. "I feel as
if I have a hand in all of this." She giggled in a ladylike manner and
overcome by her sweet friendliness, I came around her desk and
hugged her.

"Thank you, Miss Cardin. You are an angel. It's hard when you are
new and don't even have a telephone yet. You have been immensely
helpful to me." I grinned back at her. "As a matter of fact, I plan to
name my first girl-child after you!"

She trilled coquettishly and hid her laugh behind a lacy handker-
chief. "My lands, you don't want to do that to a baby! I was christened
Eulalie!"

I looked startled, then recovered. "Eulalie is a little, um, old fash-
ioned. Maybe I can modify it a bit...how about Lallie?"

She blushed suddenly. "You know, Gianna, I did have a bit of a
romance in my life. I was engaged – well, nearly engaged – to a wonderful young man long ago. He went off to war and was killed in
Burma." Her eyes misted. "He called me Lallie."

"Oh, Miss Cardin..." I was nearly tongue-tied with a strange and
lovely emotion. "It will definitely be Lallie then." And we said goodbye with me promising to be back in a day or two.

I had never lived any kind of communal life, and supper at 52 Brookside Drive was a new kind of event for me. There were ten boarders seated around a vast round table in Mrs. Lovatt's dining room. The table was set beautifully, with a lace cloth and a bouquet of flowers in the middle. She had lovely plates and heavy silverware set at each chair and I counted that ten people would be seated. I came in first.

"Oh, Miss Lewis," Mrs. Lovatt greeted me. "How'd ya do today?" I told her and she nodded, all the time plopping sugar bowls and spoons on the long side board server. She nodded, approving of my industriousness. "You're a go-getter, I can tell."

"Can I help? What can I do?" I gestured. "I'm used to helping with meals."

"Well, ain't that nice of you." She thought for a moment. "You can put the salt and peppers on the table...there are four sets, just space them...yes, that's fine." She rubbed her back for a moment and looked at the big wall clock. "It's almost six...I set everything out at about ten after. The boarders all work and most of 'em work until five, come home, wash up and are hungry right about now." She tipped her head toward the kitchen. "You can help me set out the fruit cups. Just put them in front of everyone's place." We went through the swinging door and into the steamy, delicious-smelling kitchen. "It will be a little confusing to you tonight, meetin' everyone, but you'll get to know everybody right quickly. My boarders are a nice bunch and you'll fit right in." I hefted a tray with ten fruit cups and went back through the doors to set each of them down.

I tried to set the names and the faces straight, but I must admit that the first evening *was* confusing. I sat next to, on my right, a red-faced, elderly man named Jonas Witherspoon. "In jewelry, little lady. Fine jewelry. You want a nice gold piece, maybe a neck-a-lace, you come to me." He winked. "I'll give you a special price."

On my left was a thin, vinegar-mouthed woman, Mrs. Stringer. She had small eyes and an even narrower point of view of the world. She lectured me from the start and I could tell that she didn't like my free-swinging hair or my ready smile. She told me that she worked for H. J. Pharmaceuticals. Oh lord! The same place as my nine o'clock interview! Mentally, I scratched this company off my list. I'd go to the interview, but if Mrs. Stringer was any example of what I'd find there, I wasn't buying.

Next around the table were two young women, about my own age. Janice DeCarlo was bright-eyed, voluptuous with a jutting bosom and raven-black, beautifully styled hair. She was a secretary in the law offices of Solomon and Solomon, in downtown Harrisburg. Jill Cleveland was a short, dynamic young woman, with long brown hair done up in pony-tail. Jill worked as a guide at the Harrisburg Museum of Art. I thought I could be friends with either or both of them.

Then, across the table, sat Mr. Horace Mastermind, a retired naval man who loved to play chess. When Horace found that I knew nothing whatsoever about chess, he dismissed me and fell to eating his meal. Next to him sat a good-looking young man by the name of Glen Anderson. Glen wore round spectacles and had a brush cut. He was an auto mechanic and a fanatic about English cars. I noticed that Jill gave him her rapt attention and hung on every word that he uttered.

Next to Glen sat Virginia Megani, a well-groomed older woman who, I think, was divorced. I never quite heard that night if she was employed, not much about her. She was pleasant, but didn't much join in to the general chatter at the table. And next to Virginia was Anthony Blenkinsop, a great name if I may say so. Anthony was a fledgling attorney-to-be and worked as a law clerk in the same law office as Janice. It seemed to me that Anthony cast yearning glances at her between passing the mashed potatoes.

Sitting next to the rat-trap mouthed Mrs. Stringer and rounding out the table, was another young man. His name was Aaron Coleman and Aaron was studying to become a doctor. From the chatter, I gathered that he was often absent from the table, due to staffing at Harrisburg General Hospital. Aaron looked as if he could use fattening up. He was very cute, in a boyish, eager way, and I could tell that his female patients were going to adore him and mother him.

There was one boarder missing. His name was Tom O'Hare and I learned that Tom was a stand-up comedian from Michigan. He also worked at a food service job so make the rent while he waited to be discovered. He, too, was often absent from the communal meals, due to his job and his availability, at a moment's notice, when a comedy gig opened.

Naturally, there was one more spot that was vacant. And that was for the next new boarder, who would be a woman, according to Mrs. Lovatt's sexual separation rule.

The meal was excellent. We started with the fruit cup, which was fresh fruit, not the highly colored canned stuff, and then waltzed into the main meal; stuffed pork chops with mouth-watering gravy, the aforementioned mashed potatoes, oozing butter, pattypan squash and creamed spinach. Mrs. Lovatt was also a superb baker, I was happy to see, with two big baskets of corn bread adorning the center of the table. Mmmmm-*mmmm*! And for dessert, she baked a peach shortcake that made my heart sing. I resolved to hang around in her kitchen and learn just how she made all of these delights. My mother had been an indifferent cook, except for a few easy Italian specialties, thus, I really never learned how to bake or make a decent dinner. Like everything else in my early life, I was cheated in culinary prowess too.

Conversation at the table was general and informative. As the new kid in town, I was asked a lot of questions, all of which I managed to answer without any trouble. I had learned early on in my life of deception, that people really want to talk about themselves, so it was easy to turn the conversational ball right back. "And where did you grow up?" was easily answered by just saying Idaho, and then me leaning forward and returning the question.

Everyone spoke briefly about their day, and the weather, the baseball scores, a bit of politics, and the suspension of the local park superintendent who had absconded with several thousand dollars and the wife of the local selectman, rounded out the evening.

After dinner was over, I was the only one who lingered to help Mrs. Lovett clear the table. She was almost scandalized that I insisted on helping her, but I told her that "my mother would shake me if she saw me walk away and let you do all this work." She patted me on the shoulder and said that I was a good girl, but she drew the line at me helping to wash the dishes.

"You shoo now," she gave me a good natured pat on my behind. "You can sit in the lounge and watch television with some of the others or go to your room. Whatever you like."

I asked her about having a telephone installed and she told me how to go about it. I thanked her for the magnificent meal and asked if I could watch her cooking and baking. She was flabbergasted that anyone would be interested in such a thing. "Whenever you like, Miss Lewis. Whenever you like."

I asked her to call me Gianna and we parted on a very amicable note. I went upstairs, re-arranged my small store of clothes and belonging, and made a list of the things I needed to buy:

An electric alarm clock

Bath toiletries, shampoo and soap

Toilet paper (or did that come with the room?)

A notebook so that I could write down cooking instructions and recipes

Some thank you notes. I wanted to send one to Mrs. Cardin

And the things I needed to do:

Get a JOB!!!!!!!

Get a telephone.

Get a new driver's license for Pennsylvania

Then, I read the rest of the newspaper for a few moments, turned off the light, and, in my new identity of Gianna Lewis, fell asleep.

My dreams were interrupted by the ringing of the telephone. Startled awake, it took me a few seconds to realize that I wasn't back in my girlish bed at 52 Brookside Drive, safe in the bosom, and what a bosom it was, of the enviable Mrs. Lovatt, but in a smallish apartment in New York City. Gianna Lewis was long gone…And so was Gianna St. Clare.

"Hullo," I slipped quickly into my newest role.

"Vivian?" I didn't recognize the voice. It was a male, husky and deep.

"Yes?"

"Good morning! This is Kenji." My heart took a happy leap. Kenji! "Remember me?" Oh, yeah, I remembered him big time! "Am I calling you too early?"

What does one say when one is wakened by a phone call? "Oh, no, Kenji. I was just lying here, getting myself geared up for the day." I hope my voice sounded a bit sleep and a bit sexy.

"Great. I'm sorry that I missed our breakfast rendezvous yesterday. We've all been working flat out and I just got home from a two-nighter."

"Can I ask you how it is going?"

"Bad. Sad. I don't know how anyone else can possibly be alive in the rubble, but, you know, we've gotta keep digging."

"I'm so…what can one say? So sorry. So sad, so upset. All those poor people. The ones I worked with, had coffee with, the ones I was just getting to know. All gone." I thought of Zachary. How had he died? Crushed when the plane hit? Buried alive? Burned to a crisp? No wonder my voice sounded teary.

"It's a bummer. I can't even begin to explain how it is down there." Kenji's voice also sounded a bit teary, and then he brightened up. "But life does go on. Are you still all right to go out for dinner tonight? I don't want to force you if you don't feel up to it."

I tried not to sound too eager, but heck, I was really looking forward to seeing him. "I'm just fine. How about you, though. Are you too pooped to go out?"

"Nah, I'm going to sleep for a while and then I'll be OK. What time is good for you? Six or so?"

"Six would be brilliant. I'll be ready. Where are we going? I mean, I don't care where we go, but how shall I dress?"

"Just wear something casual. I'm taking you to one of my favorite places, but it's not a fancy kind of place." He laughed and my toes curled. "I'm not a very fancy kind of guy."

"I'm looking forward to the evening..."

"Me too. See you at six."

I then jumped out of bed, noticing that my bones and aches were a little better. I showered and looked at myself in the bathroom mirror. The bruises and black and blue marks were starting to fade, turning a horrid shade of pinkish green. My nose, which had been mashed all over my face, was returning to some semblance of its former shape, although it really didn't look to me like my old nose. The hair was a wild and red as ever, curling even more furiously in the dampness of the bathroom. On the whole, I looked OK. Not much like I used to look, but OK.

The telephone rang again and I pulled a bath towel around me, sarong style, and padded out to answer. A buzz....I thought it might be a good idea to get one of those new phones with caller ID, maybe then I could trace these hang-up calls. The phone rang again and I snatched it up, angry and hostile. How dare this person harass me!

"Miss Morrison? Vivian Morrison?" Another rich, plumy voice, but no one that I recognized. "My name is Robert Rossi. I'm an attorney with the law firm of Gurall, Rossi and Matta. We represent...uh...represented..uh...represented, uh...Clausen & Chase."

Even the attorney seemed a bit rattled by all of this. "Yes, Mr. Rossi. I was hoping that someone would call."

"You know, Miss Morrison...It *is* Miss Morrison, yes?" I nodded into the phone and then realized that I needed to answer. I told him that yes, it was Miss. He continued: "Yes, thank you, Miss Morrison. I don't know what's happened to you since the disaster on 9-11, uh, were you in the building?"

"Yes, yes I was." I was going to be careful here.

"Well, you are one of the few employees who survived." Even though I already assumed this, I couldn't stop the audible gasp that burst from the throat. "I'm sorry, Miss Morrison, I know this must be very difficult for you. At any rate," his voice changed from hushed and reverent to businesslike. "We'd like to have a short meeting with you to discuss how this tragedy will affect you in the future."

"Affect me? Goodness, Mr. Rossi, it will affect me all my life!" I heard his indrawn breath. "And how will it affect me according to you? Legally, I mean." I really wanted to know. I mean, I was floating in this limbo, being taken care of by Operation Relief Recovery and the Red Cross and having people feel sorry for me, but this sort of thing could only last for a short while. The real world was out there…changed, but still out there. "What is going to happen? I mean, do I have a job?"

He harrumphed, uncomfortable. "I'd like to discuss all of this in person. I don't know if you were injured…?" His voice held a professional question, "Or if you are able to come to our office…?"

"Yes, Mr. Rossi, I was injured. I spent a few days in hospital. I was also seen by a doctor with Relief Recovery. I had a lot of minor injuries, broke my nose, and have a concussion, but I can certainly gear myself up to visit your offices. What time is convenient?"

"Can you be here at eleven? We are on Fifth Avenue, near 38th. Please take a taxi and get a receipt. Our office will reimburse you when you get here."

We hung up and I thought I needed the chew of a bagel to give me strength for this new ordeal. I dressed in jeans and a button-up shirt and went to Bernie's. Before I left my building, however, I had my daily session with "*A to Zed*" and looked in the section for the law. I learned that a lawyer was called a *solicitor*, court case documents are called *briefs*, and that a solicitor's office is called his *chambers*.

At a few minutes to eleven, I arrived at the august offices, ahem, I mean chambers, of Solicitor Robert Rossi. I dressed carefully, with a button-up blouse, a modest skirt, and a pair of low-heeled shoes. I left my face bereft of makeup and made sure that my hair looked as bushy as possible. As I entered the chambers, I even limped a little.

Mr. Rossi was a charming man, with pepper and salt hair, a hearing aid, and a sharpish grin. His handshake was firm and his blue eyes held a calculated twinkle. I could see that this twinkle could change in a moment to skewer a hapless defendant. He seated me with a tender solicitousness and asked if I wanted any refreshment. I smiled at him in a timorous way and asked for a cup of tea.

A buzzer summoned one of his minions, and the tea appeared almost immediately. It was in a china pot and was accompanied by a small silver sugar bowl, a silver pitcher of milk, and a dish, which matched the teapot, filled with lemon slices. I was impressed and said so. "I find it very difficult to get a good cuppa here in the States. You Americans make marvelous coffee, much better than any in England, but one doesn't find real tea in evidence here." I gave myself a slice of lemon and sipped, waiting for him to start.

He shuffled some papers on his desk, harrumphed, and got down to brass tacks. "Tell me about your experience on September 11th."

I recited my story and he sat back, listening carefully, but not writing anything down, his beautifully manicured hands templed in front of him. When I got to the part about Operation Relief Recovery, he uncapped a pen and made some notes on the yellow pad before him.

"And how are you feeling now?" I must admit, he sounded sincerely interested.

I told him that I was still rather bruised and battered, that my head ached, with continual pounding, dizziness and abominable pain and that my memory was elusive, especially with regard to the time just before and after the disaster. "I can't remember much about the people I worked with...It seems like a curtain is in front of me...the doctor thought that perhaps I was trying to block out what I couldn't bear to remember...friends...co-workers... I wake up at night; I'm in a panic, afraid that I can't get out of a burning building. It takes me hours to go back to sleep, and then, only with the help of a sleeping pill and a pain pill." I hunched towards him. "Am I the only one left? I mean, is there anyone else who is still...?"

He eyed me with sympathy. "Only you and two others that we have been able to locate." My face asked who. "One of the men in the mailroom, a Santana Rivera." I shook my head carefully. I didn't know a Santana Rivera. "Mr. Rivera was at the Post Office when the planes hit." Lucky, lucky Mr. Rivera, I thought. "And one of the C&C outside salesmen, a Wayne Zatorsky, who was in Arizona on a sales call. Do you know who he is?"

"No. I don't know either of them. But there were so many people....*No one* left? No one except me and the other two?" I think my voice held a note of panic.

Mr. Rossi's eyes misted. Genuinely misted, I think. I guess he knew a lot of the top brass there personally. Mr. Clausen Senior and Mr. Chase. Probably Jake Clausen and maybe even Zachary. "Not that we can find. The plane hit their floor directly. I think many of them died on impact. I'd like to think that they were spared...the fire...the collapse." I began to cry. I didn't mean to, but I couldn't help myself. I saw them, Zachary; Krissie, who had just learned that she was, after so many years of trying, pregnant; Laura that I sometimes ate lunch with; the fat guy who could always fix the copier, no matter how jammed it might become; Rollie and Sherman, the two guys who came around every week with the football or baseball pool; all of them, screaming and gasping and trying to throw themselves out of a window to escape the flames. Oh God, oh God! I thought of Zachary's wife...And was glad, yes glad, that she didn't know that he had planned to leave her. Poor thing, I was able to realize, she'd be able to mourn him wholeheartedly, instead of remembering him as the cad he was. It almost made me laugh out loud. Almost.

Rossi was talking again. "Did you see anyone in the building? Or anyone outside that you knew?"

"No," I said in a dull voice. "Only that woman in the lav." Upset as I was, I still remembered my British dictionary. "I can't remember her name...maybe it was Joanna or something like that. She died right away. A big piece of glass cut her head and parts of the ceiling crushed her skull." My eyes turned inward, remembering. "There was blood and parts of her brain and...and...I panicked....There was no way that I could have saved her!" My voice, of its own accord, got shrill and louder. "I only wanted to get out...to get out." Mr. Rossi watched me with aching sympathy. I wasn't acting at all. I was a pitiful wreck. "It was bloody horrible. Horrible." I wrapped my arms around myself, chilled and shivering. Mr. Rossi poured me some hot tea and I grasped the cup in both hands and forced myself to drink it down.

I took a deep breath and tried to stabilize myself. "I know how incredibly lucky I am, I mean, why me? Why was I allowed to live?" My eyes beseeched him, but, of course, there was no answer that we mortals could fathom. "Why did it happen at all? How can people *do* this to other people?" And again, there was no answer. I reached for a box of tissues that was on Rossi's desk and gently blew my nose, sniffed and gave him a watery smile.

He rubbed his chin. "Well, I'm sorry that you went through this kind of hell, but I am thankful that you, and the two others, are miraculously alive and able to tell us a little about what happened." He shuffled the papers on his desk. I ascertained that Rossi was a man who was seldom without the right words for any situation. But this situation seemed to be a little bit different. "Now to business. We, of course, represented C&C when they were still...um, viable...and I suppose we still represent the company now, even though they are no longer, um, ah, in business, so to speak. I understand that you were a new employee, right? You were there how long?"

"Only about twelve weeks, sir."

"Yes, well...Of course, as the company is, um, not, um, you know..." The words seemed to desert him. Tough words. Perhaps *blown out of existence* would have been a good way to say what he was trying to say, but maybe a wee bit too indelicate. "Ah, at any rate, there will be some sort of remunerative sum that will be coming your way. I don't exactly know what it will be...these matters are so far out of ordinary business that special rules...special considerations will have to be written." He looked at me and I fidgeted on the chair. I wanted badly to go home now. "I am authorized, however, today, to give you a check...an amount which will be the first part of some settlement, yet to be decided." I stared at him. "Yes, um, ah, I have here a check, um, made out to you, um, for the sum of, ah, twenty thousand dollars." I must have gasped, for he looked up at me and smiled. "This should see you through the next few weeks until, ah, we can come up with some sort of payment that will be satisfactory, ah, to all concerned." He handed me the check and asked me to sign a form. "Did my secretary reimburse you for the taxi and tip, plus the money to return home?" I nodded, mute and unable to speak. "Ah, good, good." Rossi now looked uncomfortable. It was obvious that he was through with me. I stood up, leaning hard on the arm of the chair to help myself arise.

"And may I ask you, are you representing me in this matter? Or should I get my own solicitor?" I saw his head whip around. Now I had his complete attention.

"What do you mean?" His frown could freeze the skin off a banana.

"Well, I don't quite know where to go...I mean, the money is nice to have, as I don't have a job, but what about all the rest? My injuries? What else? I don't know...?" I wrung my hands in agitation. "What's going to happen to me...?" I wasn't going to let him off too easily.

"My dear Miss Morrison. Uh, although we represent the company, we have your best interests at heart. After all, you are one of the very few people who, um, got through this alive. Do you know that there are some companies that aren't even paying their employees' salaries while all of this mess is being cleared up? Horrendous!" He threw up his hands. "Unwise! Can you imagine the lawsuits?"

I kept still and watched him. He pulled himself together, tugged on the bottom of his expensive vest, and assured me that, no, there was no need at all, at *all*, to involve another attorney. Not at all! Gurall, Rossi and Matta would be in the forefront of whatever was going to take place, representing my interests as a, um, former employee of Clausen & Chase. He walked with me to the elevator, his hand hovering just above my shoulder. I made sure that my limp was exaggerated, and staggered slightly as I went into the elevator.

"Please call me if anything...*anything*...is amiss. If I do not hear from you, I will contact you in a week or so to let you know, ahem, how things are progressing. Yes, progressing."

"Thank you, Mr. Rossi. I appreciate you looking out for me. Ta for now." The elevator door closed on his handsome, slightly worried face.

Safe in the back seat of the taxi, I gaped in wonderment at the check in my hand. Twenty freaking thousand dollars! Holy shit! I asked the cabbie, a Mr. Zarook, to take me to Bloomies, so that I might find a suitable casual garment to bring awe to Kenji's cute little slanted eyes. As we clashed through the ever-calamitous New York traffic, I folded the check and put it into my handbag. Funny, wasn't it...all of a sudden there were huge sums floating all over the place. All the money from Operation Relief Recovery, this check today (with promises of more...more), all the money that Ivan was going to collect, all the money that people were donating...so much money. It was just...odd, that's all.

I wondered if I should feel like a criminal, not because I had switched identity with Vivian, but because I was reaping so much in monetary benefits. I tried to justify it all in my mind. If I had really died, then Ivan would be getting just what he would be getting with my fictitious death. If I had left the building as myself, then I would be getting just what I was getting now as Vivian, the weekly stipends from Operation Relief Recovery and the huge handout from Rossi. Vivian, the real Vivian, on the other hand, would be getting – I mean her next of kin would be getting, um, whatever it was that the next of kins were amassing, probably a stupendous amount similar to Ivan's.

These mental gymnastics confused me…if I were alive and Vivian was dead…But I *was* alive and she *was* dead…Ah, screw it all. Pressing my hands gently to my temples, I decided to forget about what was right and what was fair. I *was* deceiving everyone, but then, I always had, hadn't I? After all, I'd gone through most of my life blithely getting rid of myself. And now, did I have any self left?

At six o'clock, Kenji's eyes were awed, or at least that's what he said in both words and gasps when he saw me. I had bought a darling casual suit, with yellow cropped pants and a matching short jacket with a yellow and white striped tee shirt underneath. On my feet were new white boat shoes, and a new saddle leather shoulder bag completed the ensemble. "You look like a buttercup," he gaped. I grinned. "And your poor face looks almost normal." His ham-sized finger touched the tip of my nose, so gentle that I might have not felt it at all, except for the jolt of electricity that went from my nose, down to regions south of my beltline.

Kenji himself wasn't looking too bad either. He had on fresh-pressed light blue denim pants, a white tee shirt that hugged his glorious shoulders, and a red knitted sweater wrapped around his neck, just like the male models do in the Ralph Lauren ads. His feet were clad in well-worn, but highly polished deck shoes. "And you look like you are about to step onto your yacht." I returned the compliment.

I was stunned when, reaching the street, I saw his car. I don't know what exactly I might have expected. A jeep? A pick up truck? Nah. Sitting at the curb, dazzling pedestrians from six blocks away, was a Ferrari! Blood red. Be still, my beating heart! "What a car!" I gasped inadequately. He shrugged and tried to look modest. "Bloody marvelous! Brilliant!"

As we whizzed down the street, he explained that he'd always wanted a Ferrari, and, when the time came to get a new car, said to himself, "Why not?" Why not, indeed.

"And I don't even have to worry much about the arrest-me-red color," he joked. "No cop is going to give another cop a ticket, capeesh?" I nodded, happy to be in this marvelous machine, happy to be with him.

We went down to SoHo and pulled up to a small, unobtrusive restaurant. A dilapidated sign proclaimed that we were in front of Liberty Sushi. "Like sushi?" he asked. I nodded. It was the right answer. Kenji beckoned to two teen age boys who had materialized, salivating over the Ferrari. "Can you two keep an eye on this for me?" Awed, they nodded, nearly speechless. "OK. You can sit in it while we eat. When I get out, I'll pay you." The boys' eyes were round with reverence. "But only you two guys inside the car. Understand?" They nodded, his slaves for life.

Over drinks, we shared information. I gave him my best version of the lies that I had been living and in turn, he told me about his life. "My mother was born in Japan. She fell in love with an American during the war. He was a Negro. A black man." Kenji watched me carefully, but I only toyed with my crispy noodles and took another sip of my saki. "Although they loved one another and he wanted to marry her, he was killed before they could make it legal. She was bereft; grief stricken, and then she found out that she was pregnant." He fiddled with his cup, turning it this way and that. I sat quietly and let him find the words. "She had me, all alone. Fortunately, there was a kindly American doctor in the hospital and he helped her to get some benefits, even though she wasn't married. He must have been a very nice guy, because, she told me, it was very hard to get anything, even if you were married."

"Were you brought up in Japan?"

"For a few years. Then, there was a program sponsored by some American charity to bring the wives and others like my mother to the United States. She had no other family, so she took advantage of the program and came to New York."

"What did she do when she got here?"

"The Japanese Family Council helped her to find a place to live." He laughed. "It wasn't fancy. It was a small apartment over a restaurant in the Japanese section of Mott Street."

"I thought Mott Street was Chinese."

"Mostly. At the end, near the bridge, there are a few streets that are Japanese." We lived there, me going to school, learning English and Japanese, and my mother working as a seamstress in one of those hot and dusty sweat shop places that make cheap clothing."

The waitress, who seemed to know Kenji, arrived with a "full boat" filled with delectable pieces of sushi and sashimi. We both dug in.

"Tell me about yourself as a boy."

"It was tough at first. I wasn't really Japanese. I look sort of Asian to you, perhaps, but in a Japanese community, I stuck out like a Martian. I took a lot of crap from the bigger kids, was sort of shunned, got called a lot of names, which I won't bore you with, and even got beat up once or twice." I made a sound of sympathy. Then Kenji started to laugh. "Don't feel too sorry for me. I began to grow. You know, most Japanese are shrimps. My mother told me that my father was a huge man, big and brawny, light-skinned for a Negro, with enormous feet and enormous hands." Kenji held up his huge mitts and I felt a crawly, warm sensation again. All I could think of was that childish little ditty that girls sometimes say. You know, the one about "Big hands, big you-know-what".

He continued, "And when I began to grow, I filled out. Big shoulders, and my muscles began to bulge a little." I shifted a bit on my seat, trying to keep my erotic mind from making pictures. "No one messed with me from then on. Man, I was the king!" He started to laugh. "All the older dudes, they all wanted to be my *friend!*" His hand lay on the table, between us and I touched his finger lightly with mine. He sucked his breath in and took my whole hand into his. We sat like that for a few moments, until the spell was interrupted by the waitress bringing us a bowl of edamame peas.

"So then what happened," I popped an edamame into my mouth, savoring its salty taste.

"So then, my mother decided that I should be educated. She went to the Catholic Church that was on our block. She told her story to Father Norton, one of the priests there, and she swore that I was worth the price of rubies. I was smart, talented, and should, somehow, be sent to college. Father Norton was a good guy. He asked me to come and see him and then he talked with my teachers. I mean, my mother had no money, practically none at all. She'd worked her whole life to give me a clean and decent home and to buy me clothes and football shoes and all the rest." His eyes were soft. "She's a mo-mo."

"A mo-mo?"

He laughed and his strong white teeth gleamed. "A Japanese word. It means peach in English. My mother is a peach. A saintly peach." He ate an edamame and continued. "She talked them into sending me to NYU. Not the most expensive of educations, but a damn good school. I was interested in law enforcement, so I took a degree in Criminal Justice, took the police exam after graduation, and started as a patrolman." He chuckled. "In this day of Affirmative Action, can you imagine how happy they were to get me? Ha! Two birds in one! A chink *and* a boogyman!"

"So how did you progress?"

"I did OK. I beat the streets for a year, then got lucky one night and foiled a big robbery. I caught the men, tackled both of them and was sitting on the bumper of their getaway car when support arrived. They were trussed up like Christmas turkeys, lying on the sidewalk in a puddle of rain. The loot, more than seven hundred thousand dollars worth of jewelry, was sitting in a heap next to· them. Their guns were sitting neatly on top of the jewels. Man, were those two robbers pissed at me!" He laughed again, a joyous sound. "And my buddies from the station. They just couldn't get over it. There was nothing for them to do! I had it all wrapped up! Ha! I got a commendation and a promotion all in one. The Department sent me back to school to learn detective work and I am now on the Narcotics Squad."

"Your mother must be bursting with pride. I know I am."

"Yeah, she's proud, all right, but she yelled at me for not waiting until I had more help. She's smart, my mother. She realized that I was one lucky bastard. Everything went right for me. But it could have been the other 'way 'round. I might have wound up with a bullet in my head, bleeding all over the sidewalk."

"Have you ever been shot at?" I was fascinated. Despite all my skirting around petty legalities and my horrible experiences with Joey, I'd never been in any danger or in trouble with the law.

"Couple of times. Never got hit, though. My partner, Lenny…you remember him?" I nodded yes. "He got hit in the leg two years ago. We were in the middle of a big drug bust and one of the guys had a pistol hidden. Luckily," Kenji knocked on the tabletop, "The bullet went through his calf and didn't hit any bone. Lenny told me it hurt like a sonofabitch." Kenji shook his head. "I don't want to ever get shot."

Our waitress collected the denuded boat. "How about some dessert?" she asked. I was going to say no, but Kenji asked me if I'd ever had green tea ice cream.

"No. Green tea ice cream?"

"Mmmm. It's the best." He asked for two dishes.

And it was… delicious, cold and melting with an indescribable subtle flavor. "This is marvelous! How did you ever know about green tea ice cream?"

The waitress joined in his laughter, "Dummy, I'm half Japanese!"

"Duh," I said and they both laughed harder.

The car was just as we left it, with two boys inside, patting the upholstery and stroking the dashboard. "Everything OK, fellas?" Kenji queried. They nodded, full of the importance of minding a treasure, even thought it was temporary. "What are your names?" Kenji asked.

The boys told him. "Live around here?" They nodded in unison. "OK, next time I see you, I'll take you both for a ride. I promise." The boys leaped in joy. Kenji gave them each a ten dollar bill and they ran off, calling back, "Thank you, Mister. Thank you."

We drove away and Kenji took my hand in his. I was emotional and almost started to cry. Why? Because of 9-11? Because of Kenji? Who can say?

"OK, my little English chrysanthemum, where to next? Would you like to dance? Take a walk? What?"

I already knew what I wanted to do, but, being a girl, wasn't going to blurt *that* suggestion out! "Maybe some dancing?"

"Right on, sweetheart." I wiggled at the endearment. "I know a nice spot." And we roared through the deserted streets to a place hidden between an Italian delicatessen and a liquor store. The club looked deserted from the outside. Only someone who'd been there before would know of its existence. We opened the door and were admitted into a dark hallway. Someone was playing a meandering version of "Stardust". A wraith appeared out of the shadows. "Evening, Kenji," the wraith said and led us to a smallish table, tucked into a secluded corner. As we sat, both of us facing the dance floor, our thighs touched and Kenji casually put his arm across the back of my chair. I bit my lip in anticipation.

There were a few couples dancing. We watched them for a moment, then Kenji picked up my hand again and brought it to his lips. He kissed it, a fleeting kiss and again, I shivered.

A waiter appeared. "What'll it be, Kenj? Wine? Got some marvelous armagnac, if you're so inclined." He tipped his head to me. "Evening, Ma'am."

"Armagnac? Sounds lovely."

"You want, you got." He smiled down at me. "Bring us two." The waiter tipped his head again, this time with approval and disappeared for a moment, reappearing with two ethereal balloon snifters with a gold liquid at their bottoms. We touched glasses, gazing at one another and then sipped and I thought the top of my head was going to fall off!

"Bloody hell!" I gasped, choking on the fumes of the brandy. "Amazing!"

"I presume that means you like it." He chuckled, as if I'd made the best joke in the world. Then, as the piano morphed into the first notes of "Moonglow", he held his hand out to me and pulled me onto the dance floor. I put my arm up to his shoulder and our bodies melded. The music, the man…it was marvelous. I gave myself up to the sensation of drifting, my entire body a'tingle, while the sublime music washed over us. Kenji pulled me closer and I could feel his heat and desire. I moved away slightly and looked up at his face. He smiled, a lazy smile and then bent and kissed the top of my head. I moved my hand to the back of his neck and reveled in the feel of his skin. Wooo-eeee.

The evening ended as it was decreed and I woke up the next morning with Kenji's kiss on my face. "Hey, mop head of mine. I gotta go." He stood back and searched my face. "You know, you look completely different without your glasses on." He peered at me. "Kinda younger…softer. But I adore you, glasses or no glasses." He bent lower. "I'm due at Ground Zero in an hour and I have to go home to get dressed." I tried to stifle the note of alarm his remark about my glasses caused me. I blew him a kiss. He bent to ruffle my hair. I smiled up at his gorgeous face, reached for his shoulders and pulled him down hard. Off balance, he toppled back onto me and…well, he was a bit late for work, I presume.

I made myself a cup of coffee and sat, watching the traffic go up and down the street. Was this love? Maybe. Maybe it was just lust. All I know is that I wanted him back in bed again. I pushed the image of Oliver's face out of my conscience and for some reason, felt a little guilty.

After I dressed, I decided to go to the bank, deposit the obscene check that Mr. Rossi had given me, and snoop into Vivian's safe deposit box. Perhaps, in it, I might find the solution to the mysterious person who kept calling and hanging up. I checked the address of the branch of the Chemical Bank where Vivian had her account. It was only about ten blocks away. As the day was bright and sunny, I walked. Perhaps it was because of last night, but I felt better than I had in ages.

I signed the back of the check, using my finest duplication of Vivian's simplistic handwriting. The teller gave a small gasp at the amount of the deposit, and, when I asked for an officer to let me into my safe deposit box, she called for one of the managers right away. I was led down a short flight of stairs and into a smallish room without any windows. I was handed a card to sign. Again, I did a "Vivian Ann Morrison" with ease. I produced my key at the bank officer's request. We both went into a vault-like strong-room, and proceeded to unlock, me first and then the officer, the box that was numbered 467. He slid the box out, then handed it to me and showed me into a cubicle, again without windows, with a chair and a table and nothing else in it. I put the box onto the table, and when I turned around, the bank officer had left the room, closing the door behind him. The door had a lock on it and I turned the knob so as to be sure of complete privacy.

I put the key into the lock and pushed the button that unlatched the top. The top swung open and....geez Louise! I'd never seen so much money in my life! I sat down, stunned...too stunned to even breathe. I touched the stacks of bills, all hundreds. There must be...thousands and thousands of dollars! I took out the bundles, counted one and then multiplied the total by the number of bundles. What the hell *was* all of this! How could anyone, much less a clunky individual such as Vivian...how could *anyone* have this much money*?*

Might they be counterfeit? A joke of some sort? I took each bundle out, there were twenty six of them. The bills certainly looked real enough. I took two hundreds out, one from one bundle and one from another. I'd read somewhere that you couldn't smear a real bill. I gathered some saliva in my mouth and spat twice, one goober on each bill. Then, I tried to smudge the printing. The bills stayed unsmudged. Was that a true test, or was it only one of those urban legends? So that I could be sure, I took the two bills and put them in my purse.

I upended the safety deposit box; shaking it to be sure I'd seen everything in it. Ah! At the bottom, there was a faded picture of two children sitting on a stone wall. A boy and a girl. The boy was perhaps six and the girl maybe four. They were staring at the camera, solemn and stiff. I turned the photo over, but the back of the picture was blank. Who *were* they? Vivian's illegitimate children? Vivian and her brother? And why were they in Vivian's secret stash?

Sighing, I repacked the money, put the photos back on top, and re-locked the box. I opened the door and called for the bank officer. Together, we went back in the vault and entombed the box once more.

CHAPTER TWELVE

I did a bit of shopping, bought the New York Times and went back to my apartment…ooops, my flat. For two nights in a row, I'd been wined and dined royally…and even a bit more than that for last night. Tonight, I would stay home, do my hair and my nails and maybe read a bit. The blinking red light drove me to the telephone. One message from Oliver. He was devastated that my license had been lost, and apparently lost while on his watch. How could he make it up to me? Lunch today perhaps? Call him by noon. It was nearly two o'clock. A little late for lunch.

Second call was from Kenji. Just checking in and to tell me that he'd had the best evening of his life last night. He'd see me at breakfast tomorrow morning. I could hear the smile in his voice. I smiled back at the answering machine.

Third call from my tormentor. Heavy breathing and then a click.

Fourth call from the divine Doctor Giggi. Could I come in for a check up Monday at 1:30?

I called Dr. Giggi's office first and confirmed the appointment. I had no way to reach Kenji and certainly no way to reach the breather, so I called Oliver. His plumy voice came onto the line. "Oh, Queen Ann, I'm so sorry that I missed you today. I want to….excuse me, can you hold a moment?" I acquiesced and dangled the phone from my ear as I opened the morning paper. Naturally, the paper was filled with news of Ground Zero, although I did notice that a few other items were creeping back into the first few pages.

As I flipped through the paper, I tried to gauge my feelings about Oliver and about Kenji. Here were two guys, as different as chalk from cheese, both handsome, both seemingly interested in me.

Oliver: Any girl's dream. Handsome, debonair, dresses like a fashion plate. Kind and funny, too. Obviously wealthy. Obviously smart and successful. Preppy type. Neat, superbly clean. A person who did a lot of good for his fellow man. He made my heart beat, made me feel warm and fuzzy.

And Kenji: Gorgeous, strong and a definite he-man. Great body and great use of same. Makes me laugh and smile and get hot all over. Exotic. Funny and a marvelous dancer. Street smart and street sexy. A policeman, for goodness sake...keeping our city safe. Keeping drugs out of the hands of kids. Working his ass off trying to find people or bodies in the most dangerous place that I could think of.

And how did I feel? Hmmm...so far, so good.

Oliver's voice broke into my reverie. He sounded angry, but not at me. "I'll call you back in six minutes. I have a situation here to deal with, OK?"

"I'll be here, Oliver. Take your time."

I sat back on my sofa and spread the Times out. As I turned to page 16, a picture jumped out...It was *me*! I gasped. *Me!* Avidly, I read the caption under the photo: Gianna St. Clare, Fort Lee, New Jersey. Beloved wife of Ivan St. Clare. Died, September 11, 2001.

A shock wave hit me and I couldn't breathe. My mouth hung open and my eyes glazed over. The newspaper fell to the floor. Dead! I was dead!

The telephone's ring jolted me back to reality. I let it ring, and ring, and ring, and ring. I simply couldn't take my eyes off myself. The phone whimpered to a stop and the answering machine clicked on. Oliver's voice asked where the heck was I...and to pleased call him as soon as I came back from wherever it was that I went to. I barely heard him.

I picked up the paper again. The entire space of page 16 was devoted to obituaries. Obituaries of the people who had been murdered when the planes hit the Twin Towers. "Oh, my God!" I whispered. "Oh, my sweet Jesus Lord."

The thumping in the vicinity of my chest gradually subsided. I devoured the photo again. It was one of me that I had given to Ivan very early in our relationship. Before I realized what a mistake I had made once again. I read the caption again and then, as my shock abated, was able to read the rest.

"Gianna was the light of my life. She was an angel and I cry every night for her. I pray that her death was swift and merciful. Everyone who knew her adored her. She will be missed by friends, neighbors and her fellow workers." From her loving husband, Ivan.

Memorial service to be held on September 21st, 2001 at eleven o'clock at the Unitarian Chapel, 236 Davis Avenue, Fort Lee, New Jersey.

Amazing! I was having a funeral!

I think I was still in a state of shock as I began to giggle. Maybe I could *go* to the service. I'd wear my glasses and a shawl, or headscarf and I'd hide in the back rows. No one would know I was there. My giggles turned into full fledged laughter and I laughed and laughed, hysterical, until my howls turned into howls of grief. Grief for the woman that I had been. Grief for what I had done. Grief for all the others who had been incinerated. Howling, animalistic, unstoppable grief.

The sobs subsided bit by bit. Snuffling, I was able to think. I realized that I had gone through most of my life killing myself. And now? Who was I? Did I have any self left? Was I still Gina Sottosanti, the sad and abused little girl who saw deceit as an only way out? Was she still somewhere within me? Was I still Gina Josephs, a young girl trying to learn how to survive? And who had stupidly and ignorantly thought that love had come her way? Had I been wrong to cast her off and become the more educated, perhaps wiser Gianna Lewis? Who the hell was I now? Nobody, I sniffed. Nobody at all.

When I could cry no more, I sat, slumped in the sofa, drained of all emotion and energy. I think I fell into a deep stupor, for when the telephone shrilled again, I saw that it was past five o'clock.

It was Oliver again. He almost scolded me in his worry. "Where were you? I was so concerned when you didn't answer. I had horrific visions of you somehow fainting away from your head injuries, lying alone and dying. I almost came over. What is wrong?"

"Nothing like that, Oliver. Thank you for your worrying. If I had been lying alone and dying, it would have been swell if you had come over." My tone was dry and bantering. I don't think he quite got it. Ah, well, we can't all be wits, but to give him some slack, he had no idea that I had just contemplated going to my own funeral. Contrite, I continued, "I went out for a moment (here I was, lying again...) and never noticed that you had left a message. I'm sorry. All is well." I tried a silly laugh. It seemed to come out OK. "I apologize on the Queen's new hat. Now, what's up?"

I'd made him laugh. Distracted him. "Oh, we had such a situation here today. Mervin, my assistant, just quit. Got into a screaming match with our head of accounting. It seemed like World War Two was being re-enacted right here in front of my desk. They started to throw things, get physical. I almost called the police." He sighed, now sounding tired and dejected. "In the words of that nincompoop, Rodney King, 'Why can't we all just get along?'"

"What a bloody shame! The police! What bloody happened? (was I overdoing this bloody stuff?) How did you get them calmed down?" I was glad to talk about someone else's crisis and put my feet up on the coffee table, settling back.

"Maybe tomorrow I can laugh at it all. But right now....Geez, Annie, my love, it was awful. I guess Mervin overheard Sarah making fun of his homosexual activities. I think she was very graphic about some stories she had heard about him flitting around, looking for true love in a gay bar men's room. She was really nasty. The entire office was listening to her and laughing. Mervin screamed and threw an armload of files at her." He sighed again. "Then Sarah snatched Mervin's toupee off his head. One of the other people in the office called me at that point and I went into the room and told them both to get into my office fast. They were yelling and screaming and I shut the door so that we might try to get it sorted out. Fat chance. Mervin tried to pick up the phone to call the Civil Liberties Union. He said he was going to...I believe the quote was...'Sue the cunt off you'." I started to giggle.

"Wish I'd been there!"

He laughed too. "I guess it was the stuff that Academy Award performances are made. She grabbed the phone and began to hit him on his now bald head." I giggled even louder. "She had his toupee in her hand and she threw it on the ground and jumped on it. He took my water carafe and emptied it over *her* head. Then he began to pull her hair, screaming that now she would know how it felt. Christ! You couldn't write this in a book. No one would believe it. They weren't paying the slightest attention to me. Finally, I had to get physically between them. Sarah scratched my face with her nails. I have two big bleeding lines on my cheek. Mervin kicked me in the shins." He groaned. "I had to fire them both and threaten to have the police come and arrest them both for assault and battery. Sarah told me that she quit and Mervin told me that he was going to sue me and my grandchildren down to the 50th generation."

"So then what happened?"

"Well, Sarah left, after upending every paper on her desk. Then I sat down with Mervin and we had a long talk. I guess I saw his point. He'd really been provoked. I asked him to take the rest of the day off and think about it all. He's going to come in on Monday and we'll pow-wow and perhaps I can see my way to letting him keep his job. I want to talk to our attorney and see where I stand. I'd like to keep

Mervin. He's a great employee and I think he was somewhat an innocent victim. Maybe I'll have to fine him or some such. But I don't
want Sarah anywhere near here again. Geez!"

"You need a drink. Maybe two drinks!"

"Yeah…All I want to do now is take three aspirins and go to bed.
Unfortunately, I have a meeting tonight, and then an appointment tomorrow that I can't get out of. But…and this is why I called
originally…Are you free Sunday day? Uncle Gerald is having a high
tea party at his country home in Greenwich."

"Greenwich, Connecticut? That's where a lot of the C&C people
lived."

"Yeah. They've been having funeral after funeral there. I think
there were more than a hundred victims who came from there. One
family, I think I read, lost both their mother and their father. If you feel
you'd rather not go…maybe it will upset you…"

"No. No. I was just…it doesn't matter. I'd love to go to a high tea.
I've never been to a high tea before." Ooops. "I mean I've been to a
high tea at, um, Harrod's in London. I've just never been to a high tea
at anyone's house. Uh, nobody really does that any more in England.
They just call it supper. Ham and eggs, sandwiches, scones and clotted
cream. Will it be like that, or will it be like Ascot?"

"More like Ascot, I think. Uncle Gerald fancies himself a man
about town. We're to wear fancy clothes. I have a pair of white flannel
pants that I once wore to a cricket match. I'm wearing those, and a
striped shirt, an ascot, for God's sake and a straw boater hat."

"Is it outside? It's a little cold for straw hats."

"Oh, Uncle Gerald does things in a big way. He has a tent worthy
of Barnum and Bailey. Big heaters, an orchestra. You could probably
wear a bikini and be comfortable." His voice warmed. "As a matter of
fact, why don't you wear a bikini? You'd be a big hit."

"Bloody cheek," I countered in a brilliant riposte. "I'll find something Ascot-y. Thank you, I'd adore high tea at Uncle Gerald's on
Sunday. What time?"

"I'll pick you up at, oh, maybe ten. We'll take the back roads and
stop for coffee on the way. I want to show you around his estate before
everyone gets there. I think you'll be impressed. I am, each and every
time." He chuckled again, "Wait until you see the Safari Room."

"I await with baited breath. You sound a lot calmer now."

A deep sigh. "I don't know what I'm going to do without Sarah, as
bitchy as she was. I have so much paperwork…." Another sigh.

"Could I help? I can do filing or whatever…I mean, I don't know anything about your business, but I can certainly remember the alphabet."

"I hadn't thought….would you be up to it? Maybe help until I can get someone else? Our files are in a mess. No one can find anything. If you just did that, you'd save out lives. I promised that we'll get someone else in a day or two." He sounded so grateful, and after all, darling Oliver had done so much for me. "Are you sure it wouldn't be too much for you?"

"Let's try it for a day or two. I have to see Dr. Giggi on Monday afternoon. Suppose I play the pampered new employee and arrive at the office at nine and leave at one? If I feel OK then I'll try a few more hours on Tuesday and we can see from there."

"Have I told you that I love you?" His tone was bantering, but there was some underlying thing there. I have to admit that my own heart thumped and I felt a glow warm up my heart.

"You'd better. I'm only doing this because I want to see Mervin and how he looks on Monday. Toupee or no toupee? Which will you wager on?"

"I say toupee."

"You're on. A quid either way."

"Whatever a quid is, I'm on."

We bantered a bit and then hung up. I felt a lot better. All that feeling sorry for myself made me feel a little silly now. Silly and hungry. I went out and trotted to the local pizzeria around the corner. It was dark and I didn't want to walk too far, but Mauritzio's was handy and, so I understood, very good. Three slices with mushroom and extra cheese and I was feeling much, much better.

I ordered a small 'za to take home with me, just in case I got the munchies a little later that night. I held the warm cardboard in my arms and walked back around the corner. I wasn't in an observing mood, and thus, I didn't look closely at the slight gentleman in the fedora hat who was standing across the street. I went up the stairs and let myself into the apartment.

I kicked off my shoes and snapped on the TV. Brit Hume was opining on FOX, and I turned the stove on for a nice cup of tea. I loved tea. It was so….refreshing. I know I sounded like some Lipton commercial, but tea was *different* from coffee. Coffee you needed in the morning. It got your mo-jo going. Tea, on the other hand, was soul food. Comforting when you were sick, or chilly, or needed a little boost. I picked out a Constant Comment bag and was pouring the hot water into a mug when my doorbell rang.

Who could it be? Oliver, maybe? Or perhaps, Kenji had been able to get away from his work for a moment. Honest, I had no premonition of danger at all. I opened the door, and gasped, reeling back, at the gun that was pointed at my head.

Most of us view violence, murder, and mayhem from the friendly side of a television or movie screen. We read newspaper accounts of horrors from the safety of our kitchen tables. We shudder and squeal in fright when Janet Leigh gets butchered in the shower. But how many of us actually experience, first hand, true terror?

Up to 9-11, certainly not me. And even 9-11, as incomprehensibly devastating as it was, seemed like something that happened in an awful dream. I was in it, it was happening, but I didn't fully understand, until later, just how dangerous it had all been.

But a gun in my face...I have to admit that I wet my pants. I was paralyzed.

The gun wavered. The little man holding it, the small, slight man wearing a fedora hat that I had glimpsed, changed before my eyes from a menacing murderer to a bundle of confusion. His grey eyes widened in surprise, his thin lips rounded in an 'O', and he backed up a step of two. "'Oo the 'ell are you?" he croaked.

"*Me*?" I squeaked, still scared shitless. "Who the hell are *you*?"

His eyes narrowed. He looked behind me. "Where's Vivien? Where's the bastard?"

"I'm Vivian!" I gestured to the vicinity of my chest. Who was he? Did he know the real Vivian? Oh Sweet Baby James, what was happening!

"Bloody hell, 'oney, you may be a lotta bleedin' things, but you ain't Vivien Morrison." He waved the gun. "Don't try to take the mickey outta me. Get back. We need to talk." He was *English*! *English*!

I backed up and he came in with me, shutting the door behind him. The gun was still out, pointing in my general direction, but you could tell that the heart had gone out of him. Whatever he was expecting, I wasn't it. Oh, God! Not now! Not someone who really knew Vivian! I backed carefully into the sofa, bumped my legs and sat down. He stood in front of me, uncertainty obvious. "Where is 'e?"

"Who?" I was confused. Who was 'he'?

"Vivien." His eyes darted, expecting to find someone else hiding behind the desk. "Where is the murderin' bastard?"

"Vivian? But *I'm* Vivian." Maybe if I said it over and over, he'd believe me.

The little man began to laugh. His high pitched giggle was almost hysterical. "As I said, you ain't Vivien."

My stark fear had faded, replaced by annoyance. How *dare* he come in here like this! "How do you know I'm not Vivian?" The best defense was a good offense, no?

"Henc, Henc, Henc." He laughed, a dry sound that came out of his nose. He looked almost ill, frail and grey. His hat was too big and came down on his ears. His overcoat hung on his thin frame. If he didn't have a gun in his hand, I'd almost feel sorry for him. However, he did have the gun. "Give it up, lady. You ain't Vivien, because Vivien is a man."

"A *man*!" I know my mouth hung down to the floor. "A *man*!"

The old man smiled, a tired, sad smile. "Yup, a man. A bleedin' man. Vivien Morrison. The fucker. 'e married then murdered my poor sweet dead daughter."

"I...I...I don't understand..." I groped for my sanity. A man! A *man*!

"So who are you, really?" He leaned back against the desk. "'is woman?"

"No...no. Oh my goodness. What a mess...." A few things began to make sense. Vivian's clunky shoes, heavy make-up, her manly ways, the studded belt, the clothes....A *man*! I began to see some piece of sanity in this situation. A man. Of course, a man.

I put my hands up to my head and my breath whooshed out. "Sit down, whoever you are. We need to talk."

He watched me for a moment and then nodded, felt behind him for the chair and sat down. I sensed that he really needed to sit. He was so thin...so unsubstantial. "Before we start, do you want a cup of tea? I was just making some for myself and the kettle is hot." His eyes brightened and he nodded, giving in. Some vicious murderer, huh!

I got up and rushed into the kitchen. I thought he might follow me. Thought he might be afraid that I might try to make an escape somehow. But he didn't. I made another large mug of tea. I used an English Breakfast bag for him. Seemed right, somehow. I put a jug of cream in the tray, the two mugs, some sugar packets, a spoon and a box of graham crackers. I carried the tray back into the main room and he was still sitting where I had left him, slumped in the chair.

I put the tray on the coffee table. He didn't move. "Are you all right? Are you sick?" I crouched down beside him, worried all of a sudden that my burglar/murderer might be ill.

He roused himself slowly. "I don't understand any of this." His face was pitiful. He dropped the pistol on the coffee table.

"Come on, drink up. Have a graham cracker. Please" I watched him anxiously as he held the cup up to his lips. His hands were blue-veined and trembled. He put the cup on his knee and munched a bit of· cracker. "Great. That's better."

I sat back on the sofa. "Are you all right?"

He gave me a peculiar smile. "I'm a little off my feed. The tea is good, lady. I'm sorry....I don't know ....I guess I made a mistake. I thought..." He took another gulp of hot tea.

"Eat the rest of the cracker. How long has it been since you ate?" Here I was, fussing over him like Florence Nightingale. A man who had just stuck a gun in my face. He coughed and told me that he hadn't had much of anything today. "I'm going to give you a piece of pizza, OK?" He smiled again, this time sweetly, and nodded.

I went back to the kitchen and put two pieces of the pie into the microwave. Two minutes and it binged. I put the slices on a plate, took a napkin and a fork...perhaps the English didn't eat pizza out of hand...and went back to my visitor. He was sitting, hands dangling, the teacup empty, three crackers gone. I fussed around him, pouring him another cup of tea, adding a spoon of sugar and a drop of milk. "Drink some more. Then eat the pizza. Then we'll talk. Oh, Lordy, do we have a lot to talk about."

He wolfed the first slice down, then nibbled at the second. His tea disappeared. He held the mug out to me. "Can I have another cuppa?"

I nodded. This was the most peculiar tea party since Alice in Wonderland. I lit the burner and got out two new teabags, waited until the water boiled and made two more cups. I retuned to find him sound asleep in my chair. Gently, so as not to wake my attacker, I set the tea-cup down. I curled myself up on the sofa, watching his face, and drank my own tea. Now that I was able to observe him, I noticed more...his coat was shabby, worn at the cuffs and collar. One button was hanging by a thread. I resisted the impulse to get my needle and thread and fix it firmly. There was something about the old coot, now that he wasn't sticking a gun in my face, that brought out some motherly feelings in me. He was clean shaven, with craggy eyebrows and. well, what kind of hair? I didn't think I could lift off the fedora and peek. His shoes were clean and polished, but the leather was cracked and the heels worn down. He looked like some elderly clerk, a bit down on his luck. Maybe he really was a burglar? Wait! What had he said? A *daughter*! Vivian had murdered his *daughter*! Wait! Wait! Married and *murdered*, he'd said! Shit, he was Vivian's father-in-law. Oh, gee whiz.

What was I going to do? My mind was nearly be-numbed. What was the story here? And Vivian – a man! Unbelievable. All of this, just un-believable.

My visitor blinked, opened his eyes and gave a hunted jump. He watched me for a moment, fearful…and then slumped back. "I guess I wheezed off."

"You seemed tired. Do you want anything more to eat?"

"No, ta, lady. I think I've made some kinda terrible mistake." Shamefaced, he touched the gun and blinked at me.

"Not really….Listen, what's your name? I don't know what to call you."

"Will…I'm Will MacGillivray. London born and London bred, al-though my family came from Scotland originally." I waited and he continued. "Vivian was my daughter…our daughter, Annie and me." My face showed my confusion. I thought he'd said that Vivian was a man? "Hee, you in America don't call men Vivien. But in England, we have two kinds'a Vivians. The girl is Vivian with an 'a', the boy is Vivien, spelled with an 'e'."

"Ah!" I said, beginning to understand a little, but only a little.

"Yes," he said, nodding at me. "Our daughter was Vivian, Vivian Ann, really, and she married a Vivien." I gave him an encouraging look and he continued. "Our Viv, she was the apple of my eye. Annie and me 'ad been married for many a year and had no kiddies. Then, when we had almost given up, along came Viv. She was the sweetest little girl you'd ever know. Bright as a penny, sweet to her Mum, a love. She got the best of everything we could manage to give 'er. I worked for the Underground, and I took the third shift so that I'd get a bit more lolly. Annie stayed home so as to be there when Viv came home from school, but she took in extra laundry too and did odd jobs, cleaning for other ladies and such so that we could save a bit extra for Viv's schooling, So the we could send 'er to a good school. She did well. Got her O levels and then went to a secretarial school. She was determined to make somethin' of 'erself. Ah, we were right proud of 'er, we were. And then she met Vivien, the bleedin' bastard, and 'er life went downhill. Oh, she loved 'im," His thin hands went up in protest. "But from the start, An-nie and me knew 'e was a bad one."

He drank a little. Holding the cup, he told me more. "They got a council 'ouse not too far from where we was living. Viv was 'appy at first, and then, we noticed that sometimes she didn't come around. We think she was being punched about. Once or twice we saw bruises, black 'n' blue marks. Viv laughed it off and told us that she was just clumsy, but we knew better." I winced, thinking of my own childhood beatings…and then of Ivan…

"She was such an 'appy child. And then, after…she seemed to grow smaller…not to laugh…not to visit 'er Mum as much. It was all wrong, I tell you. But she stuck it out. Vivien was a lout. A layabout. Never seemed to have a job. Oh, one was allus coming, some big thing, just around the corner. So Viv went out to work, so that they could pay their rent and 'ave food on the table." He stared into space. "Wasn't right. Wasn't right." He shook his head, then reached up and took the fedora off. As I might have suspected, his hair was thin and sparse, and lay across his freckled skull. He held the fedora tightly in both hands and put it carefully on his knees. "Anyroad, one day, Viv came and told us that she was gonna 'ave a baby. She was that 'appy, I tell you. And Edwin was born and she was 'appy for a few months. She couldn't work, mind you, and Annie and me tried to 'elp as much as we could. Vivien…'e was never around. Alllus at the pub, or out with 'is mates. Spending all 'is coin, and never giving 'er anything. Fair was to break our 'earts, I tell you.

"And then, all of a sudden, 'e 'ad money. I dunno how, but 'e was flash. Now I know better, I know that 'e was burg'lin 'ouses. Stealing. 'ed gotten in with a bad bunch. Easy-peasy money. And 'e got away with it, too." His face got longer and even more lugubrious.

"Once in a while, I thought that Viv was gonna leave 'im, come 'ome to us, but, then 'e talked 'er around. She didn't 'ave to work anymore and maybe she was 'appier. I donno. "

"What happened then?"

"She got caught again. 'ad a baby girl, named 'er Annie, like 'er Mum. Them kiddies was beautiful, just beautiful. Sweet and loveable, just like their mother. Made a fellow's 'eart swell with pride, it did. Annie and me, we loved those tykes like you wouldn't believe. Bought Edwin a train set and Little Annie a golliwog doll."

He hunched back in the chair; his eyes began to water. "And then…one day, Viv and Edwin and Little Annie disappeared."

"Disappeared?" I almost dropped my mug. "What do you mean, disappeared?

He shifted on the chair. His voice dropped and I had to lean forward to hear his whisper. "They were gone. Gone. Nobody knew where. All their clothes were gone. Vivien, 'e said that they'd left 'im.

Left 'im? Where would they go? They'd come to us, wouldn't they? No, we knew somethin' wasn't right. There's no chance that Little Annie would have left 'er dolly. Never."

"What did you do?"

"I went and spoke to Jimmy James. 'E's the police chief in our village. Good chap, but there was no evidence that anything bad 'ad happened to them. Jimmy tole me, 'Will, I know 'ow much store you and Annie set by Viv and the kiddies. And I know that all wasn't well with 'er and that Vivien. And I even know deep in my 'eart of 'earts that Vivien was mixed up somehow in that bank robbery over in Sturenden, but…'"

Will spread his fingers out, nearly upsetting his tea. "'But what?' I says to Jimmy. And Jimmy tells me, 'I got nothing to show that anything suspicious 'appened to them, Will. Sometimes, the ladies do strange things. Viv wouldn'ta been the first wife to leave a nasty chap like Vivien, right? I 'ad the lads look around their 'ouse. No blood, no struggle, no bodies. There isn't much else I can do. And Vivien, for all I can't take to the waster, five other men swear 'e was in the pub at Puddleby with them all evening, the night Viv and the children ran away.' And then, 'cause Jimmy sees I'm that upset, 'e tells me that 'e'll put out a bulletin asking for assistance in locating Viv or the children. It was the best 'e could do, 'e told me."

"How old were the children, Will? When they disappeared, I mean?"

"Edwin, 'e was seven and the baby was five."

I knew then. Knew who the boy and girl were in the photo in the bottom of the safe deposit box. "What happened then?"

"Annie, my Annie, that is, she sickened and died. Juss withered away. No 'eart left in 'er, you see. She knew, as I did, that the bastard 'ad killed them. Killed them in cold blood and buried 'em somewheres. Somewheres so that no one would ever find 'em." He bowed his head and when he lifted it again, I saw the tears that couldn't be contained. I thought my own heart would break.

"Oh, Will. Oh, how awful."

"Vivien tried to come to Annie's funeral, but I told 'im that I'd die before I let 'im in the same church with my Annie. I thought that 'e was going to push by me, but maybe something in my face made 'im stop. I never saw 'im again, although people told me that 'e was allus whoring around and allus 'ad a lot of money. I knew Jimmy was keeping an eye on 'im, but nothing ever came of it all. Then, about a few months later, Vivien also left the village. 'E said 'e was going to Ireland, so I 'eard."

"But he came here," I blurted, before I could think about it...

"I know, I know," Will nodded his head. "But before we get to 'ow you fit inta all of this, I gotta tell you the rest. I'm a sick man. I ain't got long to live. It's me 'eart. It's tickety. Bad tickety." He held his hand to his chest. "I gotta tell somebody. Before I die and the tale dies with me." I nodded and sat back, shocked and enthralled by the story.

"Jimmy 'eard through the police grapevine that the bastard 'ad joined up with a big gang in Ireland. Gang called The Bully Boys. They was going 'round terrorizing old ladies and stealing their jools, mebbbe sometimes conking 'em on the 'ead. Jimmy put out feelers, but nothing came of it all."

"As fer me, I got made redundant when the Underground consolidated...I was ready to leave anyway...I didn't 'ave anything to save for anymore. I'd gotten a bit put by and a good pension, after all. I worked for more than thirty-five years with them. I got to thinking. They 'ad to be somewhere, the bodies, I mean." I sucked in my breath again. "And where would they be? I 'ad my suspicions, but no proof, ya see. So I 'ired myself out as a jobbing gardener. Did yardwork around the neighborhood. I was respectable, worked 'ard and didn't charge folks much. I 'ad more work than I could manage. But the job I wanted, it was at the council 'ouse where Viv 'ad lived. That's the place I wanted to be able to dig in, you see." He looked up at me and my eyes grew huge. Dig in?

"Yes, missus. I 'ad my thoughts, didn't I? In the garden." He paused for a long moment. "And that's where I finally found them." He must have heard my moan, but he doggedly kept on with his story. "They was buried deep down, covered with a tattered blanket, all their bones 'eaped together." I put my hands to my mouth, trying to stifle the gagging sound. "'E'd butchered them, cut their throats, didn't 'e? They had their 'ands tied behind their backs and they was all thrown 'igglty-piggle in the dirt, covered all up and the bloody bastard 'ad planted some flowers over them. They was in 'is way, you see. They was just in 'is way."

"Oh, Will," I mourned inadequately. He gave me a look that spoke a million words. Or maybe only one.

"Jimmy Johnson apologized. 'e couldn't tell me 'e was sorry enough. But there was nothing 'e could do. Couldn't of made any difference even if they'd been found the day after. They were dead, weren't they? No one could a brought them back to me. We 'ad a fine funeral for them and buried them decently next to my Annie. At least they could rest in the peace of the churchyard now. Poor buggers. Poor little buggers." He broke down, bent his head and sobbed. I sobbed too and got up and put my arms around him. He felt like bird bones under my arms, frail and unsubstantial. And then, he began to cough. His body shook and he retched and a bloody sputum came out of his mouth. He was embarrassed and tried to wipe his lips with his sleeve. I grabbed a napkin and helped him and then eased him back onto the chair.

"Do you need a doctor? What's wrong?"

"I 'aven't long on this earth, lady. I 'ave consumption and a bad 'eart and I'm going to die soon. I don't give a tinker's dam...I 'ave nothin' at all to live for, only to take whatever revenge I can on that bastard. The last thing I wanted to do, even if it took all my strength, was to find 'im and make 'im somehow pay for 'is sins. I know God will send 'im straight to 'ell, but I want to do my part first."

"How did you find him here?"

"Jimmy got on the 'orn to Ireland and now they began to pay attention. They couldn't locate Vivien Morrison, but they learned that a Vivian Ann Morrison 'ad applied for a visa to the US of A. I figured that 'e 'ad just switched over to Viv's identification. 'oo would notice the 'a' or the 'e'. Most people would just think it was a spelling mistake." I nodded grimly, knowing how easy these things were. "And I guess, when 'e got 'ere, or mebbe even while 'e was in Ireland, 'e changed 'is appearance, let 'is 'air grow, dyed it red and became a woman. Good disguise, eh, lady?"

"Good enough to fool everyone here too, even me, and I knew him."

"You knew 'im?" He revived, sitting up with alacrity.

"I worked with him, only I thought he was a she...a very manly she." I began to laugh. "The people at work thought she was a lesbian!" His eyes goggled and his mouth opened wide. I recognized the feeling.

"A...les...lesbian! Bloody cheek! I'll be dipped!" And then, God bless his soul, he began to laugh with me. Creaky chuckles and then a roar of delight. Then he stopped. "But...but where is 'e now?"

My own laughter stopped too. "He's dead, Will. Dead under tons of rubble and fire and brimstone. He died in the World Trade Center on September 11th."

"Dead." The word came out in a long hissing sound. "The fucker is dead...'scuse me, ma'am. Are you sure?"

"I saw him die. It was, um, very final and very traumatic. He's gone. I'm sure he's also gone to a permanent place of fire and brimstone. I'm positive that God has punished him as much as possible. The bastard!"

He pulled himself upright. "I wanted to kill 'im. I wanted to be the one. I wanted revenge on 'im." He began to cough again. I started up towards him, but he waved me away with a weak hand. "But 'ow...'ow...why are you...? "Ow do you fit inta all of this?"

"Let's have one more cuppa. Maybe another slice of pizza and then *you'll* sit back and *I* will tell you another story."

It was well after midnight when I put Will into a cab and sent him back to his, as he called it, "bed-sitter"...a new word for me to memorize. Poor lamb, he was so exhausted that he left his pistol on my table.

I had talked for maybe an hour, told him everything, from the slums of Chicago to my new identification here. He laughed, he cried with me, he sat amazed. At the end, we agreed to meet tomorrow and I would treat him to a huge lunch. I promised that I would bring him the photo as well as a big surprise. I didn't tell him about the stash of bills, but I intended to give him all of the money. I didn't need it, after all, I had the munificence of Mr. Rossi's firm, plus all of the money that Oliver had paid to me. Maybe Will wouldn't live too long, but I wanted to make sure that he lived the rest of his life in splendor. He could maybe erect a garden or some sort of lovely memorial for his daughter, his wife, Edwin and Wee Annie.

CHAPTER THIRTEEN

I yawned and climbed into bed. I was exhausted, physically and emotionally. Who could believe today?

After one hour of staring at the dark ceiling, my eyeballs felt like they were stuffed with sand. I couldn't sleep for beans. I sat up...maybe I'd had too many cuppas, I chuckled to myself. I needed a warm glass of milk maybe. I padded again to the kitchen and warmed some up, poured it into a wineglass...it felt a bit more elegant that way...and leaped back under the comforter.

Incredible, wasn't it? While I was impersonating Vivian...no, Vivien, he had been impersonating his dead wife. Geez Louise! I had thought that I was unique, that no one else could have been so duplicitous, but perhaps, all over the world, people were pretending to be someone else. Well, there had been Ivan....

I had dressed in my best suit and taken the bus, first to Penn Pharmaceuticals, where I had a decent, but boring interview and didn't see the thin-lipped Mrs. Stringer at all. The job would be a well-paying one, if not one that would dazzle and amaze. If nothing else turned up, it would at least give me enough money to get myself settled while I tried to find a more interesting position. The pleasant woman who interviewed me told me that she would call me at Mrs. Lovatt's number (as I had told her that I hadn't had the opportunity to get a telephone yet) within three days to tell me if I had the job or not.

Satisfied, I trotted to the next interview. The bus left me off at the beginning of what looked like a meandering country road. The driver told me, "That architect woman's barn is about a half mile down. Ya can't miss it!" He grinned and waved as he took off. I walked for ·about ten minutes, enjoying the fields and flowers. There were only a few houses, none with numbers, only names like "Winter's End", "Glen Boston" and "Ardmore Acres". The driver had said a barn, hadn't he, and yes, there it was, just around the next corner. A big stone barn with a magnificent driveway, with wildflowers growing in a riot everywhere. Cool! I walked toward the door, my feet crunching on the gravel and rang the bell. I heard melodious chimes and in a twinkling, the door was opened by what looked like an elderly pixie. She was short and round and had bushy white hair, twinkling eyes and a pair of spectacles that looked like the ones Santa Claus wore.

"Good morning, I'm Gianna Lewis and I have an appointment with Miss Pedersen."

"Well, good morning to you." The pixie twinkled even more, if possible. Then she began to yell. "Hey, damn you! Get away from the bird feeder!"

I jumped. "Shooo!" She flapped her hands and then ran into the yard, waving her hands and yelling at the biggest cat that I had ever seen. "Goddam cat! Get the heck outta here!" She aimed a kick at the cat. The cat, turned and waited, clearly enjoying this game, and when the pixie was almost upon it, turned and melted away into the shrubbery. The pixie was sweating a bit. She came back, wiping her face and muttering cat-type obscenities.

"So you're Gianna? Sorry about that. Come on in." She whipped around once more, trying to see if the cat had come back, and then huffed herself into the barn after me. I went through the door and then stopped in amazement.

"Son of a gun!" I exclaimed. "What a magnificent place!"

The pixie grinned. "Like it?"

I goggled. "I *love* it!" I was in a wide hall, with a ceiling that reached about fifty feet into the air (I learned afterwards that it was exactly fifty-seven feet from the flagstone floor to the top of the pitched roof). The hall then opened into one huge room with a massive stone fireplace at one end. There were soft, glowing oriental rugs scattered on the flagstones…and mind you, I had never been in a place that had stone floors before either. The furniture was odd, all peculiar modern pieces in bright colors. Some of the chairs looked inviting, and others looked as if they would pierce your backside if you sat in them. One chair was shaped like a big, cupped hand. All around the perimeter was a low, divan-thing, with scattered cushions, one more delightful than the next. A table, made from a huge clock face sat in front of the fireplace. "Gee whiz" was about all I could say. Then I turned a noticed that there was a balcony running mid-way, all around the room and two wide staircases, made of logs, climbed up to it.

"I live here and work here too," the pixie said. "I'm Hedwig. Hedwig Pedersen." And she shook my hand with a grip as hard as the flagstones.

There was a small office tucked under the balcony at the side of the room. The kitchen was under the balcony at the back and there was a luxurious bathroom off to one side.

"Oh!" I cried with delight, as I discovered that a stream ran through the house and three or four bridges were placed throughout so that one could leap over it to the other side. Miss Pedersen asked me if I minded the occasional frog.

"We have a screen thingamajig so that animals can't get in through the stream, but once in a while, a frog gets through. Nothing else, mind you, but froggies." I assured her that froggies would be taken in stride and she laughed and took me upstairs. In the front of the house was the office area. A big loft-like room (it was once where they kept the hay) held three drawing tables, chairs, computers, file cabinets with long, thin drawers, assorted stuff that architects used, I guess, and two nice men dressed in jeans and shirts. I was introduced to them: Tom Catalano and Len Sizitsky.

The balcony narrowed and ran to the back of the barn where Miss Pedersen had her private living quarters, one big bedroom and bath for her and one small bedroom and smaller bath for any guest who might come along.

Sunlight poured through the windows and also through the huge skylights that had been built into the ceiling. It was enormous....I gaped anew and said, "My, it's just like living in a barn!" Miss Pederson guffawed and whacked me cheerfully on my back. I felt that the job would be mine in an instant. I liked her that much.

Evidently, the feeling was mutual. She asked me a few, perfunctory questions, wanted to know if I was open to learning her architectural computer systems and asked me if I could start the day after tomorrow. Salary? Oh, whatever I thought was right.

"I need, not a secretary, not a bookkeeper...but something more intimate. Like a good buddy. I don't give a hang about your typing. I presume if you're here, that you can bang out a letter or two, yes?" I nodded, swept away. "And I figure any fool can add and subtract, right?" I nodded again. "You might come into the city with me and help me pick out curtains one day. You might measure walls, you'll take irate clients to lunch and jolly them along for me, you might go out in the garden and pick tomatoes, chase the cat away, fill the bird-feeder, do payroll, make me go to the bank and be sure that I deposit 10 per cent of each commission check into my retirement account…and you can yell at me if I balk…those sort of things.

We parted on a cheerful note. The guys came downstairs and shook my hand. "See you on Wednesday, OK?"

"OK."

I did go to the interview at the grocery cooperative, but my heart just wasn't in it. After Hedwig and the boys, anything else was anticlimactic. So, then, I was employed. One huge thing to cross of my list. I spent the rest of the afternoon shopping for the small things I needed, bought myself three pair of khakis and a few casual tops, a pair of sneakers and a corduroy jacket in a lovely shade of green that made my shiny brown hair look like a valuable antique. I was all set.

My new job was the talk of the dinner table. The Pederson barn was a local attraction and everyone wanted to hear if it really had a stream that went through it. Mrs. Lovatt had done herself proud again. This time, a savory vegetable soup to start with, then fried chicken that made me want to weep. The chicken was nestled with sweet potato chips and fresh from somebody's garden peas. The dessert was a sour cream cake[1], loaded with walnuts and cinnamon. "I got the recipe from Mrs. Stelman, a Jewish lady that I met at the fish market," Mrs. Lovatt informed us. "She gave me a brisket recipe that I may try some night." Full to the top of our ears, we all nodded with happiness.

After supper, Anthony Blenkinsop joined Mr. Mastermind at the chess set, Aaron, Jill, Glen and Janice went to the movies, and I sat and watched "The Alamo" on the television set with John Wayne. I mean, John Wayne was in the movie, not on the couch with me. Oh, and Mr. Witherspoon and Mrs. Lovatt joined Mr. Wayne and myself. Mrs. Stringer and Virginia went to their respective rooms, and Tom was still on the comedy circuit.

After a mind-blowing breakfast, enough to make you want to go out and till the north forty acres, I used Mrs. Lovatt's telephone to call and get my own telephone installed. It would be put in on Friday, and Mrs. Lovatt assured me that she would be there when they came and let them in. "You can leave the deposit money with me."

Then I walked to the Harrisburg Mercantile Bank and opened a checking account. I was able to deposit the entire vacation check in my

---

[1] See Recipe at the end, you'll love it.

account, as well as transfer the smallish sum that had formerly rested in the bank in Ohio.

Life in Harrisburg tootled along. I loved working with Hedwig, as she asked me to call her. She was a fascinating old bird, one of the only women students to actually work with Frank Lloyd Wright at his "Waterfall House". She told me grand stories of growing up in the depression, studying at Cooper Union in New York City and trying to find a job in a time when experienced men were reduced to selling apples on the street.

"I found a factory that needed a bookkeeper. Shoot, I knew jack shit about keeping books, but I schmoozed him, lied through my teeth and made him think that I had a lot of experience. He hired me, and paid me bupkas. But bupkas was enough for me to live, and so I went along with the job. Much of the work was only common sense. But some of it, golly, I didn't know what to do. So I went to one of the other bookkeepers and pretended that in my old job, we did bookkeeping by the Morton method."

"What's the Morton method?" I was hooked.

"Shoot, who knows," she roared. I just made it up. And then, when the bookkeeper showed me how *they* did it, well, honey, anyone could copy once they were shown, so I was able to do almost anything." She guffawed. "And I was always careful to tell them afterwards that their method was much, much more efficient than the Morton method."

"You are a hoot," I praised.

"You know, Gianna, anyone can do anything, if only shown how. That's why I look for a bright, eager person to work with me. I can teach you anything. All you have to do is be interested and remember. Shoot, you could learn brain surgery in a month or so. Hell, anyone could!"

Her philosophy was original and seemed to work. I stashed her wisdom in my collection and the Morton method has stood me in good stead all my life.

I did learn a great deal from her. We both took lessons on CAD-CAM, the architectural computer design systems, we both went to design studios, and she showed me how to use color and patterns and how to successfully work with the fussy, wealthy clients. I soaked it all up and loved it.

In my spare time, I visited Eulalie at the Library and occasionally took her out for a lunch treat. She was a charming woman and her life, as one of Harrisburg's oldest families, was a history lesson in itself. I buzzed around Mrs. Lovatt's kitchen and she even let me do a bit of

cooking once in a while. Hedwig was right. Any fool could learn how
to cook if she paid attention and tried. Oh, I had a couple of disasters,
such as the time I forgot to put any sugar in the chocolate birthday
cake I made for Glen. And the time I used a stewing hen to make fried
chicken and no one could possibly bite into the rubbery mess. But I
persevered and found that, most of the time, the boarders never knew
if it was me or Mrs. Lovatt that made the meat loaf. I even showed her
a few of the recipes that my mother had made: *Vitello piccata, pasta
fagioli, manicotti,* and *biscotti.* I suppose Rose hadn't been all bad. Ha,
just mostly bad.

I got along tolerably well with my fellow boarders. Mrs.
Stringer and I never really rubbed along, but the rest of them, even
the elusive but hysterically funny Tom O'Hare, were fine people.
Jill and Glen got married later that year and we threw them a rous-
ing reception. They moved out after the wedding. Mrs. Lovatt was
firm. She didn't have married people. We got new boarders and life
at 52 Brookside Drive continued as usual with a little different cast
of characters.

And then, one day Hedwig and I went to check on how the
Weinstein house was progressing. The Weinsteins, Dr. Saul and his
wife, Deirdre, were two of the biggest pains in the ass for whom Hedwig had ever performed miracles. Dr. Saul was a dentist, not your
ordinary, fill-my-tooth dentist, oh, no. He did cosmetic dentistry, generally to the rich and famous. I have to admit that his own teeth and
those of the delectable Deirdre were dazzling.

They had purchased a mountain-top chunk of land in Salisia, a
wealthy suburb of Harrisburg. Hedwig had been bestowed the honor
(beating out considerable competition) of designing their aerie. They
had fallen in love with her barn and wanted something similar, only
much, much bigger and much, much more…well, more.

Hedwig had shoved off all other work to the capable Tom and Len
and devoted herself to their dream. Design after design after design
had been done and discarded. Not quite large enough, not quite osten-
tatious enough, not the sort of thing that would have their friends and
enemies grinding their teeth (thus, perhaps needing a visit to the dentist?) over. Finally, after months of design work, the plans had been
finalized and approved. The end result, naturally, didn't resemble
Hedwig's marvelous home at all. *Her* barn was a place of delight, it
looked natural, tucked into its gardens and each and every object or
piece of furniture was obviously chosen because it was loved, not cov-
eted. Some things matched, some didn't, and the result was a poem.

The Weinstein's monstrosity had lost all of the charm. It loomed huge, too big even for its mountain; the rooms were caverns, filled with the wrong furniture, the wrong colors, the wrong décor. Hedwig was physically sick over the job. She wailed that she should never have been associated with such barbarians. Much of my time was spent giving her pep talks. "Just get it finished, darling. Get it over with."

"People will see it and think that I'm like that!"

"No, people who matter know you and your work."

"This supposed to *be* my work! Great Thor! What a mistake I made! Shoot!" And she grabbed at her hair and made it look even worse than it generally did.

The Weinstein house, "Eagle's Crag" they called it, which just goes to show you, was nearly done. Hedwig and I had gone up there to check the installation of the tapestries…"Does her highness think she's creating Versailles?" was Hedwig's moan, when she saw the incredibly tortured hangings.

"Never mind. It's her house." I soothed.

"Agggh!" was Hedwig's answer.

There were five men, struggling mightily, to put up the tapestries in what was called "The Great Hall". The walls were so high that there was staging set up and we watched, openmouthed, our heads tipped back, as they fastened the offending drapery to the walls thus destroying any probability of finding any beauty as one came into the house. The screaming colors and convoluted designs snatched one's eyes to the tapestry, and one completely missed the vista of light and space that a good entryway should convey. Even I, with very little design knowledge, knew instinctively that we were witnessing a horror that could only be bought by too much money.

We wandered, disconsolate, through the rest of the house. Hedwig had done her very best; some corners, a few windows, and a glimpse of a charming spot in the soon-to-be-finished garden snuck up on you, even amid all this …mess. But overall, crap. We walked outside, breathing fresh air at last. "At least she hasn't shitted up the landscaping too much." Hedwig stopped to sniff a bed of lavender that had just been installed. "I hope she doesn't try to mess with the outdoors."

A disembodied voice came floating over a hedge newly planted *gunnera gigantus*. "Nah, she's ruining it even as I'm planting." We jumped. A head popped up. A handsome head of tumbled brown curls. A vision. The head had blue eyes in a sunburned face. A white-toothed grin saluted us, perhaps a client of the good Doctor Saul? The vi-

sion spoke again. "Look at these," he gestured to the *gunnera's*
magnificent leaves. "Gorgeous, but gone in a few weeks. And then
she'll call me and bitch because there's a wall of dead leaves here. I
tried to explain: perennials, that's what she needs, but no. She just
looks at what the short term effect will be and choses annuals!" He
sounded scandalized. "I mean, annuals have their place, but not
when you want a continuous effect." He came through the *gunnera*,
wiping his filthy hands on his backside. "Hi, I'm Ivan and I do
plants."

Hedwig and I introduced ourselves. I could see that Hedwig, never
too old to oogle good-looking male flesh, was impressed. Ivan continued, his tone aggrieved, "Instead of mass plantings, which I am
pushing, she wants formal rows of flowers. Nothing as stupid as a row
of tulips marching in a straight line. But, whatchagonnado? She's the
money. Makes me want to puke. But it pays the bills." He laughed.
"And how is she annoying you ladies?"

Hedwig launched into a diatribe and the two of them commiserated
about giving up ideals for crass moolah. As they talked, I observed
him more closely. Hunky. Wide shoulders. I was always a sucker for
shoulders. He wore a sweat-stained denim shirt and dirt-stained jeans,
a pair of sturdy boots and a red-patterned bandanna around his neck.
Toothsome, I thought.

We sat on a stone wall, which even Deirdre's money couldn't ruin,
and shared icy bottles of beer that he produced from a capacious knap-
sack. He was charming. I should have known to beware that much
charm, but...I didn't have a great track record of clever love affairs,
did I? He worked as a landscaping manager for Tri-State Landscaping,
the firm who, fortunately or unfortunately, was servicing the
Weinstein circus. He was born in France, but had come to the States as
a young boy. He'd been educated in England. Loved horticulture and
was enjoying working his way through the United States. "I've done
landscaping in Connecticut, Virginia and now here. I'm single
(whoopee, I cheered) and have no dependents, so what the heck, I can
do just as I please."

He intrigued me. I was certainly attracted to his good looks, his
debonair lifestyle and his background. He was attentive to me, but certainly just as attentive to Hedwig. I thought then that perhaps he was
intrinsically polite. Now I knew better that it was all a contrived act.

Hedwig and he were in the midst of a deep conversation in which
she described her barn. Ivan's ears had pricked up like a jackrabbit.

"Can I make a date to come and visit you? I'd love to see your home." She agreed gladly, always happy to show off her masterpiece. "Great," he enthused. "How about on Friday? I try never to work on Friday and I certainly am not going to let this place mess up my weekend." Hedwig thought that Friday was admirable. Ivan then turned to me, "Are you working on Friday?" I nodded. "Great, then I'll come over just before noon, you can show me around and lunch is on me."

"Oooh, I haven't been dined by a younger man in a donkey's years," Hedwig, as always, said just the right thing. I grinned and said that a good lunch on a Friday was just the beginning of a good weekend. Ivan gave me a long look that curled my toes and went back to shoveling soil. We went back to the office.

I actually went out and bought a new outfit for Friday's work. I was smart, wasn't I? So when Ivan rang the chimes, I answered the door in a green exotic-flower print sundress. My hair was shining clean and hanging down my back, clipped back on one side by a tortoise shell barrette. Leather sandals and bare legs completed my ensemble and from the look on Ivan's face, I'd spent my money well. Hedwig wore her usual baggy corduroys and a paint-stained tee shirt. She looked marvelous.

Ivan didn't look too shabby either. He had traded his work clothes for chinos and a red and white checked shirt. Yum, I thought.

He adored the barn. Well, who wouldn't, but he *appreciated* it too, and made intelligent observations with his connoisseur's eye. Hedwig always enjoyed compliments on her home, but even more when the appreciator knew what he or she was talking about. We left at about one, with Hedwig blithely giving Len and Tom the rest of the day off. "Shoot," she said, "If we two are going to fart off the day, then *everyone* can fart off the day!" No wonder we were all her slaves.

He was driving a new Land Rover. "Love them," he enthused. "Great for work. You can haul tons of manure, and then, they look nice when you're hauling two beautiful women to lunch." I'll admit, I was beginning to fall.

He drove us into the countryside, to a small town that he'd discovered. The town was inhabited by many Greek immigrants and we stopped in front of a *taverna.* "Probably the only Greek place in all of Pennsylvania. Sure hope you like Greek food." We assured him that we did and we went inside into a cool and dim low-ceilinged room. Trestle tables were set up and we chose one near a window. Ivan knew the owner and joshed with him for a few moments, while the owner cast an appreciative eye over both Hedwig and me. A pretty young girl, dressed in a blue and white apron brought us little dishes of olives and grape leaves rolled around a spicy meat stuffing. *Dolmides*, she said, and then she brought out pita bread and a mouth-tingling cucumber and garlic sauce. *Skordelia,* she instructed us. I dove in and when she came back with the menus, asked her how the cucumber stuff was made. Easy, she said. Sour cream, cucumbers, mashed potatoes, oil and garlic, all pounded together. I vowed to wow them back at 52 Brookside Drive.

"Tell me about where you live," Ivan prompted and I did, giving him a thumbnail sketch of boardinghouse living. He said that he had a small house on the other side of Harrisburg, but was contemplating buying a piece of land near Red Bear Lake. "Maybe we can trade," he appealed to Hedwig. "I do landscaping and you draw me paradise." She laughed and said we'll see.

We stuffed ourselves with *moussaka*, delectable skewers of lamb, and finished up with a supercalifragilistic dessert called *galito-bourikos*, a glorious confection of semolina pudding, cinnamon and crackling *filo* dough, baked and drenched in a syrup of honey. I actually put the nearly empty dish up to my mouth to lick up the last vestiges of the syrup. I thought Ivan would choke with laughter. "Lord! But that was good!" I exclaimed.

We lingered over another cup of the sweet, sticky coffee that, I suppose, Greeks enjoy, drowsy and replete, happy that none of us had to return to an afternoon of work. Ivan drove us back to the barn, and then offered to take me back to 52. He hugged Hedwig, said that he'd see her next week at the Weinstein abortion, and we waved to her as she moved slowly, stuffed with too much good food, up the path to the barn.

"Do you want to drive around a bit?" he asked, giving me a sideways glance.

"Sure. It's a beautiful afternoon and I am free, free, free."

We turned back towards the countryside and drove slowly down back roads, aimless and going nowhere in particular, our talk easy and comfortable. I liked him more and more and it seemed to me that he was enjoying himself, too. After a few hours, we reached a crossroads with an ice cream stand at one corner. "Have you room for a cone?" He asked.

"I never thought I could stuff one more thing down for a week, but," I considered, "Greek food must be like Chinese food. Yup, I'd love one." He hopped out of the Rover and came around to my side, opened the door and helped me out. As I climbed down, my sandal caught on the floor mat and I fell, literally fell, into his arms. It seemed inevitable that we kiss, and we did, a long, lingering kiss loaded with promises.

"This is incredible," he murmured. "I can't believe that I feel this way. We hardly know each other but yet, I know that I have been waiting for you my entire life."

Well, what girl could resist this, coming from a handsome, virile hunk that one was half in love with anyway? Certainly not me. And he didn't kiss or hold me delicately like Aiden had, so maybe it was safe to go ahead and fall for him. And I did.

It was a whirlwind romance and perhaps I should have been more cautious, but I had been seeking love for a long time and I welcomed it with open arms and eager lips. Hedwig was delighted, "I feel like a doting mother. You two are made for each other. I'm tickled pink!"

And I finally learned just what all the commotion was about. I didn't need any books to tell me about complete satisfaction and delight. No wonder Aiden had puzzled me. He never...well, nevermind Aiden. It was better to forget that entire episode.

Naturally, I had to make up a lot of background to fill Ivan's natural curiosity about my childhood and early years. I built myself a loving family, unfortunately all deceased now. They'd been in a car accident, I told him, and all my aunts and uncles were gone now. I had been an only child. I embroidered a little more, but tried to keep the story simple and as believable as I could. As I had learned, if people had no reason to doubt your story, they didn't.

Ivan told me more about himself. He had a father still living in England, and we would visit him as soon as we were married. And we'd be married soon, he promised. I glowed. I know that I was a pretty girl, I could see that in the mirror. But his love made me even more special. We'd honeymoon in the Virgin Islands, he declared, so I was to get a passport as soon as I could. He told me more about the boy he'd been, the little village where he'd grown up in the wine region of France. His cousins, who owned a huge vineyard there and the fun they'd all had as children. Then, his father, who was a doctor, had an opportunity to come to Boston to do consulting research. How his mother had resisted, but packed up in the end, bringing him over on The Queen Mary.

"I was the pet of the ship. Nine years old and running all over the decks, up into the Captain's Quarters, wearing the Captain's hat and even steering the boat, with, of course, some firm, adult hands held over mine." My eyes misted as I had a vision of Ivan, in a small sized sailor suit, grinning as he held the ship's wheel.

"We had a beautiful mews house in Cambridge. My father went to the University hospital and lectured, and my mother joined a bunch of civic organizations. Naturally, we all spoke English as well as French and I quickly lost my accent mixing with the boys at the private school I attended."

"When did you decide to go to England?"

"I, I must modestly say," his eyes twinkled, "was a superb student. My professors thought that I should take a test to be admitted to Cambridge. I passed with flying colors and went over to England. Unfortunately, my mother had a heart attack during my first year and died suddenly." I touched his hand in sympathy. "My father was devastated. He no longer wanted to be away from Europe and so he applied to a hospital in London and, naturally, was accepted with dispatch. I was happy to have him nearby. I rowed for Cambridge, got my Blue and after graduation, decided to go to the States and see what my future might hold."

"Do you miss you father? Do you see him often?"

"I go over three or four times a year. I miss him, but he has his own life there now." He laughed gently. "He even has a new honey. She's a very wealthy widow and the two of them are always busy, traveling, going to the theater. No, he's fine and we enjoy each other's company when we see one another, but go on with our own lives when we don't."

"Would you ever consider going back to England to live?"

"Would you?"

"Why not, if that's what you'd like." Oh, I was so happy. My life had finally become what I subconsciously had been yearning forever.

We saw each other nearly every night, except for a few nights when Ivan was too tired or working. When I didn't see him, I went to the movies with Eulalie, or out for supper with Hedwig. As I said, I was deliriously content.

There was only a moment or two – well, maybe three or five - of discord. We went out for dinner a lot and once in a while, I felt that Ivan had too much to drink. And when he did, he became surly. I didn't want to be a shrew or a nag, so I tried to overlook this small problem and see only the bright side of our relationship. And most of our relationship was very, very bright.

One night, when Ivan was too exhausted to join me, I sat at 52 Brookside reading and passing the conversational ball around with old Mr. Witherspoon. Naturally, all of the boarders had met Ivan and all of them were looking forward to being invited to our upcoming nuptials. Old Vinegar Stringer came in and looked oddly at me. "Not out with your Lothario tonight?' she queried in a tight voice.

"No, he's had a long day and went to bed early." I smiled up at her, my own happiness making me tolerate her better than I had before.

"Indeed," she said. "Home early. Then it couldn't have been him that I saw at the restaurant this evening, could it?"

"Of course not," I protested, indignant. "Why would he be in a restaurant?"

"Why indeed." She seemed to find something amusing in our conversation. "The person I saw was with a young woman. Maybe it wasn't him." A peculiar sound bubbled out of her mouth and she then wished me a good night and went up the stairs.

"She's a bitch, she is," Mr. Witherspoon commented. "Take no notion of her spite."

I agreed and dismissed the matter from my mind.

CHAPTER FOURTEEN

I awoke much refreshed; my memories of Ivan faded. Today was going to be a banner one. First, breakfast with Kenji and then my visit to Will. I was excited. Will was going to be so surprised and thrilled. I know that money didn't mean anything to him, but it would be fun to see his sad and tired old eyes get big and maybe he could do something back home with it that would ease his grief.

I showered, surprised at how well my body was recovering. I looked pretty good for a woman who was having a Memorial Service in a few days. I had to laugh. As much as I had hated Ivan, I saw the huge amusement in him collecting thousands and thousands of dollars for my death, and being lionized for being the epitome of a grieving widow. As I dried my hair, I mused over the deaths at the World Trade Towers. I wondered if anyone else had done what I had done. Was there someone…a henpecked husband, a man who was drowning in debt, a woman, perhaps like me, who was trapped in a horrible marriage…was there anyone else who had upped and walked away, never looking back at the ashes of their deceit?

And me…who would have thought that it could get so complicated? I had no idea that Vivian…for I would always think of her as a chucky, red-haired woman…Vivian's real life could have been so twisted as it was. Tch-ing over the strangeness of life and tsk-ing over the laugh that Fate must have when she, for surely Fate was a female, saw what we humans did to one another, I dressed and went to Bernie's.

Kenji, Lenny and the two policewomen were already there, almost finished with their breakfasts. Kenji's face lit up when he saw me and he stood and kissed me on the cheek. Lenny looked amused and sort of uncomfortable. Carmencita and Jessie nudged one another and grinned. I grinned too. "I'm starving. What's good?"

They all had to leave before I finished. "We're off Ground Zero for now. The searchers are finished." We all looked somber. "We're back on Narco." Kenji told me.

"We're back on Angel duty," Lenny said with a great deal of satisfaction in his voice. "I've got a feeling in my big toe that we're gonna get the sucker this time around."

"What sucker?" That was me asking. They all knew already.

"He's called The Angel," Jessie told me. "Top drug lord in the City. No one really knows who he is, but we'll get him." Her pretty face was grim and her eyes showed a great distress.

"He's at the top of layers and layers of small potatoes. We catch the street dealers, the peddlers, the junkies and even the distributors, but we can't get a handle on him." Carmencita added. "He's smart, slippery and slick, the bastard. But one day, one day soon, he'll slip up and we'll find the chink in his armor." She looked over at Jessie and the two of them exchanged a determined glare.

"We always get our man," Lenny assured me. His voice was dry.

"Are you sure it's a man?" I asked. "Could this person be a woman?"

"Possible, but we don't think so." Kenji's handsome face was grim. "I'd hate to think a woman could so callously endanger the lives of thousands of kids...sell stuff to get them hooked. I believe he's a man." He looked towards his cohorts for confirmation. All of them nodded.

"Why is he called the Angel?"

"That's what the street calls him," Carmencita answered. "Also, we got the name confirmed from a junkie who was dying. He didn't know the Angel's real identity, but he knew what he was known as. The Angel, huh!" she spat out. "Ought to be called the Devil!"

"OK, group, let's get cracking." Lenny unwound himself from his cup of coffee and stood up. The rest followed suit. "See you in a day or two, Vivian Ann," he called back to me. Kenji loitered for a moment.

"I'll catch up with you in a second." He came over to my chair and rubbed his hands on my shoulders. "Hi, sweetheart. I've missed you."

"Mmmm, me too." I put my hand on top of his hand.

"I've got duty the next couple of days. Can I see you on Tuesday night?"

"Certainly. What do you want to do? Can I cook dinner for you?"

"Oh, that would be great. He bent down and kissed the side of my neck, nibbling a little. "It was so good the other night. You were so good. I...I really...well, we'll talk more on Tuesday."

Lenny's head came back into the door. "Yo, Lover boy, come on!" He winked at me and withdrew.

"I gotta go." He gave me a tiny squeeze. "Bye."

"Bye, Kenji."

Anita shuffled over. "He likes you. Nice boy." She put my plate down. "Them others, they was teasing him before you came in. He was jumpy, watching the door for you, made a disappointed face at every other person who came in." She chuckled. "Too bad I'm so blamed old, and my bunions hurt, else I'd give you some hot competition."

I left Bernie's and hurried to the bank, went through the rigmarole of the safe deposit dance with a new bank manager, a woman this time, collected the photo from the bottom of the box and took one of the bundles of hundred dollar bills with me. One bundle would fit into my purse, but there was no way that I could carry all the money with me at once. Next time, I'd come back with a small suitcase and give the rest of the money to Will.

I took a taxi downtown to where his "bed-sitter" was located and found myself on a seedy street near 12th Avenue on the West Side. A laconic man at the desk told me that Will was on the third floor, Room 390, and I went up the stairs, wincing at the stale smell of urine and keeping well away from the fly-spattered walls. Will would be able to move to a much nice place, maybe a hotel, I happily mused. I'd take him to some good restaurants and fatten him up, poor thing. He looked like he could use a good bit of mothering.

I knocked at the door of 390. No answer. I knocked again. Had I made a mistake about the time? Had he been so tired that he'd forgotten that I was coming? I knocked once more. Then, some creeping notion of dread beset me. Was he ill?

I turned the knob and the door opened under my hand. "Will? Will? Are you OK?" I opened the door. The room was dim and still. I saw him, still asleep in his bed. I turned the light switch on, calling gently, "Will! Wake up. It's me, um, Vivian."

He was lying in bed, the covers tucked up to his chin. I called his name again. He didn't move. Worried, I crept to his side. I shook him gently. "Will?" And then I stepped back, aghast. He was...gone. "Oh, Will...not now! Not when we've found each other. Oh, no! Nooooo!"

I touched his thin cheek. It was cool. Had he had a heart attack? Or had his poor, sick heart just given up? He looked peaceful, asleep. I sighed. Was it a miserable joke of Fate that snatched him away? I hadn't wanted him to die. I wanted to cart him back to England, triumphal. I wanted him to shout to the newspapers and his police buddy that the murdering scum Vivien had been struck down by the hand of God. I sniffed. God was working in weird ways these days. Could anyone think that He had allowed all that mess to happen just to punish Vivien Morrison? I sighed again, dejected. Whatever had happened to Will, he was clearly dead. Poor, sad Will.

A tear fell on the sheet. I guess it was mine. Oh well, I was glad that at least Will had died knowing that Vivien had been taken care of. I patted his limp, cold hand and tucked it back under the coverlet, as if to keep him warm. "Oh, Will!"

What should I do? Call the manager? Call the police? I thought quickly. No, neither of these would be good for me. I couldn't be involved with the police. Who knows what he might have told them…who knows…? And as for Will, well, it really didn't matter much anymore, did it?

I looked quickly around the room. There wasn't too much stuff of a personal nature. A picture of a happy young girl, a mother and a younger, contented Will was on his bedside table, together with a cheap alarm clock and a bible. In the closet, two pair of shoes, shined, but well-worn, three pairs of pants on hangers, one tweed jacket and the overcoat that he had worn last night. The fedora was on a shelf. There was a dresser with a comb and brush on top, together with some toiletries and a wristwatch. With my fingertips, for I had seen all those television shows, I gingerly opened each drawer. Top drawer held his wallet, some handkerchiefs and some bath articles, second drawer, his underwear, clean but old. The third drawer had an assortment of shirts and the bottom drawer, two cardigan sweaters. On the desk was a book…*The Complete Sherlock Holmes*…and a couple of crossword puzzle books, a few pencils in a cup, a Gideon bible and a New York City telephone book.

I eased the desk drawer open and found a shabby attaché case. I pulled it out and sat down on the room's only chair. It was his file about his search for Vivien. There were newspaper clippings, creased and yellowed, a birth certificate for Vivian Ann, some photos of her and her children, copies of Irish newspapers with articles about several robberies and then the stories in the British papers about finding the three bodies. I held the documents in my hands and thought furiously. I couldn't leave these here. No. I took them and the bedside photo, made sure that there was nothing else…well, incriminating, and shut the attaché case.

I went over to the bed and bent down and kissed Will's forehead, smoothing his sparse hair and thinking that God could have waited a day or two before He decided to call Will home, couldn't He have? Ahhh, I wasn't big on depending on God these days.

And then I shut Will's door quietly. Someone would come eventually, and there was no reason to think that anyone wouldn't know that he died peacefully and naturally. I walked down the stairs, through the lobby and back into the streets of New York.

Was I suddenly a femme fatale? Here I was, an ordinary woman, pretty, but by no means a beauty, masquerading as another woman. Something was very strange about it all, wasn't it? And here were two men, so different, and each seemed to be attracted to me. And I was attracted to both of them.

Shouldn't I just relax and enjoy it all? After all, I'd fallen in love three times before, and three times before, I'd been knocked down. First by the despicable Aiden, who used my youth and innocence to fuel his base desires, the swine. And then Ivan, who hurt me, hit me, abused my soul, and frittered away tens of thousands of dollars. And then Zachary, who convinced me to hope for a future of love, and then changed his mind. Again, my musings turned to the enigma of God. Had God punished Zachary by immolating him? But if that sort of logic held true, why had God allowed Ivan to publicly become the world's most devoted windower? The numero uno chest beating mourner, poster boy for false bereavement, fooling everyone but me, and then giving him zillions of dollars? Unless God had something really big waiting for Ivan later on. One could only pray.

After all, Ivan had been the worst....

Our marriage was set for the first Saturday in June. We planned a simple ceremony, with a local Justice of the Peace officiating in the lawn behind 52 Brookside Drive. I asked Eulalie and Hedwig to be my attendants, and they were both thrilled to pieces. Ivan was having his boss, Dan Sargeant as best man, with Randy Corke, one of his landscaping co-workers, as an usher. I was not going to be bedecked in satin and lace with a tulle veil, it just wasn't me. Instead, I found a beautifully cut suit, in a heavy, cream-colored silk. It looked lovely and felt right. I told my handmaidens to wear whatever they liked. Somebody sneaked me the information that Hedwig was going to appear in a Norwegian caftan that her family has sent her from the old country. I thought she'd look spectacular. Eulalie had a rose-colored number with a fichu collar that she thought would be "suitable".

"Anything you want, Eulalie. You'll probably knock the spectacles off Mr. Mastermind and Mr. Witherspoon."

"Oh, I certainly hope so, dear," she answered.

Mrs. Lovatt insisted on doing the food, and told me it was her wedding gift to me. Naturally, all of the boarders were invited, together with Janice and Glen. Tom and Len and their wives, Marie and Marsha, would be there, as well as a few of Ivan's other friends and the people that he worked with. I hoped that it would be a sunny day and didn't worry about too much else. I felt serene and sure. Pretty sure, anyway. The only uncertainty continued because of a few more scenes caused by Ivan's drinking. We'd had two huge fights over it all, but each time, he managed to convince me that he would reform.

Mrs. Stringer continued her slightly sardonic digs at me, but I made it a point to ignore her. She never again mentioned anything about Ivan and any other woman, but I often caught her looking at me with malignant amusement. Oh well, we'd never, ever liked one another from the very beginning. And I was marrying Ivan and would be going away from 52. I'd probably, with luck, never see her again. She couldn't hurt me any more.

Saturday was beautiful and the wedding was perfect. Janice caught the bouquet and announced that she and Anthony would be the next to get married. It was a happy surprise in the middle of a happy day. Even Old lady Stringer's sour puss couldn't get me down, although I noticed, during the reception, that she had buttonholed Ivan and was hissing at him. His face looked angry. I'm sure she annoyed him as she annoyed everyone else.

We said goodbye to our guests and drove away in the Land Rover. "I've never been to the Virgin Islands!" I was on a high. "I'm going to find a deserted little cove and we can go skinny dipping! What time does our plane leave?"

"Uh, we're not going to go there. We're going to, uh, a hotel near Hershey." Ivan's face was red and he was clearly uncomfortable.

"What?"

"I, uh, I just…look, we just don't have the money to take a trip like that!" He was angry, embarrassed and angry.

I was stupefied. We had *planned* the honeymoon, *talked* about it endlessly. I thought that we had reservations, plane reservations, hotel reservations. I had packed bikinis and beach towels. What the hell? "But, Ivan…" I began, trying to keep my voice steady. "I don't understand."

"Look, Gianna. We're just not going. Don't bug me any more about it!" I sat still. I didn't want to spoil our day. I blinked my eyes fiercely, trying not to dissolve in to tears. We drove in silence for about an hour and then came upon a lonely motel just off the main road. A blinking sign under the "Vacancy" sign read "Lounge" in wavery red neon. .He stopped the car.

"Let's stop and have a drink." I didn't want to. We'd had enough to drink at the wedding. Maybe more than enough. But, to keep my marriage day happy, I opened the door and let myself out.

The lounge was one of those places that you only see in a B movie. Seedy. Run down, with seedy, run down people at the bar. Most of the men were truck driver types and the women looked emaciated. The two of us, in our post-wedding finery, looked as out of place as two husbands at a Tupperware party. Nonetheless, we took a booth.

"Order me a rum and coke," Ivan told me. "I'm going to register."

"Here? We're staying *here*?" I was aghast. "To*night*?"

"Just shut up," he snarled and left me there.

A waiter drifted over. "Whatchwant honey?"

"A rum and coke…weak, and a…a.." Should I join him and drink myself into a stupor? "A martini, please."

He brought the drinks and said, "That'll be ten-fifty." I paid him. Ivan came back and slouched into the booth. He took a huge gulp.

"Pisswater!" He got up, took his drink with him and went over to the bar. I could tell that the traitorous waiter told him that I'd ordered a weak one. He gave me a murderous look and the bartender shrugged and poured more rum into the drink. Ivan nodded, and came back.

"What the hell are you playing at?"

"Me? What am *I* playing at? What's happened? We have enough money. I've been saving for months. What are we doing here in this flea trap? This is our *wedding* night!"

"Yeah, and what a mistake that was." He tossed off the drink and returned to the bar. This time, he came back with a larger glass. I toyed with the detestable martini. I hated martinis. He drank it down again, not even looking at me. I began to cry. A few patrons nudged one another and watched us, like a cat watches a fish swim around in a glass bowl.

"Ivan what's wrong? Let's go our room and talk."

"Sure baby, after all, this is our night of nights, huh." I just couldn't believe it. He'd simply changed before my eyes. I got up and he went back again to the bar. Some money passed between him and the bartender and he returned, carrying a paper wrapped bundle.

We went through the flyspecked lobby and into a small, wretched room. I prayed that the sheets had been laundered. I'm not overly fastidious, but this was more than I could bear.

Ivan dumped the bottle out of the bag and made himself another drink. In a flash, he'd downed it and poured another. "You want one?" he asked waving the rum at me. I shook my head.

"I'm...I'm going to bed." With as much bravado that I could muster, I got my nightgown out of my overnight case. The beautiful, sexy, pale green nightgown that was supposed to be the beginning of our first married night together. I didn't want to put it on...this was the wrong kind of place and Ivan was all of a sudden wrong too. But, it was all that I had with me. Everything else was packed in my big suitcase in the back of the Rover, the suitcase that was supposed to be going with us to the Virgin Islands. I sidled into the bathroom and locked the door. I thought I heard him laughing out there. I undressed and put on my bridal night finery, brushed my teeth, put out the light and went back into the room. Ivan was sitting on a chair, drinking steadily and the television was showing a re-run of "Happy Days". I slid under the covers, squeamish, hoping against hope that no insect was under the sheets with me. He didn't even turn his head.

I put the pillow over my face and began to sob, as quietly as I could. Then, exhausted emotionally, I fell into a restless sleep.

I was jerked back into the night as Ivan ripped back the covers and began to maul me. "Don't! Don't do this!" I screamed. "Please, Ivan, please!"

"Please, Ivan, please!" He mocked me in a nasty falsetto voice. "Shut up, bitch. Spread your legs. After all, we're married now." And he slapped my face twice, first one way and then the other. I screamed again, and he crushed me, putting his sweaty palm over my mouth. "One more sound from you, Gianna, and I'll knock you senseless. Got it?"

I nodded, frantic and terrified. He took his hand away. His weight was suffocating me and I could feel his arousal. I tried to push him off. He was heavy and strong and horrible. He hit me again, this time harder and I gasped. My head was reeling with pain and I felt as if I were going to be sick. He ripped my nightgown off, pulled my legs apart and mounted me. I was dry and frightened and he hurt me dreadfully. I tried not to struggle. I was helpless under his unrelenting rooting. I lay as still as possible, praying to some God to save me from this madness. But God was busy that night, paying attention to somebody else's problems.

Finally, grunting, he fell off me and passed out into a stupor. I gathered my wits as best I could and crawled into the bathroom. In the mirror, a horror looked back at me. My hair was in ruins, my face bruised and battered, my breasts were bitten and scratched and my eyes…my eyes looked as if I'd seen the fires of hell. Joey had been despicable. But Joey had hated me. Ivan had vowed, only a few hours ago, to love and cherish me forever. I went back into the bedroom, took the motley bedspread off the bed, wrapped myself in it and slept on the floor. I know now that I should have left him there, taken his money and the car and gone to the police, but I was still hoping…hoping that this was some kind of mental lapse for him, and that tomorrow, he'd be the bright and smiling man that I married.

A week later, we came back to Harrisburg to Ivan's little house. He went back to work and I went back to work. Tom asked me where was my tan? Had we spent the entire honeymoon inside? I told him that there was a problem with the reservations, that we had gone instead to a hotel in the mountains. I smiled widely as I told my lie and something in my face showed him that everything was wrong. Tactfully, he backed away and no one ever asked me anything again about my honeymoon, not even Hedwig.

We barely spoke, Ivan and I. Some marriage. I was sad, but determined to see if I couldn't work it all out. Then, a week later, I learned that the Range Rover was being repossessed. Ivan had never made any payments on it. 'We're moving. Get packed. We gotta get away before they come for the car," he ordered. Again, I should have run screaming anywhere. I could have gone to Hedwig's, I could have found a safe haven with Eulalie, or Mrs. Lovatt, or even a total stranger on the street. But I was so shamed that I quietly put all our belongings in a suitcase again, packed all the wedding gifts in a cardboard box and left Harrisburg with my beloved husband, without even saying goodbye to some people that I loved and respected. I was a coward and I was ashamed of myself.

But because I was more of a coward than ashamed of myself, I did nothing and let all those wonderful people think…what did they think? That I had just been an ungrateful woman and forgotten all of them?

I bought myself a magnificent hat for the event at Uncle Gerald's, a lovat-colored felt with a wide brim and a pheasant feather sticking out of the ribbon. I wore a liberty print skirt and a long, sable-colored cashmere sweater, high polished leather boots and I fancied that I looked as if I were going to a fox hunt. Oliver arrived looking like an extra in The Great Gatsby movie. His cheek had two long scratches down the side, courtesy of the barking mad Sarah, but it only made him look a bit more rakishly attractive. We stood for a moment, admiring one another, then laughed and got into the car he had rented for the day. It was a long, low slung antique racing car, a Loganda, I think it was called, and we looked so stupendous, we couldn't stand it!

It was a beautiful fall day and we rode with the top down up the Saw Mill River Parkway towards Greenwich, Connecticut. The wind roared past us and conversation was difficult. I enjoyed the scenery and the autumn leaves changing color as we drove north. In about forty-five minutes, we stopped at a small inn and had coffee and brioches. Then, we whizzed up the Merritt Parkway and into Greenwich.

Greenwich, Connecticut is one of the wealthiest towns in the country. A beautiful, bucolic place with huge mansions and park-like estates. Oliver slowed the machine down and showed me the Round Hill Country Club, Indian Harbor and then we went into a private area called Belle Haven. "Lots of movie stars and famous people live here," he informed me. "Diana Ross, Mel Gibson, Ron Howard, um, ah, that blond, hunky movie actor that won the Academy Award last year, um, what's his name?" He shrugged, unable to dazzle me further. "And Cokie Roberts, that tennis player, Ivan Lendel, Angela Perillo, that Italian actress, Tom Seaver, The Helmsleys, lots of them."

"I can see that you'd have to be a movie start to afford these kind of houses...my goodness, look at that!" I gasped as we passed a house as big as Buckingham Palace on our left. "Geez Louise! It's a bloody palace!"

He patted my hand and then picked it up and held it. "Just wait until you see Uncle Gerald's little spot. He calls it Summerfield."

"Ah," I said. "Almost the like the princess on Howdy Doody."

"Huh?"

"You know, Princess Summerfallwinterspring." He began to laugh.

"You are one priceless woman, my Annie Laurie. I hate what happened to you, but I am so glad that you came into my life."

Thus warmed, we turned into a magnificent Belgian block driveway. "The stones came from Wall Street when they dug it up to pave it."

"No shit!" I goggled.

"None at all." We pulled up with a swoop to the front of the house. My word! It was lovely. An old Georgian mansion, with ivy crawling all over it. Huge. Amazingly imposing. Not that I noticed things like that, ha ha. It was so…stupendous…it much have cost a fortune!

Uncle Gerald came out to greet us before we could even reach to pull the enormous brass bell-pull. He hugged me and shook hands with Oliver. "My word, my dear Vivian Ann, you look eons better than when I saw you last, trying on underpants in the hospital!" I blinked. Uncle Gerald had evidentially had a good head start on the champagne. If I remembered correctly, he was embarrassed to see me trying on *anything* in the hospital! What a swell-a-gant, el-e-gant party this was going to be! I duly admired the bell-pull and Uncle Gerald whispered loudly that he'd stolen it from the Taj Mahal. Actually, I believed him.

Our outfits were admired. Uncle Gerald was dressed in jodhpurs, with puttees wrapped around his skinny shanks and polo boots on his feet. He had a gold embroidered rajah's jacket buttoned across his waist. On his head, naturally, was a red turban. He looked, well, extraordinary, which, I think, was the impression he was striving for.

He ushered us in, grabbed two glasses of champagne from a hovering waiter…" Oooh, champers, brilliant!" I gushed in my best Brit voice. Uncle Gerald then took us (me really, Oliver had been through this dog and pony show all his life) on a tour of the place. We started at the top, where there was a room full of mirrors with no surface or wall in a straight line. A place one had better stay away from if one had anything at all to drink. Very disconcerting. Then to a room with walls all made from blackboards. I was invited to chalk some epitaph, but declined, saying that I hadn't had enough booze yet.

The next floor held the guest rooms, each done in a singular style: One as a sultan's harem, one as an underwater room, one as a jungle, one as a circus, and so on and so forth. The bathrooms were beyond belief, each matching the décor of the bedroom it served. I have never seen so many bidets in my life. (Actually, I had seen very few bidets, but I am often prone to exaggerations when my senses have been so overwhelmed). And they were overwhelmed, my senses, that is. This was one of the most amazing houses one could imagine!

Then to Uncle Gerald's private rooms. We were only shown a few, the Safari Room, the Gold Room (it defied mere mortal description), the Moon Room, his trophy room and his private, rather naughty, art collection. I spent some time at a later date trying to figure out what his own bedroom might have been like, but Oliver told me that I could never, ever come close to the reality.

The public rooms on the main floor were sumptuous, eclectic and fun. This certainly was a house made for parties.

The tent had been set up just past the terraces. It was the size of Miami, only a little warmer, due to the vast heaters that blew tropic air. There were at least a hundred tables, all set with chintz tablecloths, silver etageres and dainty china tea cups. Waitresses, dressed like Mrs. Hudson of 21B Baker Street, dispensed elaborate silver tiered servers, filled with scones, clotted cream, finger sandwiches and strawberry fairy cakes. I clapped my hands and told Uncle Gerald that it was just like Christmas at Harrods's, only more. That seemed to please him.

Elegantly dressed guests began to drift in. I lost Oliver early in the day, but managed to converse with lots of the *cognosgati*. I met a lovely couple who lived down the street, Doctor Marco Sabatini and his wife, Opie; a man named Robert who had two sons, both named Robert; a tall, lovely woman named Debbie Higgins who ran a riding stable; two opera singers from the Met; a ballet dancer from Paris whose name I never caught; Ambrose Finch, Greenwich's Police Chief and his date, a lady named Mallory. I understood that Mallory's husband had been murdered by a serial killer years ago and she also was the cousin of the aforementioned Opie.[2] I tried to remember everyone's name, but I think my brain went into overload. There was a snake charmer, complete with three cobras; a 98 year-old woman who told me that she had backstroked the English Channel; an aide to President Bush; President Bush's cousin, Prescott; three gatecrashers from Greenwich High School who came in on a dare; a radio disc jockey named Jake, a Maharini; two nuns from St. Mary's Church; oh, it was a glorious affair.

And then, Oliver found me, mellow with wine, sitting on the floor, playing One Card Silly with Uncle Gerald, one of the waitresses, a man who was supposed to be a jewel thief and Leona Helmsley. He hauled me to me feet, took a loving look at my flushed face, and pronounced me ready to go home. Muzzy, I agreed.

---

[2] Please read The Ice Floe for the whole story

Uncle Gerald and I kissed and I was bundled into the Loganda and driven home. As I recall, I sang show tunes all the way. Oliver took me up to my apartment, let me get changed, and then tucked me into bed. He kissed me on the lips gently. I was in the mood for more, but Oliver, bless his blazer buttons, was really a gentleman that evening. He laughed, tousled my hair, and told me that we would save all that for another time when I might remember how nice it was going to be. I think I cried a little and then fell into a stupor.

The alarm clock woke me at 6:30. I sat bolt upright and my head nearly fell off. I crawled to the bathroom and scooped four aspirins and some water into the dry cavern that used to be my mouth. "Wooo! That was some party!" I muttered softly. I managed to take a shower and the hot water and the analgesics did their work. I felt I might survive.

CHAPTER FIFTEEN

I managed to get to the offices of Operation Relief Recovery on the dot of nine. Oliver greeted me with narrowed eyes. "Are you OK?" He grinned.

"Perfectly fine," I smiled and the effort hurt.

"Want some coffee?"

"Is a bear Catholic?" I gripped the hot mug and sipped the plasma. "Oh, much better." I touched the two scratches on his cheek. "You are my very favorite American. That was a marvelous party. Your Uncle is barking mad, but interesting, if you catch my drift."

"I think...I hope...I have inherited a bit of his eccentricity."

"And thank you," my eyes dropped, "for your lovely company last night." I appreciate it. I mean it." I was uncomfortably embarrassed.

"I kicked myself all the way home." Oliver's face was pink. "Sometimes, I'm my own worst stupid fool enemy."

"No, Oliver. You were nice. Wonderful and nice. You made me feel...cherished. Thank you." His face came closer and I tipped my face up to meet him. My heart was beating a savage tattoo and my brain was mush. Was this what I had been waiting for my whole life?

"I should....Oh, good morning Mervin." We sprang apart as a tall, thin man with a cap of glorious auburn curls came into the office. I tried not to stare. "Uh, Mervin, this is Vivian Ann Morrison. Annie's one of the 9-11 survivors that we have been assisting." Mervin bent over my hand. I had a hard time keeping a straight face wondering if the toupee would fall off. "But today, she's going to assist *us* filling in temporarily until we get a replacement for Sarah.

"The bitch..." Mervin started, but Oliver held up his hand and Mervin subsided, breathing heavily through pinched nostrils.

"Junie!" Oliver called and an attractive red-haired woman with oversized harlequin glasses appeared. He introduced me, again using Annie as my name, and asked if Junie could take me around and show me some of the basics while he and Mervin had a short meeting.

Junie showed me the office and explained a little about how ORR, as they called it, operated. She sat me at a desk, showed me their filing system and asked me to file folders that had piled up in an OUT basket. Idiot work, she assured me. "Just file alphabetically by last name. Sarah hated to file, but it's important that we be able to find a file when we need it, so if you can clear this mess up, you'll have the undying gratitude of everyone in the office. OK? I mean, I figure that you can file?" Her eyes questioned me.

"I'm a very competent file clerk." I assured her. "I learned the Morton method many years ago." Junie looked impressed. Aiming to please and happy that she'd given me a task that I thought I could do, I set to filing, using, naturally, the best of the Morton method. There were dozens and dozens of file, all seemingly related to the lucky people, like me, who had somehow survived the tragedy. After a while, the filing became monotonous. I became a little curious and so I opened and perused the file of one Anthony Ginise. Mr. Ginise had been a waiter at Windows on the World. He had been sent to check on a shipment of frozen pastries on the loading dock, and thus, has escaped death. He had been caught in rubble, however, and was still in Beth Israel Hospital with a broken hip, ankle and crushed lung. I noticed that he had been paid two thousand dollars a week as his temporary stipend. I nodded. There was a Mrs. Ginise and two little Ginises, so I know ORR had helped them as they had helped me. There was a billing sheet from good ole Dr. Giggi, who had been seeing Mr. Ginise every day in Beth Israel. I was fascinated to find that Dr. Giggi charge $350 per visit. Boy! No wonder he had looked so sleek. I eyed the half-done pile. There were more than a hundred files yet to be put away. If Dr. Giggi saw half the people in the file folders half of the time he saw Mr. Ginise, Dr. Giggi must be doing Ohhh-Kay!

Junie came in to see how I was progressing. She was admiration itself when she saw how much I had done. "Thanks, Annie. You just can't imagine how tough it is when we can't find a file. You've done more than snippy Miss Sarah ever got done in a week." She invited me to take a break with her and led me into a nicely appointed staff room where hot coffee, tea and assorted pastries and fruit were laid out. Naturally, she introduced me to all as Annie. I chuckled to myself. Unwittingly, Oliver had given me yet *another* pseudonym. Actually, I liked the name Annie much better than Vivian. Even from the start, Vivian would not have been a name of choice for me. And especially now that I knew what I knew about the real Vivien. Oh well, in the future, I would acknowledge anyone who called me Annie and maybe manage to encourage it. Maybe I could start by stating that my family had always used my middle name. Hey, if you're gonna lie, I had discovered, pick yourself an excellent lie and emphasize it every time. I'd see how it all went.

The ORR staff was nice. We sat and chatted, sipped tea and coffee and munched on platters of goodies. Junie had been with ORR for three years. "Great place to work. Oliver is a peach. If I weren't happily married, I'd jump his bones." She giggled. "Everybody thinks he's swell. Heck, even my husband Paulie thinks he's a peach." She asked me about my ordeal and I told her an abbreviated version. She told me that I was lucky. Completely sober now, I agreed.

Oliver joined us. He held a dollar in his hand. "Did I say that Mervin would or wouldn't have a toupee? Do I owe you a dollar or do you own me?"

"I simply can't remember. Whatever. It's worth a few shillings to me to see his dandy new coiffure. That mop on his head is *some* hairdo!"

Junie and Oliver started to laugh. "Shhh, don't let him hear us or he'll start all over again. This one is a brand new toupee. His old one was brown and straight."

My explosive laugh brought coffee out through my nose.

"Can you have lunch?" Oliver asked me. "It's almost noon and I hear you have done wonders for the file mountain."

"I use the Morton method." My eyes twinkled, but I didn't explain. "Can we do it tomorrow? Remember, I told you that I have an appointment with the good Dr. Giggi at one and then, as I am feeling a bit sore and tired and my head is aching a bit," Oliver refrained from even a grin and I found myself appreciating him more and more, "I plan to go home and rest after seeing him." Junie looked disappointed. "Oh, I'll be back tomorrow to finish the pile and do anything else you might need."

"May God bless you, Annie" she intoned with sincerity. Oliver's face showed a tiny bit of puzzlement. "I'm going out for rasta food, boss. See you tomorrow, Annie. And thanks."

"She calls you Annie-my-pet-name too?" I grinned and jumped in at the opportunity.

"Actually, many of my friends have called me Annie since ever so long ago."

"Really?"

"Indubitably." I gave him a saucy look. "I was such an adorable baby that the name Vivian was seen as too grown up for me." I winked and he guffawed. "Even my mother called me Ann or Annie, although my father never wavered from the Vivian thing."

"Ah-ha! I knew that instinctively!" Oliver managed to look proud and bashful at the same time. His face was so sweetly contorted that I almost went over and kissed him. Almost. "And all my Anna-Banana, Queen Annie, Annie-Laurie and what-not were all due to my instinctive brilliance!" He grinned and shook his head in admiration of his own intelligence. I thwacked him on his shoulder and he hugged me. I felt pretty good, even though I'd added yet one more lie onto the mountain that rode around on my shoulders.

I stopped by the bank and put the stack of hundreds back into the safe deposit box, together with the photos, the documents from Will's attaché case and the gun that Will had left on my table. I didn't quite know what else to do with all of these things. I didn't think I should throw them away or destroy them, but...I didn't want them in my apartment. The documents and the gun filled the box to almost overflowing and I had to lean hard on the top to get it to shut properly. As I locked the box, I said another prayer for Will. I wondered if someone had found him yet. I could try checking the newspapers, but he was such an insignificant little man, I doubted that they'd waste space on him. I made a vow that someday, when all of this was over, I would take a trip to England, find Inspector Jimmy James and tell him the entire story...well, most of it anyway. I'd see to it that something, *something*, was done in memory of all of Vivien's tragic victims. I promised myself that I wouldn't spend any of the money in the safe deposit box on anything else but some kind of memorial for Will and his family.

At the doctor's office, I waited only a few moments before Sister Bertrille came to get me. "How are you feeling, Miss Morrison?" She asked. "We were all praying for you." I assured her that her prayers were working as I was much better than when I first came here. The name badge pinned to her starched bosom proclaimed her as being a Mrs. Bunting, and she showed me into Dr. Giggi's inner sanctum. I

appraised the sleek office décor with newly opened eyes as I thought
of the dozens and dozens of folders and how many visits at $350 a pop
had gone into these glitzy rooms.

He was seated behind the polished desk. Today, he was wearing a
black turtle necked sweater and looked like a handsome version of Sa-
tan. He was immaculately barbered and his black eyes softened as he
welcomed me. I felt a bit unworthy about the nasty thoughts I'd been
harboring about his excessive charges. He was probably worth $350 a
visit and more.

I sat down. "You look marvelous! I had to look hard before to see
your beauty underneath all of those bruises." I preened a bit, I'm
ashamed to say. "You're a radiantly different woman." He leaned forward as if I were the only thing in the world to him today. "How are
you feeling?"

"Ta, much better. I'm now able to wear my own frocks and not
hospital clothing. My bruises are subsiding. The horrid aches are
nearly gone. My nose is still a bit tender." I touched it and he winced
with me. "I'm still having bad headaches; I can't remember a lot of
things that happened that day. I think the whole episode is blocked for
me. I...I'm still upset and my sleep is still poor. I got so emotional
when I read about some of the people I worked with...their obituaries.
I find myself bursting into tears at some trivial matter..." I spread my
hands in supplication at his desk-altar. "But all in all, I'm managing to
rub along."

"We must get you feeling better. I'm glad to hear that your body is
doing well," He gave my body a swift look. "And the terrors and the
memory will adjust themselves in time." He got up from his chair, walked
around his desk and sat in the chair next to me. Our knees were almost
touching. Again, he leaned to me. "I have two prescriptions for you, one
for pain, if you need it and one to help you to sleep. Perhaps a glass of
wine at bedtime might help." I thought back to yesterday's bacchanalia
and grinned inwardly. Oh, yes, indeed, a little champagne had helped me
to sleep very well. My only problem had been in getting up.

"Thank you, Doctor."

"Please, call me Paul," his voice touched down to my belly button,
it was so velvety and rich. "And, if I may, can I call you Vivian?" His
hand rested, just for a nanosecond, on my knee. He hadn't really
moved, but somehow, he seemed closer to me.

"Uh, well, most of my friends call me Annie. But of course, uh,
Paul, I'd be pleased if you used my...um, my name." Let's see how
this Annie thing progressed.

"Annie. A lovely name." Oh he was smooth. So smooth. "And here is my card with my private telephone number on it. I want you to call me, day or night, anytime, when you feel upset or need to talk." He smiled, and looked sincerely, oh so sincerely, into my eyes. "I'm there for you, Viv...uh, Annie, anytime you might need me. For anything. Anything at all."

"Uh, I will. I'll call..." I felt dizzy and lightheaded. I wondered if he was trying to hypnotize me. It could be working. I leaned a little bit forward, a little closer to him...and the buzzer on his desk rang, a strident sound that jerked me back.

"Yes, what is it?" Dr. Giggi..uh, Paul, sounded annoyed.

"Oliver Church on Line Two."

"Ah, yes, Oliver." He smiled again at me. "You know Oliver, don't you?"

Ah, yes, I said to myself. "Of course. He's my super savior."

"One moment." He reached for Line Two. "Oliver, my boy. How are you?".....Yes, certainly......By the way, I have the lovely Vivian, um, Annie Morrison here...You are? Ah, good, good..." Paul looked at me in a new way. "She's doing well...better than expected...Of course, time will mend a lot of things. Yes, yes." His obelisk fathomless eyes smiled at me, and I wouldn't have been surprised if he had twirled his moustache. He twisted towards his desk, picked up a gold pen and wrote something down on a pad of paper. "I'm sorry to hear that. I'll stop in and see him when I make my rounds...The AMA dinner Tuesday night? Of course. I think we're at the same table...I look forward to talking with you, Oliver....I'll tell her. Goodbye." He swiveled back. There was an avid speculation now in his glances. He turned his spotlight back on me. "Oliver, good man. Good man. Tells me you did a bit of office work for him today."

"They had a crisis situation and I was able to help. I, um, lent them a bit of a hand, actually. I carried the ball for about three hours. I felt almost tip-top afterwards but I was a little tired."

"I don't want you to overdo anything. You take it very easy and pamper yourself." I nodded, meek and mild. "Annie, you've become very precious to all of us...I mean, all of the people who...well, we *care* about our patients." His mellow voice droned on, but the spell was broken. He patted my knee again and then asked me if I enjoyed opera.

"Opera? I don't know...I like Pavarotti and such..." It was obvious that I wasn't an opera buff. "I've been to the Opera House at Covent Garden to see some light operetta, but, don't know much about it all."

I hoped against hope that Covent Garden was the right thing to say. I sneaked a peek at Dr. Giggi to see if I had goofed. He was looking down at his hands.

"I have some tickets for an upcoming performance at Lincoln Center...I don't know the date," he rummaged on his desk..."Where are those..? Ah, well, let me see if I can find them and I will call you next week. I want to see you here again in about ten days and I'll try to firm up the date...I think they are doing a Verdi compilation with James Levine conducting." I raised my eyebrows and tried to look intelligent. Was he asking me for a date? He harrumphed. "We'll talk soon." He rose and I rose too. His hand rested on my shoulder and he turned me towards the door. As we walked out, his hand moved to the small of my back. I suppressed a surprised look as he walked me to the desk.

"Helen, please make another appointment for Miss, um, Morrison. A week or so. Thank you." He bowed over my hand and for a moment, I thought he was going to kiss it. But he didn't. He just winked and reiterated. "Remember. Any time, day or night."

I said, "Ta Ta." He left me, presumably to mesmerize the next female patient.

Helen, without any expression whatsoever, made me another appointment and wished me good day. I reciprocated and went shopping.

I picked up the newspaper and bought Chinese take out for myself. I was starving. Sesame riblets, two scallion pancakes, a small order of pork lo mein and a big order of shrimp with lobster sauce. I eyed the stack of little boxes with anticipation I put them away in the fridge. There. That should keep the wolf from the door tonight.

My blinking telephone message system told me that my solicitor extraordinaire, Bob Rossi, had called while I was out. I rang him back.

"Oh, Miss Morrison. Good afternoon. I was checking to see how you were doing. How are you feeling?"

"Better, Mr. Rossi, thank you. As a matter of fact, I was at the doctor's when you called."

"And his report?"

"Decent, my dear solicitor. Decent. My bruises are fading, the pain is better, but my nose is still tender and my emotions, sleep pattern and memory are still troublesome." There, that would make him think. "And the dear doctor gave me a stronger pain reliever prescription and some sleeping tablets."

"Ah, well, sounds like you are on the mend." A hopeful sound in his voice.

"It will take some time, I was told."

"Ah." A bit of deflation there. "Well, I want to assure you that I am working hard to, um, get matters rolling."

"Matters?"

"Matters. The Insurance Commission is hard at work, drawing up guidelines for remuneration."

"Really? And precisely what does that mean to a gel like me?"

"Well, uh," He seemed nervous. I wondered why. "There is a large pool of money involved. From various sources, you understand." He cleared his throat. "Insurance money from the people that insured C&C, contributions in the millions to help victims' families and people such as yourself, who were injured in the disaster. Federal monies. It's a confusing thing, legally. Then there are the airlines and the airport security firms…were they in any way at fault here?…these kind of matters need to be thrashed out before the money can be distributed. Difficult, difficult." He confided, "Does a person who died who made, say two hundred thousand get as much as a, say a porter, who made two hundred dollars a week? What happens if the deceased has private life insurance? Should that amount be deducted from the final amount?" he sighed. "Definitely difficult."

"Ah, always money. Amazing how grief is assuaged with cash." I could hear his gasp.

"Well…well, there are practicalities, you know, my dear Miss Morrison." He was a little huffy. I think I had insulted him in his mercenary soul.

"Oh, I understand perfectly."

"Ah, the check I gave you…?" I could hear the delicacy in his phrasing. "Is it sufficient for your current needs?"

"At this moment, yes." I could almost see him slump in relief. "But, naturally, there is the future."

"Of course, Miss Morrison. Of course. I will continue to represent you and do my best to see that you are fairly treated. I'd like you to stop by the office in the next few days to sign some papers for me. Is tomorrow or the next day good? About noon?"

"Tomorrow at noon would be fine." I figured Oliver wouldn't mind if I took my lunch hour to visit Rossi. Rossi agreed and then harrumphed and asked me if I could join him for lunch afterwards. I was startled and I suppose the surprise showed in my stammer that no, I wasn't able to have lunch. He made light of the whole thing and I stared with great suspicion at the receiver in my hand. Lunch? What the heck was going on?

He made some small conversation while I wondered what his fair share of all this gelt would be. I didn't think that we knew each other well enough for me to give him a heart attack by asking just yet, so we said our goodbyes and hung up.

I settled on the couch and spread the paper out. The fires were still burning at Ground Zero. Money was pouring in, but now, the intended recipients (me? Ivan?) and those that were in charge of disturbing the money (Bob Rossi?) were in turmoil. No one could decide just how to split up all this munificence. I shook my head in disbelief. Wasn't it amazing that a thing like money could set neighbor against neighbor? I turned the page. Ah, here was a story about Kenji and Lenny's nemesis, The Angel. I folded the page and read avidly.

POLICE SEEKING THE ANGEL OF DEATH
By Elizabeth Kenney
New York City:

Police Commissioner Hans Jacques asks the help of every NYC resident to assist in the apprehension of New York City's most wanted drug lord, a man only known as The Angel. There is a $500,000 reward payable to the person or persons who are instrumental in The Angel's capture or death.

"This man is directly responsible for at least six hundred drug-related deaths in the City since 2001, when we realized that he was the kingpin in NYC's drug trafficking. He is a shadowy figure to us, using layers of street drug sellers and distributors, filling our city with cocaine and ecstasy and those illicit poisons that kill our children and those who are addicted or too weak to resist the blandishments of a cheap high. And then, when the poor addict is unable to get out from under the monkey...heck, the gorilla, on his back...or her back, lots of these children are young women...the price goes up for the next hit. The addict, with no possible way to support their habit...young girls and young boys too, some as young as nine years old, turn to prostitution, robbery, or even murder to get money for the drugs," the Chief explained.

"There are those of your out there who have information. You know who on your block is addicted. Perhaps you even know the name of the dealer who lives next door. Help us, we beg of you, to get this piece of garbage off the streets and out of our fine city."

The article went on to tell stories: stories of lives ruined, families ripped apart, dead children found in back alleys with needles still in their veins...all horrors, all brought about by the greed and corruption of people who could care less about what their poisons did to others.

I found myself fascinated. Here was a huge problem, a nasty, horrible, disgusting situation, and I knew...personally knew...four of the men and women who were out there, putting their lives on the line to catch this filth. I wondered what horrific things they'd seen...and then I shuddered. This kind of underbelly was something that few decent people ever got to see, much less think about every day. My admiration for Kenji and his fellow officers, men and women who daily faced death and then, on their days off, went down to Ground Zero to help strangers, knew no bounds.

CHAPTER SIXTEEN

M y next day at work at ORR was much of the same except that Oliver called me into his office and handed me four thousand, four-hundred dollars. It was a huge wad of cash. "This is for your last week's stipend and for next week's," he told me in his charming and velvet voice as I tried manfully to stuff all the money into my purse. "I thought, as we had begun with you taking cash instead of a check, we'd continue to do it that way." It sounded plausible...lots of money here, but certainly plausible and so I nodded. "Can we see each other on Wednesday night?" The velvet voice caressed. "We have a lot of unfinished business." I blushed, thinking of just what kind of business he might have in mind and what kind of business I might have in mind. "I'd like to take you to a show...I have tickets for *The Producers* and maybe a late supper afterwards." What girl in her right mind would refuse? No fool, I accepted with delight.

I asked if I could slip out for the appointment with Mr. Rossi. "Bob? A good man." I told Oliver that Rossi had been reciprocally effusive about him. "I'll be seeing him tonight. Of course you can go, Annie Laurie, my sweet. You're not on the clock here. As a matter of fact, we owe you a debt of gratitude that can't be paid. I'll even take you to lunch, if you can get back...no, why don't you meet me at The 21 Club at one. OK?"

Glad that I hadn't accepted Rossi's offer, I felt a soft glow of anticipation at the thought of being with Oliver once more. Was I falling for him? Maybe. But beside that, being of sound mind and good appetite, I agreed to the date. "And while you are playing at being benevolent employer, I have to leave at 3:30 this afternoon." Strike while my iron was hot. I didn't have to tell him that the reason I had to leave was so I could pick up the food for my home-cooked rendezvous with Kenji tonight. A girl can keep some secrets, can't she?

"Sure...whatever time you can give us is a gift. Why don't you plan to go home right after lunch. Are you coming back tomorrow, or have we over-worked you?"

I assured him that the file pile and I would be re-acquainted in the morn. He turned to other business and I went back to work.

I had morning coffee with the staff, Mervin and his curly new rug pouring the brew. Actually, he was a very pleasant, albeit, high-strung, man. I was a good doobie and filed my little fingers off. The pile that I had so assiduously attacked yesterday had grown again, threatening to topple out of the basket once more. I was nearly at the bottom when I came across my own file. "MORRISON, Vivian Ann." The file was buff colored, just like the rest of them, the label red. But, holy cow! It was *my* file!

Well, what would *you* do? Naturally, I opened it, sat down, and read it from cover to cover. Several things made me gasp. One was that my license, the missing, original one that had Vivien's picture on it, not my picture, was clipped to a large piece of stationery bearing the name of a firm named Bozak & Staplefield. There was nothing else on the paper, but a large red question mark My stomach felt a little queasy. Was there some suspicion about my license? Shameless, and bit annoyed, I took the paper and the license and put it in my purse.

The second thing was the accounting sheet. Oliver had given me twenty-two hundred dollars ten days ago and twice that much this morning. Even with reckless spending on a few new outfits, paying all of the bills, and saving a portion for my rent, I still had several hundred dollars left over from the first fistful of money. Six thousand, six-hundred dollars was a shitload of money, wasn't it? However, the accounting sheet showed that I had, on paper, collected eight thousand, eighth-hundred dollars. What was going on? Or did they post the next week's cash amount ahead of time. My suspicious little eyes behind my oversized red eyeglass frames narrowed. Hmmmm?

The third thing was the oh-so-good and polished Dr. Giggi's billing sheet. I had seen him twice, both visits at his office. He had never visited me at the hospital. The accounting record for him listed five hospital visits, two home visits and five visits to his office. The total for all of this care was in the vicinity of five thousand dollars…so far. I sat back. What *was* going on? What the *hell* was going down here?

I took the billing sheets, peeked to see that no one was at the copy machine, went over and made myself a copy of each. I put the copies in my purse, which was now bulging with its load of money and odd, to say the least, documents. I then filed myself back under the "M's and rushed to completely empty the FILE bin by 11:45.

I found Junie and told her what I had completed. She squealed with delight. I told her that I was leaving for the day, but would be back tomorrow to tackle additional files or whatever they had decreed was easy for me to accomplish. I stuck my head into Oliver's office and we agreed to be at The 21 at one o'clock. Before I left, I called Rossi and said that I'd be a few minutes late. After all, I had to get to the bank to deposit my money.

As I walked down the street, my thoughts were jumbled and worried. Obviously the hallowed halls of Operation Relief Recovery and Dr. Giggi, and probably Oliver were up to some real bad stuff. Was every client being double or triple billed like this? Did Mervin and Junie know what was going on? Gerald Summerfield, our eccentric and fabulously wealthy Major and head of ORR? Was that how he managed to own a house that had a Safari Room? Was that why Oliver drove such a grand car? How far did this deceit go? I chuckled to find myself indignant. *My* deceit was just fine, huh? It was only *other* people's deceit that was bad.

As I deposited my money and left the bank, headed for the glory of The 21 Club, my indignation began to fade. Were they any worse than me? Or worse than the lying son-of-a-bitch, Ivan, the duplicitous wife-beater who was professing such devotion to my memory? Was *everyone* some kind of con artist? Only some of us with bigger stakes and more ulterior motives?

Perhaps I shouldn't have included Ivan in these categories. True, he was going to reap huge financial gains from some future settlement, but he wasn't, probably for the first time in his life, lying about the circumstances. I mean, he actually thought I was dead. I think he thought so anyway…Even Ivan couldn't be aware of my own machinations, could he?

I stepped off the curb and was nearly hit by an errant taxi. He shook his fist at me and I gave him a New York salute. I climbed the curb again and walked the several blocks, musing about Ivan. One could never be sure of anything that Ivan said or did. His ability to lie made me look like Amateur Hour.

When he and I had fled the dreaded car repossessers, we wound up in New Jersey. "They'll take months to track us here," Ivan was full of glee. I found that nothing excited him like a successful con game. He was a born gambler, both with our money and with his life. Something else that I had neglected to see when he was wooing me, but, of course, he never meant for me to see it then. Now that we were man and wife, he let me in on many, many other little secrets. He wasn't born in France; he'd never even been to France. His mother wasn't dead and his father wasn't an eminent doctor, and he certainly didn't live in splendor in England. No, Ivan was born in Cleveland, the son of two trailer-trash parents who, as far as he knew, still lived in a doublewide in a run-down trailer park on the outskirts of Cleveland, and lived on welfare and handouts. Ivan, to his credit, had split as soon as he was able. He'd knocked around the mid-west, working at carnivals as a shill and then a barker. He'd operated three-card-monte games on the midways of local agricultural fairs, he'd done a spot of forgery, escaping the law by minutes by climbing out of a window and shinnying down a pine tree, he participated in a burglary or two, breaking and entering newly widowed women's houses during the hours when the said widows were attending to the burial of their recently departed. In essence, he was an awful person, much worse than me.

All his little stories, the embellishments...how he played with his French cousins, the little boy on the Queen Mary, all lies. But I had to hand it to him. He was a damn good liar. Much better than I was and much more inventive. He'd included splendiferous details, trills and exaggerations that I had never dreamed of making-up. Embellishment was his middle name, wasn't it?

And the outside world was completely fooled, just as I had been. He was a charmer when he wanted to be. The world beyond our apartment only saw the mask of Ivan, handsome, attentive, funny and, to all appearances, successful. But successful, he really wasn't. He simply couldn't hold on to a job. Oh, he dazzled them for a little while, getting employers to be impressed at the start, but, in a short while, his drinking and his laziness soon forced them to terminate his employment. And then he was broke again. I think, truly, he married me for my earning ability. Having me along meant that he could slough off, work-wise, and depend on the little woman to bring in the jack. And dumb little me, I *was* the family breadwinner, securing a job first at a small family-run restaurant in Fort Lee. There, I waited on tables, serving Italian food and wine to patrons, helped in the office, doing billing and payroll, and even pitched in once in a while helping in the kitchen. The family that owned the restaurant, the Lamonica family, loved me and I loved them. They were like the big, noisy, cheek-pinching, hugging Italian family that I might have had. They all loved Ivan too, and never suspected that his every visit to the restaurant left them with a few bottles of wine less than when he came in. One night, I found Ivan waiting for me in the office. The next day, a large amount of cash was missing. It had made its way into Ivan's pocket, and disappeared just as quickly the following night in a poker game at the Fort Lee firehouse. Embarrassed and frightened that he would be found out, I left the Lamonicas, making up a story that my doctor said that I needed a sit-down job. I don't think that they ever knew that Oliver had tread one-too-many times on my ability to shield him from the pokey.

I told Oliver that I knew that he had taken the money. He tried to bluff and lie his way out, but he knew that I knew he had done it. "How can you steal from people that are your friends?" I asked him. He only shrugged and said their money was green like the money of strangers and enemies, and it was easier to steal from your friends...they never suspected anything bad of you.

I said that I would report him to the police if he didn't get off his lazy ass and get some kind of a job. He took my threat seriously, after I started to call the local precinct. He showed me just how seriously he took the threat by blacking my eye and twisting the arm that held the phone until the bones in my wrist fractured. I was used to, by now, the black and blue bruising, but even I had to go to the emergency room to repair the wrist. The doctor and nurses at the hospital were experienced and wise in the reasons for a wife to come in to see them with blackened eye and other injuries. They pleaded with me to admit that he'd beaten me. They wanted me to report him and charge him with assault and battery. But I was three-times a fool and pretended that I had fallen over our cat, not that we had one, mind you.

My only secret triumph in our marriage was that Ivan never knew that I, too, had a lot of baloney in my background. I kept quiet because I knew, had he known, that he would hold my lies over my head and one day, use them to punish me severely. It was one of the few small victories I had during those years of misery and shame.

Ivan did find employment after breaking my wrist. In fact, he found it seven or eight times that year, and a few more times in the year that followed, as he was fired or let go from every job he took. He drank away every dime he earned, and tried to wrest every cent from my earnings. I was home-bound, helpless until my wrist healed enough to get out from the constant blows, complaints, arguments and verbal abuse he heaped on me. When I was able, I found a job across the river in New York City. My new employer, Clausen & Chase.

I started there as a file clerk, and advanced myself up the ladder to an excellent managerial position in Human Resources, complete with my own Administrative Assistant. Six months before the tragedy of September Eleventh, I met and fell in love with Zachary. Zachary and I seemed to have so much in common. I was deliriously happy. Was love, good true love, about to come my way after all my mistakes and disappointments? Maybe God was punishing me before, but I felt that now, with Zachary's love and support, I could make a fresh new start, forget all the lies of the past, and rise from the ashes of deceit into a brand new future.

The past years with Ivan had been unsupportable. I would have left him, even if Zachary hadn't come into my life. The abuse, both physical and verbal, had escalated into a constant threat to me. No longer in love with Ivan, and as a matter of fact, hating him, I was seeking a way to leave him. The nurses at the Emergency Room had seen me a few more times. They had promised discrete assistance and complete anonymity in a safe house, should I pluck up the courage to run and hide. I had made inquiries into finding a place to live and had saved what money I could – difficult, as Ivan took very cent I had and gambled it away or drank it away, - but I managed to sneak a few bucks here and there and hide it in the bottom of an antique container that I kept filled with potpourri. When I met Zachary, I was more than ready.

From the moment Zachary and I were introduced, until the morning that he betrayed me, I floated along in a cloud of love. He was the twin of my heart, he told me. We both were trapped in horrible marriages, we both wanted love and peace and happiness. Or I wanted love and peace and happiness. I never did get to find out, after the morning of September 11th, just what Zachary wanted. The only thing I learned, that fateful, horrible morning, was that he no longer wanted me.

The enormous doorman, resplendent in yellow racing silks, opened the door to The 21 Club to me. Oliver was waiting, and I was ushered into luxury once more, cocooned in oysters and caviar, men with expense accounts and women with lush furs. Big, long expensive cars, operas and Broadway show tickets. All the trappings of his lavish life style. Only now, I knew there was something definitely fishy about just how he managed to afford such a life style. Not that I was in love with Oliver. Well, maybe a bit in love. Well, maybe even a bit more than that. But not really, I told myself. Not yet anyway. I admired him, liked him, and up until this morning, respected him and his successes. Now, I didn't know quite what to think. I was intrigued, however, being a girl who had turned opportunity into um, well, *better* opportunity for myself...but didn't want to condemn him just yet...not until I found out a wee bit more about just what it was that ORR did and how it did it. Up to now, even my opportunities, as I called them, hadn't involved stealing or anything really illegal, had it? Well, had it? I shook my head, vowing to empty my mind of any and all thoughts in this vein. At least until after I finished enjoying the fifty dollar hamburger.

We parted, after a lunch which cost as much as it would to feed family of five for a month. He went back to work, or so he said, and I went to the offices of Solicitor Robert Rossi, wondering, naturally, what scam *he* was in the middle of, just like the scams that everyone I had met who was feeding off this tragedy called 9-11...including, I was sorry to say, myself.

Rossi seemed a bit less nervous. He asked me to sign a paper allowing him to represent me as a former employee of C&C.

"My dear solicitor, how much will you take off the top of whatever settlement is made for me?" I was through pussyfooting around him. He looked scandalized.

"I wouldn't be making one cent off your settlement." His reproachful eyes met mine. "The legal feels paid are a separate issue; the administrative judge that will rule on all of this will set our fees. My goodness, Vivian, you are my client! We do the best we can for our clients."

There was a discreet knock on his office door. His secretary beckoned to him, crooking her finger and intimating, with worried glances, that he had better come right away. "Excuse me, Vivian, I have to see what...." He went to the door and I watched a hurried, whispered conversation. Rossi hit himself in the head with his own hand and with a hunted expression, asked me if I would excuse him for a few moments. I was inwardly gleeful as whatever was making him so upset, nodded my assent and told him that I would read the copy of Newsweek that was on his side table. He left, closing the door.

I got up, wandered to the window and gazed down at the marvelous sight of New York City on a beautiful fall afternoon. From Rossi's aerie, overlooking Central Park, one couldn't see the devastation down at Ground Zero. One might not even remember that it existed, if one chose. I thought again of Vivien and Zachary and shuddered. I turned away from the window.

Aimless, I went to the side table, picking up Newsweek. There was a stack of files on the table, held down by a paperweight in the shape of a large golf club head. I ran my eyes over the file labels and saw "St. Clare, Ivan" on the second folder from the top. I gave a quick glance around, then slid the file out and opened it.

So Ivan, too, had signed on with the estimable Mr. Rossi. Signed on to the tune, it appeared, by the contract that I saw, of a cool million dollars, with forty percent going to the smooth and sleek Roberto Rossi. A million dollars and Ivan wouldn't sue the airlines, a million dollars and Ivan wouldn't sue the landlord of The World Trade Center, a million dollars and Ivan wouldn't sue C&C. I slid the file back where it belonged and sat down, Newsweek on my lap. The cover was yet another scene from hell, sooty firefighters lifting mangled pieces of the building, trying, with every fiber, to help their fellow man. Kenji and Lenny and Carmencita and Jessie and countless others, some who were entombed forever in the wreckage. And here was Rossi, also striving with every fiber to help his fellow man too. Just in a different way. Actually, despite all the heartaches and headaches and wristaches and cheekaches that Ivan had given me in the few years that we were man and punching bag, I was sort of glad that he was going to profit from all of this – after all, nearly everyone else I had met since the tragedy was profiting too.

And I was even happy, in a perverse sort of way, that Zachary had never told Heather that he had been cheating on her and was planning to leave her. After all, he was dead and what good would it all have done? I never met Heather, and despite hating her in a general way because she was married to Zachary, I never really meant her any harm.

I had the decency to squirm a little over this. Even though I had never *meant* her harm, I was perfectly willing to go ahead and ruin her life by running away with Zachary. Maybe there was a God who overlooked all of this mess, but I still couldn't think that He would arrange for all that carnage and death just to allow Heather not to know that her husband was also cheating on her. I sighed. Whenever I tried to philosophize over lofty matters like these, my brain turned to muzzy mush and I made no sense whatsoever. At any rate, Heather could weep and grieve over Zachary's death and her sorrow wouldn't be tarnished by his infidelity. And I hoped, sincerely hoped, that she had a good attorney who would see to it that she received a decent amount of compensation.

Everybody else was, weren't they?

I stopped at the Korean grocers, picked up baby bok choy, some absolutely luscious-looking raspberries and an armload of wickedly expensive sunflowers. At the butchers, I got four lamb chops and at the corner bodega, got a package of *polenta,* some cheese and dry sausages, crackers and a quart of extra-heavy cream. I rushed home, whipped up some *panna cotta* and put it into the refrigerator to chill. I gave the lamb chops a good dusting of Lawrey's Seasoned Salt and set them out to rest on the counter. I pureed a few of the raspberries and macerated the rest with a bit of sugar. I put out a large, heavy saucepan and filled it with water, ready for the polenta, set the little table in the kitchen, stuck the sunflowers into a large vase and took a shower, dabbing myself with Shalimar in various strategic places.

I wore a long, patchwork skirt with a green sleeveless top, a few artful chains around my neck and swingy earrings. My feet were bare. I put Andrea Boccelli on the CD player and checked the *panna cotta.* Brilliant.

Kenji loomed at the door. He looked exhausted and worried. A man overwhelmed. However, his eyes lit up when he saw me and he bent to kiss me. Three hours later, we cooked the *polenta*, the lamb chops and to hell with the bok choy. Later, back in bed, he licked the *panna cotta* and raspberries from …oh, I really don't mean to tell you all this stuff. Sufficient unto the day to say it was an extremely good evening.

Later, in the most intimate of times, we talked, Kenji telling me how they planned to trap the Angel and me giving him a more detail version of the lies that I had concocted for my background. I hoped that Kenji never used any of the resources of the Police Department to investigate me. Not really a problem, I felt. After all, why should he doubt anything I said?

Kenji told me that he'd be working non-stop for a few days. Could we see each other on Monday? He apologized, but, hey, catching the Angel was vital. I had to agree, but I hated the thought that some drug guy was usurping my time with Kenji.

In the early hours, after he left, I wondered if I loved him. I lusted for him, certainly. His lovemaking left me sleek and plaint and sweetly satisfied. The man was a definite hunk, but love him? Ahh, there was no reason to have to make any decision, sensible or not, about this. I rolled over, punched the pillow, and fell asleep.

CHAPTER SEVENTEEN

Working like this was interfering with my breakfast rendezvous with Kenji, Lenny and the ladies. I had to leave my apartment and hustle down in the subway too early to have time for a stop at Bernie's. I missed chatting with the kindly, unflappable Anita and even missed Bernie's inscrutable pancake-flipping style. However, I had promised Oliver that I would be there until he was able to find a new employee, and he had done so much for me (and perhaps for himself or Uncle Gerald) that I didn't want to let him down. And besides, I honestly cared for him a lot. Maybe not like the physical thing I shared with Kenji, but as I had only speculated on what making love to Oliver might be like, it was early days for such serious thinking. For the present, I intended to enjoy myself, not fall in love, not make any commitments for the future. Just be. I was tired of changing identities every time a man let me down. Maybe if I didn't fall in love, I could stay as I was for a while. And honestly, I was reveling in all the attention I was getting, even if some of it was because I represented piles of money to my admirers...well, not Kenji though. As far as I could see, he was the only one who seemed to be honest and wasn't using me with any sort of ulterior motive. None that I could see, anyway.

When I got to the offices of ORR, this little problem seemed to be solved. "Hi Annie," Junie greeted me. "Will you be happy or sad to leave this sweat shop? We've got a new you."

"Me? A new me?" I wondered what she would say if she knew about all the old identities I'd shed.

"Yup, Oliver hired someone yesterday afternoon. Her name is Courtney Harold. Harold, with an 'a'."

"Ah, bloody good. Can she file as well as I can? With the speed of light?"

"Nah, no one could sling them away like you," Junie laughed.

"Whew," I pretended to wipe my brow. "Brilliant. I wouldn't want to be replaced by a cheeky new lady."

"And," Junie continued, "She has a beautiful hairdo. Curls just as nice as Mervin's!"

"No!" I staggered. "I'm toast. I can bally well tell when I'm completely outshone. Where is this blinking paragon?"

"Filing! Where else?" We both laughed. I went into see Oliver. "I hear you've put me out on the breadline."

"Scarcely that, my dear Annie. I know this was all a little too much for you. Dr. Giggi was horrified that we made you work. He told me that you really weren't ready and that you could be doing yourself some irreparable harm." Oliver's face was creased with worry. "If I thought that we were making you ill...If I thought we were hurting you..." He stood up, nervous all of a sudden, and came over to me. I blinked and with no reason, my blood sang. He came closer...within inches, looming over me. His eyes held a dazed look and I think my eyes were just as dazed. My heart hammered and my soul yearned and he kissed me. Thoroughly kissed me, I mean.

"Woo," I said, when he let me go.

"Woo is right. "I want to woo you, my sweet. I want to see you all the time, my dear darling girl, but the office isn't the right venue. It's better that you aren't here."

I caught onto his jacket, swaying. "Uh." I said, with brilliance.

"You're too fragile to work right now, darling girl." His face was tender. I gulped.

"As always, Oliver, your thoughts are brilliant. I was exhausted after a few hours of work, but, I wanted to stay here and help you. Now I feel sad and mixed up. Leaving you, I mean. Like I'm being punished or some such. I'm jealous of this new filer girl."

"Oh, Annie, you sweet, silly thing," He kissed me again, softly and sweetly. And ...well, it was very nice. Very, very nice. Brilliant, as a matter of fact. I didn't mean for it to feel so good, this kissing of Oliver, but it did. My mind, trying to be sensible and practical, reminded me that I had just vowed to not make any romantic decisions just yet. And yet, and yet....I yearned for him.

There was a knock on the door. Like guilty lovers, we sprang apart, Oliver almost jumping over his desk and me backing up towards the window.

"Come in." His voice was just, slightly just, breathless.

"Hello, Mr. Church," It was a tall, pretty girl with the same sort of tousled hair-do that Mervin had been sporting recently. I saw Oliver muffle a laugh. It was the new filer girl. My competition!

"Hi, Courtney. Annie Morrison, this is Courtney Herald who is joining us." The girl smiled at me. She was very young and very sweet. I hoped that she just loved filing.

Oliver said he'd be by to get me at 6:30. "We'll have a drink before the show and then, I think, we'll go to The Russian Tea Room for
dinner. Have you ever been there?"

I shook my head no and Courtney squealed that she'd always heard
that The Tea Room was faaaabulous. Just faaaabulous. It was hard not
to like her. She seemed like a cute, enthusiastic puppy. A tall enthusiastic puppy, but very cute and certainly, she was bright and cheerful,
unlike the slightly vicious Sarah, the toupee-snatching woman. I
thought Courtney would fit in well and sincerely wished her all the
best with the never-ending files. I felt that I could trust Oliver not to
kiss her over the FILE box.

I said my goodbyes to Junie, Mervin and the rest of the staff. I
wished that I'd had one more chance to check out my file, to see if
anything else had been added, but, naturally, that was not possible.
Oliver walked me to the elevator and, as there were six or seven other
passengers, merely kissed my cheek, winked and said that he'd see me
tonight.

The drinks were wonderful. We went to a small jazz club near 47th
Street, then on to the theater where we both laughed ourselves sick
watching "Springtime for Hitler" and the rest of Mel Brook's nonsense.

I have to say that I adored The Russian Tea Room. I had blini with
the ubiquitous caviar (ho hum, caviar again), a cold soup made with
ligonberries, chicken *Kiev* and then a thin lemon pancake flamed with
slivovitz. *Nostrovia!*

And afterwards, we went back to my apartment and finished what
might have been done a few nights ago, only I was too drunk. It was
sweet and tender, blazing hot, delectable and everything that it should
have been and I'm glad that Oliver had been such a gentleman.

Again, in the sweet afterglow (was I becoming a femme fatale?
Was I having too many of these afterglows?), he asked if I might consider marrying him. I sat bolt upright, clutching my sheet to my chest,
like some Victorian virgin. "Marry? Bloody hell! What? Oliver, we've
only known each other for a few weeks!"

"I know. But I also know love at first sight. I adored you even before I met you."

"What do you mean?"

"The moment I heard your voice, I was toast. Uncle Gerald told me
that I would adore you, and he was right. Even with your broken nose

and all your bruises, I knew you were the girl for me." I gazed at him, narrow-eyed. Could he be telling the truth? He wiggled up against a pillow, took my hand in his, kissed it and continued, "I know I'm asking you to make a decision that you aren't ready to make, but I wanted to let you know how I feel and perhaps get you used to the idea that I want to be with you for the rest of our lives. You've been through a horrendous time, my darling, and I know you'll need a lot of time to absorb this, but I love you, Vivian Ann, and I'm never going to stop."

Again, all I could say was "Bloody hell, Oliver! Bloody hell!"

"Is that good, my banana?"

"It's brilliant, Oliver. Just like what happened and just like you."

He grabbed me, kissed me silly and then sat up. "I'm a wealthy man, Miss Banana. I'm also Uncle Gerald's heir. You'll never want for anything. I know you're not the kind of woman who cares about that kind of thing, but I want you to know all about me. My life will be yours and I don't want anything to be between us that isn't true and good."

What does a girl like me, who has nothing but shadows and lies in her past say to something like that? Nothing much. I just kissed him and told him that I was so honored, that I felt so cherished and that it was too early to make such a decision. At that juncture, we made love again…and then once more.

Could I take this sort of thing for the rest of my life?…Hmmm, yes. But I'd thought these kind of happy thoughts before. I'd trusted and yearned and thought I would live happily-ever-after before and look what had happened. Was God toying with me once more, punishing me by dangling happiness in front of me again, happiness that was always slightly ahead of what I could grasp? Happiness that I could never achieve?

❦

I went to Bernie's for breakfast the next morning. I knew that Kenji and crew were working, thus, I was astonished to see Lenny there at the window table, alone.

"Lenny," I called to him. "I thought you were all hard at work, catching the scum of the city."

His look to me was inscrutable. "I got off earlier than expected," he said. He looked funny. Funny-peculiar, and there were lines of strain around his eyes and mouth. He asked me to join him, but there was some strange constraint between us. We ate breakfast, each of us

exchanging general chit-chat, saying nothing at all that was personal to
either of us. He looked relived when he'd eaten and was able to be on
his way. He was almost to the door, and then, he turned around. "Listen, Vivian. Be careful."

"What do you mean?"

"Just…be careful. Don't make friends so quickly. Don't assume
that everyone is what they say they are." His thin face wore a most uncomfortable look. "You don't want to get hurt. You're too nice a
person and you've been through so much." I stared at him. What did
he mean? But he turned and was gone.

I spent the weekend with Oliver. We took a ride up to Duchess
County and had dinner with some old friends of his, Larry and Martha.
They lived in the city, but also had a country estate up in a town called
Clinton. They had taken an ancient Dutch farmhouse and restored it
into a jewel. We dined in an old country inn and their talk of travel and
good times was careful to include me. I could see that a lifetime with
someone like Oliver would include these kinds of careless pleasures
with no strife or concern for where the next meal was coming from.
But was that what I wanted? And did I care enough for him to be with
him, money, privilege or no money, no privilege? And could I trust his
love to be true? And what about the financial tangles that I had uncov-
ered? And what would he think about me and my life of deceit? Could
Oliver love me if he knew…really knew…about me and all of my lies.
Only time could give me this answer. And Kenji, a little voice prodded
me. Yes, little voice, and Kenji.

On Monday morning, only Lenny and Carmencita were at breakfast. "Jessie has the day off. Her little girl has a dentist appointment."
Carmencita told me. "It's tough to work when you're a single mother."

"Tough for a single father, too." And thus, Lenny let me see a tiny
glimpse of his life.

"Where's Kenji?" I asked, trying not to let them see that I cared.

Again, I sense some peculiar…something. The two of them looked
anywhere but at one another and I felt a sense of goose bumps along
my bare arms. I don't know why.

"He called in sick today," Lenny answered with reluctance.

"Ah," I ventured. I didn't think I should say that I planned to see Kenji that night.

I shopped for food, necessities and bought myself a new outfit for tonight. I didn't know what we planned to do, so I played it down the middle and bought a pair of tan velveteen slacks and a darker cashmere sweater with a cowl neck. I thought I could go almost anywhere dressed in them. I also stopped at a hair salon...not the same one that I'd gone to originally...and had my hair re-colored and had a new, softer perm done. I guess I was used to how I looked. I didn't get a shock when I looked into the mirror. As a matter of fact, I was comfortable with being the new me and wondered if I'd find my old self strange now. As I sat under the dryer with the hot air whooshing in my ears, I had a mental image of me, looking as I used to, coming to the door tonight and Kenji not knowing who I was. It made me chuckle. I wondered too if he, or Oliver, for that matter, would like me better as Gianna St. Clare or as Vivian Ann Morrison. I shook my head as the dryer stopped. These thoughts were bizarre, I told myself. And my self told me back: *No more bizarre than the reality.*

Kenji arrived at six. He was dressed in black pants, a black tee shirt and a black leather jacket. He was sexy- almost menacing - and for a millisecond, I stepped back, frightened. He stepped forward, hugged me and the spell was broken. I hugged him back and we kissed. I forgot about the spell.

"I missed you at breakfast," I told him. "Lenny said you were a tad bit under the weather. Are you all right?"

"Lenny talks too much." Kenji's edginess was evident. "I'm fine. Are you ready?'

Surprised at his brusqueness, I put my purse over my arm and went out the door.

It was the Ferrari tonight. Red hot car and red hot man. How could I be attracted to two such different men? Kenji, hot and sexy. Oliver, smooth as butter, wealthy, but also hot and sexy, too. Oh, such a problem for me!

I sat back, letting the baby kid leather cradle me, and stopped thinking at all. Kenji seemed keyed up, the car like a chariot under his hands, and we tore through the streets, even, at one point, going through a red light. Fortunately, we weren't killed nor did we kill anyone.

"Would a fellow cop let you off with running a red light?" I tried to keep my voice light. In his present mood, I didn't want to upset him. Perhaps he wasn't feeling well and this was his way of dealing with it. Even though we had been intimate, I didn't know him very well. Which, my little voice peeped, is why you should be careful of intimacy before you're ready for it.

"Where are we going? Or shouldn't I ask?"

He slowed down slightly and turned towards me. His face cracked a grin. "I'm sorry, babe. I've got the blue meanies tonight. I shouldn't be taking it out on you. This job…getting this bastard…is getting on all our nerves. We've got pressure like you wouldn't believe from the Commissioner, the Mayor, shit…everybody! 'Just catch him,' my boss says. Sure, boss, just catch him. No problem."

I patted his thigh. "Try to leave it all behind you for a few hours. I know it will still be there tomorrow, but perhaps you can relax and have a nice evening with me." His grin and assurance that he would be fine after a drink or two made me feel a lot better. We drove into the bowels of the warehouse district, way over on the east side, down below the docks. The streets were dark and shuttered. There didn't seem to be any business, restaurants or stores on these streets, only looming empty-looking buildings. And then, a blue lighted sign that said "Bar" pierced the gloom. We stopped right in front. It was a storefront, partially boarded up, a creepy place, I thought.

"What's this?" I kept my question easy.

"A place I go to. We'll have a drink and then we'll go for some ribs. OK?"

"Sure." Why was I nervous?

I was the only woman in the bar. There were deep shadows everywhere and the men who were there were all big, quiet men. A few of them were talking to one another and it was hard to see anything clearly. Kenji asked me what I wanted to drink. I thought perhaps a beer might be a good selection in a place like this. This wasn't the sort of place where one could ask for a pink squirrel. "A draft beer, maybe a Michelob?" He touched my shoulder lightly and went to get the drinks. I sat, getting chillier and chillier in the atmosphere.

Kenji came back, holding two beers. He set them down and then, his cell phone rang. "Damn," he said. "Excuse me." He reached into his pocket, brought the phone out and said, "Yeah?" I turned my head, trying not to listen. I hear murmurs and a few words. Words like "Shit!" and "No, this is *not* a good time!" Kenji hung up. He looked angry.

"Problems?"

"Yeah, you could say that." He picked up his beer, drained it and went to get another. I sipped at mine, hunching myself into the booth. He returned, placed another beer down and sat.

"I gotta go. Business. I'm sorry, babe."

"Shall I get a cab? Obviously, this is more important and you have to do what you have to do." Again, I was trying to keep it light, not make him feel as if he was deserting me. After all, this was only a date. He was a professional, a policeman, someone who had huge responsibilities.

"Let's go. I think...you can wait in the car for ten minutes. That's all it should take. Let's see how it all falls in place. I wish I had time to drop you off, but...this is important."

We got up and left the bar. No one seemed glad to see us when we came in and no one seemed to realize that we had gone. We got into the car and drove off. We headed, if possible, into even murkier territory. I noticed that a fog had sprung up. The air was colder and dank with the smell of the river. We were close to the western edge of the city.

I was really nervous. "Kenji. Leave me off one some well-lit corner. I can get home by myself."

"Vivian, there are no well-lit corners here. Just sit tight. I need to go and see a man. It will take me about ten-fifteen minutes and then we can relax a bit." His voice was different, business-like, clipped and a bit distant. He peered through the windscreen, trying to orient himself in the canyons of these looming buildings. I shrank back in the leather seat, worried.

The car careened across an intersection then stopped abruptly, backed up, and the tires squealed as we turned around. "I almost missed it," Kenji muttered. We stopped in front of a decrepit, crumbling warehouse. There was only one light visible anywhere, a small, dangling bulb that shed no glow at all.

"Wait here. I'll be right back. Don't leave the car." He got out, then leaned back in and kissed me fiercely. Leave the car? Was he crazy? I huddled into the leather seat, trying to make myself invisible to whatever might lurk around here. I was terrified.

I watched as his black-clad body melted into the darkness. I wrapped my arms around myself and rocked back in forth in agitation. *Come back, Kenji, come back*, I urged him. *Let's get the hell out of here*!

I heard some sounds. A door sliding open, creaking, a crash and then a shout. Then…nothing. I didn't know what to do. For once in my life, I wished that I had a cell phone. I could have called the police. But what could I have told them? And might I screw up some intricate plan? I heard another sound…was it a gunshot?

I hesitated, feeling like some B flick heroine who is repeatedly warned, "Whatever you do – don't go into the cellar!" And what does the dumb woman do? Naturally, despite the fact that the audience howls at her, she goes into the cellar! And who is lurking in the cellar? The monster, of course. And I was afraid of the monster, mortally afraid.

But I couldn't just sit here. I had to…do what? What could I do? I had no flashlight, no gun. I wouldn't be of any use to anyone in a fight? What could I do?

Whimpering, I got out of the car. "Oh, Kenji … Kenji!" I couldn't stop. I walked, trying to make no noise, toward the building and the single dangling light. My footsteps echoed, no matter how lightly I tried to step and I was sure that the monster would jump out at me any moment. My mouth was dry and my tongue suck, actually stuck, to the roof of my mouth. My heartbeat sounded like a tom-tom and I wondered if anyone could hear me coming. I got to the door and pushed at it. It slid open, creaking. I peered inside, ready to jump, to fall, to scream the place down.

It opened into a large space, perhaps it had been a factory at one time, but now, it was largely empty. The floor was filthy, littered with pieces of machinery and metal parts for I knew not what. In a few spots, perhaps where the roof had collapsed, there were oily, dank puddles. I heard a scuttling sound and shuddered. A rat? I hated rats. A rat would be just as bad as a monster. It was very dark inside, but my eyes picked out an iron staircase at the side by the wall. The wall was plastered with torn and crumbling posters. Rules and regulations, old Workers Compensation posters. I went towards the stair and listened carefully. I could hear nothing. Nothing at all. I waited. Should I go up?

My inner voice screamed at me to get the hell out of there. Perhaps my inner voice was right. I turned to go back out and then I heard a metallic sound, and then footsteps on the floor above. I squinted, trying to see anything. Anything! Then more footsteps and a shout. And then a gunshot. No doubt about it this time. It was definitely a gun.

Oh, shit, what should I do? I was so frightened, but I was more frightened to leave. Was Kenji in danger? Was this where the Angel was hidden? Like a rat in a sewer? I put my foot on the first step and hugged the railing. It was foul and greasy with iron dust, cobwebs and some other unknowable filth. I went up, slowly.

I heard another shout – was it Kenji's voice? - and then running steps, two sets of running steps. A large drum came rolling towards the top of the staircase and I cringed, frightened that it would fall on me. Ohgod! Ohgod! I climbed higher, drawn by adrenaline. At the top of the steps, I stumbled over something. I think I cried out, although I slapped my hand over my mouth to stop the sound from coming out. The shape in front of me was soft, bulky. It was a man. He was lying on the ground. Was it Kenji? Was he dead?

I grabbed for his clothes and felt rough wool under my fingers. I bent down, trying to see the face and discern if he were alive or dead. I touched more. The man, whoever he was, was bald. Not Kenji. I swallowed the dust in my mouth. Not Kenji. I whimpered. Some other person and I think he was dead. Oh, God! How could this be happening? I touched the man again. His weight, his limplessness, his lolling head. He felt dead. I let his body fall back to the floor and stepped around him. My heart was pounding so hard that I was having trouble breathing. I had to pee. I felt like throwing up. What the hell was I doing here?

There were two more shots and then I heard more running. Then sounds like boxes or barrels being thrown around. I hard someone yell, "Fucker!" and then another shot. I held on to the wall to guide me and crept forward. I heard someone say, "I'll kill you Robbie!" Robbie? Who was Robbie? The voice that yelled wasn't Kenji's. It had a Hispanic sound. *Oh, Kenji*! Where was Kenji?

And then, from outside, I heard the sound of a car or truck arrive. I saw the flash of headlamps crawl across the walls and ceiling, lighting up the room momentarily. It was another huge area, filled with racks and shelves and steel tables. The walls were corrugated iron...I stopped my frightened perusal as the headlights were shut off and I heard pounding footsteps below me. The door slid open and there was now someone else in the building too. Maybe two people. I thought I heard a whispered "Stay here!"

I slid behind a rack, melting myself into the blackness. Someone was climbing the stairs and I could hear the footsteps getting closer and closer. Again, I put both hands across my mouth, stifling the scream that threatened to erupt. The person walked lightly, making the softest of footfalls and I heard a sharp click which made me think of the guns in an old western movie. I crouched, ready for anything. I felt the breeze of his...his?...passing. Whoever it was, they had no idea that I was here, hiding. I couldn't believe that they couldn't hear my heart nor the sobbing of my breath.

The person near to me yelled. "Come on out!" The answer was silence. "Its over. Over, do you hear?" The voice...where had I heard it before? I leaned toward the sound and cocked my head, listening hard, trying to pierce the darkness. There were two sharp bursts of gunfire – this time, I could see the flash from the gun – it must be the person who had just come up the stairs. There was another metallic noise and more running. Someone was coming down a flight of metal stairs.

Oh, God! Please! I found myself babbling silently, praying... pleading for something to help me.

The familiar voice yelled again, "It's over, Angel you filth!" And then there was another shot, this time from above. I heard more running, light footsteps and then the sound of another car. Someone pushed over a rack and the sound ricocheted back and forth, combined with the sound of glass breaking. I cowered back and bumped into someone. I gasped, he gasped and steel arms wrapped around me and a hand went over my mouth. My legs buckled and I could feel myself falling. Someone was coming up the stairs and I saw a flashlight beam pierce the blackness.

My captor muttered, swung me around and suddenly a beam of light lit up Lenny! *Lenny*! He was the voice that I recognized. I tried to squirm, to fight myself free, but I was held in a ferocious grip. My captor pulled me further into the darkness. A shot rang out from above my head and Lenny fell to the floor, writhing. Convulsively, I twisted, every instinct trying to reach his body, to help him. My captor pulled me closer. He whispered, "Don't move a muscle, Vivian." It was Kenji!

Thank God, my brain said. You're safe. I nodded, to show him that I understood and plastered my body against his. We stood together in the blackness and I felt the heat from him warm my terror.

The flashlight played over the walls. I couldn't see who was behind it, but I hard more voices, yells and the stampede of more feet coming up the stairs. A woman ...a woman? ...yelled, "Police!" and Kenji's arms tightened around me. Through my fright, I prayed to God that we'd be saved from this nightmare.

The gun upstairs flashed and there was a cry nearby.

"I see her, your bimbo. I'll kill her!" a man cried. A flash of fire blinded me and a bullet hit my arm. "Ha!" Again, the exultant voice was Hispanic. "Keel her," he had said. My arm was on fire. Nothing had ever hurt like this hurt! Nothing. I wanted to scream, but Kenji's hand was pressing against my face. I groaned, but no sound came. My bulging eyes saw legs, then a waist and then a gun, held by a man – a stranger – big and rough and terrifying. He pointed the gun at me. "I'll kill her, I swear!" And he shot straight at my head. I tried to pull Kenji's body down with me, twisting away from the gun. Kenji whirled me around, dropping his hand from my face and the bullet came. I screamed. Kenji's arms dropped and I fell to the floor, scrabbling in terror. Kenji staggered a moment, and then, from below, came a fusillade of shots. I tried to push Kenji out of the way, but he twisted, almost dancing, and collapsed. Another gun went off, right by my ear and I cowered, arms over my head and then I was rolling on the floor to get to Kenji. I saw the big man fall, hit by the gun shot and then it was quiet all over with only one hideous scream from above. Lights went on and the warehouse was bright. I saw everything – Kenji on the floor, covered with blood. Lenny, groaning and clutching his leg. The big man, his head blown away. I saw everything, but understood nothing. My arm was burning and I saw the blood on my hands and bewildered and hysterical, began to scream.

A woman called to me. "It's over, Vivian. All over." Strong hands reached for me and lifted me up. Some strange man, dressed as a policeman, carried me. He took me down the stairs, trying to be careful, but bumping my head along the way.

I tried to reason with him, to urge him back up the stairs to help Kenji, but he paid no attention to me except to say. "Easy, lady. Take it easy."

I blinked in the harsh light. Carmencita...*Carmencita*... was there, dressed in a black jumpsuit, and she patted me on my face. I think she was crying. "He's dead. I'm sorry, he's dead," she told me. "We got him." All around us, police were scrambling, fanning out, guns in hand.

My policeman put me down on a stretcher that had appeared, together with a lot of other professional looking people, some of them running, some of them carrying equipment and cameras. More lights went on and there were people everywhere, men in white jumpsuits, police, EMT's, Carmencita. "I don't understand," I croaked. 'What happened? Where is Kenji?"

"Shhh." My nice policeman said, patting my shoulder. "Take it easy, little lady."

I tried to get up, tried to fight, but waves of dizziness and the pain in my arm assailed me. "What...? What...?" I babbled.

A soft dark hand stroked my brow. It was Jessie King. *Jessie?* I began to cry. I didn't understand anything, but I felt as if a black cloud was pressing down on me. Doom hovered. Oh, what was *wrong*?

"Jessie?" I whispered.

"Don't worry about a thing right now. We'll take good care of you."

"Kenji!" I wailed. "*Kenji!*"

"Shhhh. Shhh." She bent over me and she looked so sad. I tried to struggle up. She held me down, gentle and the fear grew greater.

"What happened?" My voice started as a whisper but escalated into a shriek. "Kenji...he saved me. That man...he was going to kill me and Kenji took the bullet. Kenji!" I think I screamed again.

"Vivian!" Jessie crouched over me. "I have to tell you what happened."

"Please...please..."

"It's all over," Jessie said sharply. "It's all over. We've killed him. We've got the Angel."

"But, Kenji's dead," I began to cry. "I don't care about the Angel. Kenji's dead!"

"Honey," Jessie said softly. She crouched down even further so that her face was right next to mine. "Kenji *was* the Angel, doncha see? He tried to kill Lenny. Lenny's pretty bad, but he'll pull through. You'll be fine, but Kenji's dead."

"I don't understand," I wailed. "Kenji was *good*. He was on *your* side!" I began to cry and tried to wipe the tears with my hand, but my hand didn't work. Not at all.

"No, Vivian. He was bad." Jessie's voice was soft and hypnotic, urging me to understand. "He wore a mask for all these years. Pretended. And all the time he was running the drugs, making millions off kids and sentencing them to death. He was bad, Vivian. I know you don't want to hear all of this, but you got to understand. He wore a *mask*! He called himself the Angel, but he wasn't. He was the Devil."

"Oh, no! Noooo," I screamed. A doctor came to my side.

"Shall I sedate her?"

"No," Jessie said. "She's tough. She can take it." I shook my head from side to side, hurting with horror. I wasn't tough at all. I was soft and afraid and hurt. Not Kenji! Jessie smoothed my wild hair. "She needs to know the truth. She'll be OK. I'll stay with her." She held my good hand while the doctor shrugged and began to splint and bandage my arm. I lay there, holding onto Jessie, while hot, pitiful tears ran in a path down, through the dirt, dust and sadness on my face.

CHAPTER EIGHTEEN

They tell me that the operation took about two hours. Luckily for me, the bullet only chipped a small piece of bone, and they were able to remove it without any permanent damage to my arm. In a few weeks, it would be as good as new.

Jessie and Carmencita were right there with me and stayed with me in the recovery room until they felt that I was able to cope with the truth of what had happened.

It was Lenny who had the first suspicions. He knew Kenji best, you see, as they had been partners for almost fifteen years. He told me the story himself, when I was unhooked from all the tubes and needles in my arm and could wheel myself down to his room, that at first he tried to talk himself out of believing that Kenji could be living two lives. "I loved the guy. He saved my life more than once. I thought I could have trusted him with my kids. But the money got to him. He'd been poor as a kid and I think that's why he turned. He knew the routine in and out. He knew when the raids were scheduled. He knew our plans. He knew just when to disappear, slip away, become the bad guy. Just as easily, he could put the mask back on and become Kenji Hutchinson, good cop." Lenny watched my face. "I know you cared for him and I know he cared for you. But you couldn't have kept up that kind of thing with him. He would have hurt you sooner or later, and you…you're not the kind of girl who could love someone who led a double kind of life, could you?"

I dropped my eyes. "No," I whispered. "I could never love a man who deceived me."

Carmencita and Jessie came to visit me, bearing a huge bouquet of daisies. "We knew you were falling for him. We could tell. And we already knew that it was him. We couldn't say anything or do anything. The setup was already in place. We knew that the guy who was his first-in-command, a scumbag named Robbie Momento, was going to have a showdown with him. The last shipment of cocaine was bad and Robbie had taken the heat on the street for it. We knew he was going to demand to meet Kenji to find out if Kenji had double-crossed him. We had Momento's telephone tapped and we went into action when the phone call came on Kenji's cell demanding a meeting at the old warehouse."

"Why did he have to meet Momento?" I was still unsure of what had really happened that night.

"Momento was positive that Kenji was double-crossing him. He was sure that Kenji had replaced some of the cocaine with some inert substance, maybe cut it with sugar or something. This way, Momento figures that Kenji got all the money and kept half of the cocaine. Thought he was going to re-sell it to someone else. All the dealers were hot on Momento's tail. He was the one that they dealt with and he was the one they would crucify if the stuff was bad. Momento threatened Kenji, said he was going to call the police and tell them who the Angel really was. Told Kenji that the reward was enough money for him to live comfortably. Kenji swore that he didn't know anything about the cocaine being cut. Said that he'd be at the warehouse and would explain everything."

"Why did Kenji cut the cocaine? Wasn't it enough to get all that money? Did he need more?"

Jessie blushed. I wasn't sure that a Black woman could blush, but she did. "Kenji didn't cut the cocaine, Vivian."

"Then what...I don't understand."

"*We* cut the cocaine. We knew where it was stashed and cut it. We knew that then there would be a confrontation and that we could trap Kenji"

"*You* did it?" I was astounded.

"Lenny thought it up. He was berserk when he figured that it was Kenji who was double-crossing us," Carmencita chimed in. "He just went nuts when he knew it was Kenji." There were tears in her dark eyes. "Lenny figures out the plan. That way, we had some control over what was going down." She smiled sadly at me and shook her head. " 'Course, we didn't know that you would be along for the ride. Shit! When we knew you were in the warehouse, we panicked! We had to be careful. We were happy to kill Robbie Momento. He was a bad one through and through. Can't even tell you how many good people he'd killed, nevermind how many children and innocents that he hooked."

"Who else was killed," my voice was low.

"Two of his creeps. A man named Alverez and some other guy that we still haven't identified."

"Did Kenji have to die?" My question was a wail.

"Probably for him, it was better. He'd be crucified. He'd shame his poor mother and that would probably have been worse for him." She made a soft sound. "He really loved his mother, poor thing. Even bad people love."

"Oh, Lord, I still can't believe it all. He fooled me completely. I could have sworn to you that he was straight as an arrow," I lay back, cradling my arm and wondered. Deceit…it gets to be a habit…when could he have ended it?

"Vivian, honey, he wasn't all bad." Jessie comforted me. "He loved you in his own way and he saved you from being killed. He might have gotten away if he didn't stop to help you. He had some good. He was our friend and colleague for a lot of years, until he went really bad." She signed, dejected. "I hated to believe that he was the Angel…but he was."

"Try to forget about all of this," urged Carmencita. Her face was stern. "Kenji was just human, flawed like a lotta people. Some parts of him were good and some parts of him were bad. Just like most people."

Jessie echoed her. "A little good, a little bad."

"But this kind of bad was really bad. I know everyone lies." Oh, yes, I understood about lying. I was the numero uno champion, wasn't I? But this was different, wasn't it? Wasn't it? Drugs. I'd never…never! I swallowed past the lump in my throat. "I could never have forgiven him that part. Not about selling drugs to children." My voice was tired and weak. "I understand bad, too. I've done lots of things that weren't perfect. But that part was over the line. Over any line."

CHAPTER NINETEEN

Oliver and Uncle Gerald came to see me. They were both subdued and spoke in hushed whispers. Oliver's face was grey and I saw deep shadows under his eyes. Uncle Gerald stayed for an uncomfortable ten minutes, then excused himself and tip-toed away. Oliver came near and took my hand. "I heard about what happened. I also heard that you were, um, ah, seeing this person, um, Kenneth..?"

"Kenji," I corrected him.

"Ah, Kenji." He stared at me. "Did you like him?"

"Yes. I thought he was something he wasn't, however." Oliver looked shamefaced and uncomfortable. He didn't have any idea that I had some inkling of why.

"I'm sorry about it all, Annie. I don't know much about it, but maybe, one day, you'll feel like telling me." He was kind and sweet and tactful. I dabbed at the tears that threatened to fall. Oliver gave a small cry and sat on the bed, gathering me in his arms, careful not to touch the bandage on my arm, careful of my arm itself. "Oh, sweetheart. I wish I could make it all better for you." I sobbed and sobbed against his nice blue oxford shirt. I cried for Kenji, for myself. For all the lies. Oliver held me and patted me and murmured soft, soothing words. Finally, snuffling and sniffing, I had all of my passion spent. Oliver unearthed a huge, clean hanky from his pocket and helped me to blow my nose. If you have never had one arm, your right arm, completely immobilized, you'll never know how awkward it is to do many things...for instance, blow your nose.

A young man in green scrubs came in on silent feet and delivered a tray of lunch.

"Do you need some help managing?" he asked me.

"I'll help her." Oliver took the tray and manhandled the little table that slides across one's bed. He thanked the young man and we were once again alone. He took the covers of the dishes and peered at their contents. Oatmeal and some green gelatin. "This is crap!" he exploded. I started to laugh and couldn't seem to stop.

Oliver used my telephone to call someone. He spoke for a few minutes and I heard "Champagne and chicken hash" being mentioned.

"And some custard, please," I begged him. I was dying for custard.

And until the delivery came, about an hour later, he sat on my bed and told me silly stories. We spread the food out on a towel and fell on it. There were a dozen oysters with lemon slices and cocktail sauce, hot cream of mushroom soup, chicken hash on a crispy bread shell, hot rolls and butter, a container of thin sliced, crispy fried onion rings and two dishes of baked custard with cinnamon shaken over. Three nurses and two nursing assistants came in to see what had been delivered. They left, mightily impressed.

'Well, well". It was Dr. Giggi, crisp in a starched lab coat, handsome and debonair. "I see you got here swiftly, Church." He gazed upon the detritus of our picnic and, for some reason, shook hands with Oliver. "Stand aside for a moment and let me see how she's coming along." He bent to check my dressings, feel me here and there and monitored my vital signs. Oliver stood at the foot of the bed, sipping a glass of bubbly. He had a silly sort of smile on his face. Giggi stood up. "You're fine, considering what happened to you." He searched my eyes. "Just what *did* happen to you? I only know that someone shot at you."

"I was in the wrong place and with the wrong crowd." I bit my lip. "It was...awful and I don't really want to talk about it now." Giggi's dark eyebrows went up. He seemed at a loss for words.

"When can she come home? She's coming to my place. She needs some TLC and I plan to care for her until she's better." Oliver's words were almost truculent. I watched his face. Some look passed between the two of them.

"Round ten and the entire shooting match to you, Oliver." Giggi raised his hand in some sort of salute. "She can leave tomorrow morning. I'll write the discharge orders and leave a few prescriptions which we'll fill here. Some antibiotics and some pain pills." He turned back to me. "Do you still have any of those sleeping pills or do you want a few more?" I nodded and told him that I still had a few. I asked for three or four more, just in case.

"I'll leave them at the desk with the rest of the stuff for you. Come and see me in three days. I want to check the wound and make sure that its healing. Bullets can be tricky sometimes."

"Did you operate on me?"

"No, but I made sure that you had the best that we can offer. I don't do surgery."

"Ta. I appreciate all that you did."

"I only want you to be well. Right?" He turned to Oliver. Oliver smiled broadly and nodded his agreement. Giggi made his farewells and left us alone again.

"Do you want to sleep or talk?"

"Sleep now, talk tomorrow." I yawned, exhausted in my body and in my soul.

In the morning, I was wrapped in a luxury cocoon and a wheel-chair brought me to the hospital entrance. A long limousine awaited me and Oliver picked me up and put me in the back seat. He thanked the nurse that brought me down and a large bill of some sort passed into her hand with his handclasp. She grinned at him and said, "Thanks!" Then she wished me good luck and returned to her duties.

Oliver climbed in beside me, adjusted the pillow that he had brought, put a light blanket over me and we drove to his apartment.

I was very curious to see where he lived. It was a brownstone, just off Central Park West. "Nice," I ventured.

"I only do nice," His smile sent shivers down my spine. While he made arrangements to get me out and comfortable, I mused at my ability to change my emotions. Two days ago: Kenji. Today: Kenji nearly forgotten. Was I completely devoid of real feelings? Did I have any real ability to love?

Oliver carried me up the broad sweep of steps and the door was instantly opened by a plump, elderly lady. "Kathleen, this is Vivian Ann. We call her Annie. Annie, this is Kathleen."

Kathleen cooed over me as Oliver placed me, like some precious artifact, on a couch in a light-filled room. I gazed around. It was a beautiful place, done in eclectic style, modern couches jostling with antique chairs, all done in peaceful neutral tones with occasional jolts of brilliant jewel colors. I decided that I liked it. "Nice. Did you have a decorator?"

Oliver gave me such a look. "I did it all myself. What fun would it be if someone else picked out your sheets and pillowcases?"

"Exactly, my dear Watson."

"What can I do now for you?" I heard strains of County Cork in Kathleen's voice. "Lunch perhaps?"

"Lunch would be divine. Thank you. I'm starving." I dimpled at Oliver. "After the lunch that Oliver brought to the hospital yesterday,"

I told Kathleen, "I was spoiled. The liver and onions, although nice, just wasn't up to standard." She tittered and told me that she'd be back in a jiffy.

"I was going to give you liver and onions, but maybe I'll keep it for tomorrow." Laughing at her own wit, she sailed out.

Oliver crouched at my feet. "Are you comfortable?" He touched my arm with a light finger. Even so, it felt good, almost electric.

"I'm perfect. I may never get better so that I can be treated like this forever." I took his hand in mine.

"That's the whole idea of this exercise, my darling. I hope you understand." His grin turned serious. "I want to care for you forever." He stood back as Kathleen wheeled a serving cart next to the couch. She set up a tray table for me.

"Thanks, Kathleen. I'll take over." She smiled and folded her hands in front of her.

"I hope you enjoy your lunch, Miss Morrison."

"Annie, please call me Annie." I blew her a kiss. "After all, I adore you already." She giggled again, a cute giggle for such a lady, and then left us alone. Oliver lifted the covers off the serving dishes and I sniffed appreciatively. "What do we have?" I asked with appreciative greed.

"Clam chowder. Mmmm! Beef stroganoff, noodles with poppy seeds and, oh, goody, Brussels sprouts." He rubbed his hands in anticipation and then, struck, turned to me. "You do like Brussels sprouts, don't you?"

"They are right up there with spinach and Swiss chard. I love them."

We ate, devouring her good cooking and making small talk. We both knew that a meaningful discussion was waiting for us. After lunch, Kathleen asked if we wanted dessert and tea. "I'm going to take Annie upstairs to her room. Give us fifteen minutes to get her settled and then bring up a tray." Kathleen nodded and began to clear.

I stood up, balancing with Oliver's help. He scooped me up again and carried me up the stairs. "'My, my,' said the wolf to Little Red Riding Hood, 'What strong arms you have!'" I squeezed his bicep in admiration. Like another children's story, Oliver was huffing and puffing a bit as he carried me into one of the front bedrooms. It was an attractive room, done in blue and white, and he plopped me, carefully, but gratefully, wheezing just a little, onto a freshly turned down queen sized bed. I fluffed my pillows with my good arm and nestled back against them.

"If you'll give me your key, I'll go and get some clothes for you." Oliver's face was pink. "I borrowed a few things from Kathleen to see you through the day...she's a tiny bit larger than you, but they'll be warm and easy to sleep in." He gestured to a pile of clothing stacked on a chair.

Feeling grateful and relived that the files, the incriminating attaché case, and the gun, for God's sake, were safe in the bank vault, I acquiesced. "The key is in my handbag...Here." I handed it to him. "Maybe I can make a little list before you go over. How long do you think you'll be stuck with me here?"

"Forever, I hope." He sat on the bed and began to gather me close. Soft footsteps told us that Kathleen was coming. Oliver jumped back, his face crimson.

"Here we go." If Kathleen was aware that she had just interrupted anything, she didn't let on. She held a bed tray with a pot of tea, china cups, sugar bowl, milk and a sour cream cake on it.

"Ohhh, sour cream cake?" She nodded, pleased that I was so smart. "I *love* sour cream cake. I had a landlady once, years ago. I lived in her boardinghouse and she was a marvelous cook. Almost as good as you, Kathleen." Kathleen made a pushing motion with her hand, but I could tell that she was pleased. "Her name was Mrs. Lovatt, and she taught me to cook a bit." I caught myself. I had almost said that the boardinghouse was in Harrisburg, Pennsylvania! Was I getting careless? I coughed and began again. "Her boardinghouse was in a small town near Bern, Switzerland." And now, I went into fantasyland. Why did I feel that I had to keep lying? No one could possibly care, but I just couldn't stop. "She was a Swiss woman, trained as a baker. And when she retired, she took her family house and turned it into a boardinghouse for students at the American School. I stayed there when my own parents died." I was improvising, fast and furious. "It was a jolly place, filled with students from all over the world. She had a dog, a Bernese Mountain Dog. His name was Boon and he ate up all of the scraps. One of the duties of the students was to walk him every day, otherwise Boon would have weighed a ton." I laughed with pretended pleasurable memories. "Mrs. Lovatt's cooking was plain and good. She used only the best ingredients and all the other students envied us." I wanted to stop. I wanted to cease this verbal hemorrhage of lies, but I couldn't seem to. They spilled out and curled around me like snakes.

"Do you have her recipes?" Kathleen was obviously an avid cook. My face was pink. I tried to hold back from any more fibbing. Dear God! Let me stop all of this. Lying, even on such a small thing like a recipe!

"Some of them. I do have the sour cream cake one, and this one looks very similar to hers. I'll have to drag out the recipe file...it's in storage...and we can compare recipes."

"I'd like that." She was so sweet and honest and I felt so rotten. "Now, let me go down and let you enjoy my cake." She turned. "I'm going to the supermarket, Mr. Church. Is there anything special that you want me to get?"

Oliver turned to me with a question in his eyes. I asked if I needed to get shampoo and all that and he assured me that he had all that stuff. "I guess not, Kathleen, thank you." She beamed and left us, closing the door behind.

We drank our tea and ate two pieces of cake each. It was almost like Mrs. Lovatt's, rich and thick in one's mouth, with crumbly cinnamon-sugar streaks throughout. I pushed all the stupid, stupid lies out of my head and tried to breathe deeply. Even that hurt me.

Oliver took the bed tray away and then sat back down next to me. "Are you tired, or is this a good time to talk?"

A dart of some trepidation filled me. But I was anxious to get it all over with. "Let's talk. I can sleep a bit later." I re-arranged my pillows and skootched over so that he would have a little more room. "You go first."

He leaned against my hip. "OK. Let's see." His handsome face was anxious. "I want to tell you a little more about me, Uncle Gerald and ORR." I lifted my head. This wasn't quite what I was expecting. "Uncle Gerald says that he's a Major, but he really was never a Major in the army." My jaw dropped. "Anna-Banana, if we're ever to have a life together, and I pray that we will, I have to come clean with you." I turned toward him, my mouth open. What was he going to *say*? He put his arm around me with tenderness. His face was just above mine, and he bent and kissed me, a light, butterfly kiss. I felt warm, my worries forgotten...so fast... and kissed him back. The next kiss deepened into more...and before I knew it, he was under the covers with me, shoes and shirt and all.

"Your arm...be careful of your arm," He whispered urgently, but I found that, in some cases, one could even forget about a bullet hole in one's arm.

Afterward, when he had re-dressed me in Kathleen's voluminous nightie and we were able to think clearly, we began to talk again. "Now, what was I saying before we were so rudely interrupted?" His smile was tender and mischievous.

"Something about Uncle Gerald...I can't remember..." I touched him...and then we made love again and then we slept and then it was nighttime and we could hear Kathleen making tactful noises downstairs.

Oliver got dressed and went down to tell her that we would have dinner in the bedroom. "She's smirking in the kitchen," he came back to tell me. "She's enjoying my discomfort!"

"A woman above rubies."

"You're telling me!"

Our dinner arrived with a discrete tap on the door. Scallops and bacon, then lobster in a wine and cream sauce with incredibly tiny peas and toast points. "I'll leave the coffee pot right here...I'll plug it in so that it will stay hot. There's gingerbread and lemon sauce for dessert." She arranged the tray and then turned to us, "I'll say goodnight now." And she retired.

"We should eat first, don't you think." I asked with raised eyebrows. Oliver sighed and said that he supposed so, but he'd really rather keep doing what we had been doing. We ate, stuffing ourselves, and then had a snifter of brandy.

"Let's get this blamed confession of mine out of the way. It's sticking in my craw. Look, darling, if we are going to marry, and I *want* to marry you, you've got to know all about me, even if what I have to tell might not put me in the best possible light." I nodded, mute for the first time in my life.

"OK. Uncle Gerald was in the army, but he was never a major. When he got out of the army, he hooked up with an old buddy who worked for the Red Cross. Bruce...Bruce Rarlton. Bruce was an old rascal, a charming con man who always saw a way to make himself a few bucks out of any situation. He used to be one of those guys who found things when he was in the service. You need a new tent? Bruce knew a man who had one. You need some whisky? Bruce could get it for you. He was a pisser." Oliver shook his head in admiration. "He and Uncle Gerald figured out that they could make some good money. They'd take over the fundraising for the Red Cross. They'd do a great job, raise more money than the Red Cross had ever seen...mind you, both Bruce and Uncle Gerald could coax the silver out of a dime, so they were very successful. Money flowed copiously in the Red Cross

coffers, and money also flowed, as Uncle Gerald and Bruce had nego-
tiated a good deal, into their own coffers. They really weren't doing
anything wrong, just taking a nice little profit. They took ten percent
off the top. A decent percentage, certainly not exorbitant." He watched
my face anxiously to see how I was taking it all in. I stared at him, fascinated.

"Continue!" I begged him.

"Well, in time, they decided to form their own company. They called
it Operation Relief Recovery, popularly known as ORR. Why? Because
ORR was the initials of Bruce's hound dog. The dog's official name was
Old Rapscalion Rarlton. ORR. They called the dog Orrie. See? They
thought it was a hoot!" I began to snicker! ORR indeed!

Oliver searched my face again, delighted that I was laughing, not
getting mad. If he'd only known.

When I stopped my giggles, I urged him to tell me more. He stood
up and began to pace. "ORR did so well that Uncle Gerald was beginning to be a rich man. Bruce died a few years ago. He had no other
family, so he left everything, including his own fortune and the dog to
Uncle Gerald. Orrie the dog came to live with Uncle Gerald, but he
died too; went to some happy hunting ground where Bruce's ghost
could throw bones to him. By that time, ORR was the hottest game in
town. *Everybody* wanted them to raise money for their charities. Uncle
Gerald couldn't handle all the work. He asked me, his only and favorite nephew…I had just graduated from Yale…to come and help him
out. I was delighted. What an opportunity for me!" He turned and
faced me. "We were doing fine. Money was rolling in for all the charities; we were taking our just percentage and making a fortune. And
then, we got involved in fund raising for the victims of a hurricane in
Texas." He stopped talking and came towards the bed.

"What went wrong?" His face showed me that I was right. Something changed for him. I just knew that something went wrong. After
all, I was a master of such happenings, wasn't I?

"We began raising funds. The hurricane had done some dreadful
damage and donations were pouring in. And then Uncle Gerald had an
idea." Oliver came and sat down again. He took my hand. "Now, let
me tell you a little more before I tell you about his idea."

"Um," I urged. I squirmed a bit on the bed. What the hell was he
going to tell me now? And what was I going to say?

"We…Operation Relief Recovery, that is, enjoyed a sterling reputation. Not only did we raise more money than anyone else, due to
Uncle Gerald's silver-tongued charm, but we only took ten percent.

Most fund raisers took between thirty-five and forty percent. So eve-
ryone wanted to use us. We also enjoyed a great reputation with the
IRS. I handled the books and I am, if I must say, a genius in that area.
Our record keeping was clean and we whizzed through all audits."

"And then?" What was coming? Maybe a Dr. Giggi? Maybe
someone like me?

"And then Uncle Gerald got a wee bit greedy. He figured that
we could actually overbill for services. We got more involved with
doctor and lawyers, because of the injuries and the lawsuits for the
hurricane. And Uncle Gerald got creative. Who would know that so
and so only went to the doctor five times instead of nine times?
Who would check to see that a patient got three prescriptions instead of five? Harmless, Uncle Gerald thought. He found a willing
partner with Paul Giggi."

"Aha!" I said!

"What do you mean 'Aha'?"

"I'll tell you after you tell me the rest."

"Are you still speaking to me?" Oliver's face was wistful. "Do you
think I'm a cheat or a cad?"

"Well, you *are* a cheat, aren't you? And what makes you think I
think that it's all bad. Let me hear the rest."

"How about the cad part?"

I kissed his nose. ""Let me her more. Certain cads are OK."

"All right. So then, we made a lot more money. I have to tell you
that I protested at first." He looked abashed. "Uncle Gerald told me to
go pound sand and bought me a new car. He said that if Bruce were
still alive, he would tell me to hush my duff. So I hushed. I felt guilty.
And then, as the months went by, I felt less guilty."

"Is that it?"

"No." He sighed. "Not at all. Giggi is our primary doctor, but there
are a few more. A few attorneys ..."

"Like the estimable Rossi?"

"Are you psychic?"

"Oliver, I'm a snoopy person. I'm suspicious and determined. And
thus, I learn things, you dope, you." His mouth was hanging open. I
was glad to know that I liked him just as much with his mouth open
and all his sins hanging out as I did before this hour of confession.
Maybe even a little better. After all, who was I to lecture anyone on
being a con? I jiggled impatiently on the bed. "Come on, tell me all."

"A few other professionals. Some disaster workers, some excava-
tion companies." He shook his head. "And 9-11. It was the perfect

opportunity for us. But somehow, I couldn't quite get the joy out of it
that I once had. 9-11 was something else entirely. I didn't want to keep
this up"

"I understand. I knew you guys were up to something…and I felt
bad, because of what happened. It seemed all wrong to profit from this
particular tragedy." I gripped his hand hard.

"Yeah, well, but you profited from it, too, Vivian Ann." His voice
was a bit smug. I jumped back, hurting my arm.

"*What do you mean*?"

"I don't exactly know. I…well, let me go back. I had been as-
signed to you. I knew right away that you weren't British, whatever
the hell you were, and I didn't think the photo on your license was
really you." He bit his lip and looked sheepishly at me. "You were
much prettier than the picture. There was no way that you could
change so much, become you and not the person in the photo. I got to
wondering."

"You…you…!" I was sputtering. "You knew I wasn't *British*!
With all those English words and all!" I was aghast. I thought I'd been
so damn clever! "I practiced so hard!" I wailed. "I even got a British
dictionary!" He patted my shoulder gently and shook his handsome
head from side to side.

"Nah, you weren't good enough. I didn't know quite where you
came from, but I knew it wasn't England." He grinned. "So you were
conning me a bit, my sweet, while I was conning you!"

I tried to bluster. "Well…well…I, um." He laughed harder and
pointed his finger at me.

"You're worse than I am! Where are you from, really?"

"I…oh, Oliver. Could you really love me if you knew I lied to
you?" I tried to side-step having to say anything incriminating.

"Yeah, I could." He hugged me lightly. "I mean it. I meant it when
I said that I fell in love with your voice. And when I met you…I was
almost pole-axed with adoration. I never thought such a thing could
happen, but honestly, Vivian Annie or whatever the hell your name is,
I love you." My mouth flapped. I couldn't speak.

"I confess that I took your license. I got in touch with an investiga-
tive firm that had done some business with us…Bozak and Staplefield.
I told Charlie Bozak to find out who you really were. He's tried mightily, but there wasn't much of anything to go on. I just know that you
are someone other than Vivian Ann Morrison." He touched my face. "I
don't care who you are, my sweet girl. It doesn't matter. And if you
don't want to tell me, I don't care either. I wish you would, but if you

don't, well, then I'll go on thinking that you have some good reason. But I had to tell you about me and about Uncle Gerald. I couldn't give you my heart properly if I wasn't straight with you, even, as I said, if I'd done a lot that I was ashamed of."

"Well." I said slowly. "I'll be dipped. I thought I was doing such a good job with my British talk." I made a face. "Oh, Oliver. I tried so hard. I mean, I even bought the damn dictionary and tried out new words each day." I shook my head, "I didn't fool you, huh?"

"Nope." He looked as pleased as a four-year old child.

"Bloody hell."

"And furthermore, I am leaving the firm. I have already told Uncle Gerald and he is so pissed that I think he might leave his fortune to the Flat Earth Society. I have a lot of money and I think I'm good at fund raising, but I want it to be on the up and up, the way we used to be, not like this. I'm going to form my own company. I just have to think of a name that's as good as ORR."

I began to laugh. I laughed and I laughed and I laughed. Oliver watched me uncertainly for a few moments, and then, unable to help himself, he began to laugh with me. We howled, we almost peed in the bed, we rolled, keeping my arm safe, we laughed some more…and then, gradually, we stopped. And he grabbed me (always the gentleman, still keeping my arm safe) and we made the wildest, most beautiful love….and then I began to talk.

I told him everything. Every single thing and it felt so good. I was like a faucet that gushed and gushed, spilling and spilling…Right from the start. He listened, crying with me and laughing with me, cheering me on when I left Rose and Joey, pissed at Aiden and his little boys, berserk at Ivan and his treatment of me, angry, but sorrowful at Zachary, understanding that even his perfidy didn't deserve the death that he suffered. I told him what I had discovered in his files, about poor Will MacGillivray and how I knew that there was diddling going on in the offices of ORR. And then I told him about Kenji. I think I hurt him, but he took it in stride.

"You were a victim, Vivian Ann." He pulled his hair. 'What the hell should I call you? Gianna, Gina, Vivian…*what*?" I began to laugh again and then I started to cry once more.

"I don't expect you to forgive me, Oliver. I'm not a good person. I think I don't deserve to have any decent person love me. I tried so many times, but it always turns sour. Let's enjoy each other's company while my arm mends, and then, I'll go and you can get on with your life."

"Gianna, Gina, Vivian, Annie - whoever the heck you are, you *are* my life. If you can forgive me and what I've done, I certainly can forgive you trying to do the best that you could." He smiled at me and traced a path from my nose to my mouth. A hot, blazing path of love. "I love you. I mean it. I know you don't love me, but you will. I'm a determined man and I'm going to wear you down, day by day."

"Really?" My voice was squeak.

"I promise. We'll wait a bit, get married and think up a great name for our new company. I'll give Uncle Gerald some annoying competition and he won't be able to do a thing about it! It will piss him off royally!"

"But...Oliver, I like you enormously...more than enormously. I think I do, but I just don't know if I love you."

"You will, my pet. You will." And then we stopped talking once again and put our energies into other things, for the fourth, or was it the fifth time.

ALMOST THE END

I always like stories that have a good ending. I hate to be left hanging, wondering if the murderer was caught, or who married who, or such. Therefore, for the last time, I will let you in on my private life.

We decided to settle on Annie as my new name. I was sort of used to it and it reminded me of Will's wife and all that had happened so many years ago in England. We decided that we were going to pull one more swindle, just a little one, that wouldn't really hurt anyone. We were going to ignore my marriage to Ivan. After all, Ivan sure wouldn't thank me for barging back into his newly re-compensated life. We shook hands on it. It would be the last time we fooled anyone, especially one another.

I moved out of my apartment and into Oliver's house. We married, very quietly, three months later. And, yes, yes, we did lie on the marriage license, but I feel that came under the same lie as not telling Ivan that I was still alive and ignoring my marriage to him.

Uncle Gerald was so upset that Oliver was leaving him that he capitulated. Operation Relief Recovery changed its way of doing business. Dr. Paul Giggi, Attorney Robert Rossi and all of the other old partners went back to doing business with us on the up and up. Everyone agreed that it had been a good thing, but before it turned into a bad thing...a really bad thing...it would stop. We were all rich. We didn't need to feed too greedily off the bad luck of others. I think everyone, in truth, was relieved.

I found out, by eavesdropping, that Paul Giggi and Bob Rossi had a little bet between them. The bet was me. The two of them had bet ten thousand dollars on who would be the first to bed me. I overheard...I told you that I was a snoop...them commiserating about my marriage to Oliver and lamenting that neither of them had gotten even close to 'first base with me. I suppose this knowledge should have been a blow to my self-esteem, after all, hadn't I sort of preened around when I thought that all these handsome and successful men were vying for my attention? I might have felt bad, but I didn't. I was too preoccupied with the upcoming delivery of our first child, a girl, and yes, I named her Lallie.

With some of our ill-gotten gains, we set up a program through the New York City Patrolmen's Association to give scholarships to the children of policemen who are killed in the line of duty. Lenny, Jessie and Carmencita sit on our Board of Directors. There will be no messing around with the three of them watching out!

In 2003, Oliver, Lallie and I went to England. There, we met with the now-elderly Jimmy Johnson, and donated all of the money that Vivien Morrison had stolen, with a few thousand more from Oliver and me to build a school to the memory of Will and Annie MacGillivray, Vivian, Edwin and Little Annie. At last, I closed the safe deposit box. There was no need to keep it any longer. All the money was gone.

I threw the gun into the Hudson River and put the attaché case into a bottom drawer. The little picture of the two children, I had framed and it sits on my bedside table. I look at it every day and kiss my own precious daughter. I am now awaiting the birth of our second child. The obstetrician tells me, through the wonders of modern science, that this time it will be a healthy boy.

Uncle Gerald passed away six months ago and Oliver and Lallie and I moved into the Greenwich, Connecticut house. I think that the children will enjoy playing among the mirrors and blackboards and elephant tusks.

Oliver was right. I managed to fall in love with him in a very short amount of time. We are very happy. I trust him and he trusts me. We've been through it all, and we've come out on the other side, not unscathed, but wiser people. We understand human frailty. We've taken a vow never to hurt one another and to make each other laugh at least once a day. So far, we are doing splendidly.

And one more thing, we've gotten ourselves a dog. He's a mutt, a huge, hairy, lop-eared creature, who, of course, answers to the name of Little Orrie.

THE REAL END

Mrs. Lovatt's Jewish Friend's
Sour Cream Cake

2 sticks of butter
2 cups of sugar
4 eggs
4 cups of flour
2 teaspoons baking powder
2 teaspoons baking soda
1 pint sour cream

And: For the filling and topping:

1 cup sugar
1 cup chopped walnuts
2 teaspoons cinnamon

1. In a Kitchen-Aide or heavy mixer, combine butter, sugar and eggs. Cream well.
2. In a separate bowl, mix the flour, baking powder and baking soda.
3. Add the dry mixture to the creamed mixture, then add sour cream The batter will be heavy and stiff.
4. In a small bowl, mix the sugar, walnuts and cinnamon.
5. I use a bundt pan and I double the recipe. If you're like me, grease and flour a LARGE round bundt pan. If you use only the single recipe, use a bread pan or a smaller round mold. Whatever pan you use, plop half the batter into it.
6. Sprinkle the batter with ½ of the sugar/walnut/cinnamon mix
7. Plop the rest of the batter into the pan. Smooth the top slightly.
8. Sprinkle the balance of the sugar/nuts/cinnamon on top of the cake. Mmmmm, looks good, doesn't it. Smells good too. Actually, the batter is *scrumptious* raw.
9. Bake 1 hour, or possibly more (perhaps an hour and a half), if the recipe is doubled, in a 350 degree oven,

checking to see that the top doesn't burn. If it seems to be getting too brown on top, cover cake with a piece of aluminum foil.   `

10.   Cake is done when it sounds hollow on top and a tooth-pick or cake pick comes out dry. You want the cake to be done, but not overdone, as it is best when it is moist.

11.   Enjoy and think of me.

ALSO WRITTEN BY J TRACKSLER

The Tears of San Antonio
Part 1, Una Furtiva Lagrima
Part 2, Un Di Felice

The Botticelli Journey

Murder at Malafortuna

The Ice Floe

And coming soon…

Cherubini
Worse Than A Thief
Panis Angelicus